FIRST
BULLET

FIRST BULLET

ANDREW CERONI

outskirts
press

Also by Andrew Ceroni

DAVID'S SLING
IN THE BLACK
SPECIAL MEANS
THE RED SHORE
SNOW MEN
MERIDIAN

For my mother, Joan, who
instilled in me a love for books

Our top focus—protecting our nation— must go beyond homeland preparedness. America will only be secure if we deal with threats before they happen, rather than after they happen.

Bill Frist

PART I

Attack the enemy where he is unprepared,
appear where you are not expected.

Sun Tzu, The Art of War

CHAPTER 1

Moon Palace Resort
Ocho Rios, Jamaica
Thursday, June 8ᵗʰ

Sharon Phillips sluggishly slid her eyelids open. Her brow promptly creased, wrinkling as she felt a burning sensation creeping across the tops of her toes. She glanced down, seeing her feet had slipped out of the canopy's shadow into the glare of the midday Caribbean sun. Her toes were on their way to growing crimson red. She pulled her knees up toward her abdomen where her feet then crept back into the shade of their colorful beach umbrella.

Sharon slowly shook her head and reached over with her left hand to grasp a glass, beads of moisture running down its side. She sipped the remains of her Mai Tai, returning the glass to the side table, and then reclined back against the chaise lounge. Inhaling a lungful of breezy, saltwater air, she wriggled further back into the lounge. A smile washed across her face as she gazed at the silky soft, white sand beach surrounding the both of them.

She glanced across the broad shoreline, then out to beyond the azure blue waters that stretched to the horizon. With a broad grin still across her face, she began humming the tune to lyrics now dancing through her mind… *"Down the way where the nights are gay, and the sun shines daily on the mountaintop. I took a trip on a sailing ship, and when I reached Jamaica, I made a stop…"*

Sharon's head leaned off her right shoulder to where her husband, Roy, was laid out flat on his own lounge chair. His eyes were closed…he was quietly napping. She was relieved that at least he wasn't snoring. Back in Virginia, Roy had told her that Ocho Rios would most likely be a more intimate and tranquil spot than the much more highly advertised and frequented Montego Bay, *Mo' Bay,* as the Jamaicans call it. The residents of Mo' Bay did in fact observe their own beaches and avenues bustling each day with crowds of tourists. Over time they had grown accustomed to it.

Sharon and Roy were in the third day of their seven-day vacation and so far, Ocho Rios had been just marvelous. Staying in their ocean front junior suite at the Moon Palace Resort in the middle of Main Street was an experience in luxury. Simply fabulous. Late into the night, through the balcony's open sliding doors, they could listen to the distant beat of Reggae music carried on cool, wispy sea breezes. These were tunes easy to drift off to sleep by. And now, with the proof in the pudding, Sharon knew that Roy had been spot-on in his assumption about Ocho Rios.

Roy worked in the CIA's Operations Directorate, the Special Activities Division (SAD), at Langley Center in McLean. Over a month ago, he returned from an operation in Colorado Springs that nailed a German terrorist planning to attack the U.S. Olympic Training Center there. After a violent shooting engagement during which Roy was wounded, he decided he wanted to take some time out to chill. Although his wound wasn't serious, Roy wanted to get away, to go somewhere as far as he could get from the daily routine at Langley.

With his healing complete, their choice ended up being Jamaica. And Sharon had to admit she hadn't seen Roy so relaxed and laidback in years. He was really enjoying their time alone together, a vacation on a gorgeous Caribbean Island, and the peacefulness that accompanied it.

The dinner they had last night at PG's Restaurant was terrific. The cuisine had an Italian twist to it. Everything had been very fresh and delicious. She wondered where Roy might be planning to take them tonight, so she leaned over and gently patted his shoulder.

"Yes, honey," Roy muttered, stirring awake and rolling his head toward her.

"Sweetheart, if you nap too long, you might not be able to sleep well tonight. And we have a cruise scheduled for a 50-foot catamaran tomorrow. Do you have any ideas for where we might go for dinner tonight?" Sharon asked.

"Yeah, I do. I thought we'd take a run over to a place called *Christopher's*. They're to the west of the Moon Palace off main street and right on the ocean at Harmosa Cove. The views are supposed to be magnificent. I think it's a little too far for us to walk though, so we'll drive over. A couple of guys back in the office who have been there said the pumpkin soup and coconut shrimp appetizer are superb. They also said that the grilled lobster is to die for. They advised asking to have some curry sauce added to the grilling of the lobster as it makes it extra special. Sound good?"

"Wow! Yes! What do you say we go shower up and get ready."

"Deal."

After showers and donning a new set of clothes, Sharon and Roy made the drive down Main Street to Christopher's. It was short and easy. The dinner that followed was scrumptious. Setting her knife and fork down, Sharon settled back in her chair smiling at Roy and sipping at her Chardonnay.

"This was great, Roy. Super choice. And the grilled lobster was just as awesome as your buddies said it would be. Thanks for a fantastic dinner, honey."

"I agree. It was great. I'm glad you enjoyed it, honey," Roy answered, glancing off to a far corner of tables. He seemed fixated on it.

"Roy, you look distracted, what's over there that's catching your eye?" Sharon said.

Roy had noticed a large group, maybe ten to twelve men, taking seats four tables away. They appeared Asian. No women with them, just men.

"I just noticed…" Roy began as he and Sharon both glanced upward. A tall, lean black man in a white dinner jacket had approached their table.

"Hi, I'm Kent Ormsby, the restaurant manager here. I trust that dinner was to your satisfaction, sir? Yes?"

"It was fantastic," Sharon interjected, beaming.

"Thank you. We do strive for perfection although I think perfection is a bit out of reach, actually," Kent replied.

"Well, tonight you were very close, Kent. By the way, that table over there filled with oriental men…what are they? Chinese, Japanese, Thai?" Roy asked.

"They're a Taiwanese tour group, or so they say," Kent responded.

"You have some doubts about their origin? Do you mind telling me why you have misgivings," Roy asked.

"Well, they come by here on the weekends. The same bunch. They speak Mandarin just like the mainland Chinese. There was an error in their billing two weeks ago and in my attempts to try to fix it, I needed to contact them. I called pretty much all the hotels in Ocho Rios. None of the hotels had a Taiwanese or Chinese tour group. I found that interesting."

"It is interesting. Do you know how they get here to your restaurant?" Roy asked.

"Vans. Two vans with *Coral Island Tours* and a graphic of palm trees inscribed on the side panels. After checking further, I also reached the conclusion that no such tourist agency exists on the north shore in Jamaica with such a company name either."

"That's curious."

"Right. My security people...well, they're trained to be very low key and wander casually all over our grounds. They told me that the tires on those vans are always caked with mud. Mud with a reddish tinge."

"Mud with a reddish tinge? What does that tell you?" Roy responded.

"Bauxite. They must be staying somewhere up in the Blue Mountains...somewhere near a bauxite mine. Our bauxite puts a reddish tint to the soil," Kent said.

"Bauxite?"

"Yes. Bauxite is aluminum ore. Jamaica has almost half of the world's supply, and most of it is exported to the United States. While we export our bauxite usually through the busy port of St. Ann's Bay, we're working at improving our own port here of Ocho Rios. We're dredging the harbor. Anyway, yes, the Taiwanese issue is interesting, but then again, I really didn't feel a need to investigate further."

"Half of the world's supply of aluminum ore is here in Jamaica? Wow. I wasn't aware of that. And I understand your reticence to continue pursuing a personal investigation. Thanks for sharing your views, Kent. So, they say they're Taiwanese, but there's nothing really to substantiate that, is there?"

"That's correct. But then as long as our credit charges go through as approved, I really can't care if they're from Taipei, Hong Kong, or Beijing. I'm sure you can understand me on that count."

"I do. It's curious though, why this bunch of guys would claim to be a tour group from Taiwan, stay so long here on the island, and show up at the restaurant only on the weekends. Well, no matter. Thank you, Kent, and please know that dinner, as my wife claimed, was wonderful."

"Thank you, again. Have a great rest of the evening," Kent replied as he left their table to engage another couple at their table.

"Hmmm…I'll be right back, darling. I want to take a stroll out in the parking lot and see what that bauxite-red mud looks like. I won't be gone long," Roy said, gently squeezing Sharon's hand and tapping the tabletop with his other hand's fingers.

"All right, if you must. You have that look on your face. Ever the investigator, you are," Sharon replied, smiling, and shaking her head, "Go ahead and take a look. I'll glimpse over the dessert menu," Sharon replied.

Roy leaned over, kissed her, and then made his way along the slate path to the parking lot. He quickly spotted the vans and was soon walking alongside them. He moved around one van then turned into the space between them.

Roy's fingers scanned along the edge of the advertisement with the company name on the side of one van. The words *Coral Island Tours* were surrounded by images of Palm trees.

The edge of the label lifted in his fingers. Plastic. The title of the tour company wasn't painted. Rather, it was only a large, removable adhesive label. Interesting.

"Excuse me, but what are you doing so near our vans?" A male voice blurted out. Roy turned to his left as the palm of the man's hand pushed on his chest, shoving him backward against the side of the van.

"I'm sorry. I didn't mean to offend. I was just curious and..."

"You have no business with our vans, mister, whoever you are! Please, leave now!" the man's voice rose. He reached out to shove Roy again.

"Keep your hands to yourself, mister! The fact is, you have no business shoving me either!" Roy responded. He grabbed the Chinese man's wrist, bent it, and turned it inward toward the man's chest.

The man winced as a sharp pain shot from his hand along his forearm. Bending the man's wrist further inward, Roy forced the bully of a man down to his knees, the man moaning as the pain increased.

In seconds, a blunt object thudded against Roy's right temple. Roy released the hand of the man on the ground and staggered again to the side of the van, bumping against it. He spun around to see another Chinese man rapidly twirling a set of nun-chucks, chain sticks, in front of him. This man was grinning as he spun the nun-chucks.

"You looking for trouble, are you, American pig? Well, you found it!" the second man exclaimed.

The second man moved in closer to Roy as the first man rose to his feet and approached Roy from the back. Roy swiveled, his right leg snapping sharply up and backward. His right foot caught the first man in his jaw, knocking him back to the ground. As Roy ensured his left foot was planted securely, his right leg then swept around in a high reverse kick.

The heel of his right shoe slammed into the right temple of the second man. The man groaned. His nun-chucks dropped from his hands and tumbled down just seconds before his left shoulder slammed to the ground.

A set of massive arms suddenly wrapped around Roy's chest, pinning his arms from behind him. It was a third Chinese man—and a huge one at that. This man, who was like some sumo wrestler lifted Roy off the ground and tossed him smashing into the side of a van. Before Roy could recover, the colossal Chinese giant rushed against him, once again forcefully pressing him by wrapping his thick, enormous arms around Roy's own arms and chest. The giant began to fiercely squeeze Roy, forcing air out of his lungs.

Gasping desperately to breathe, Roy abruptly arched his neck and thrust himself upward toward the side of the giant's head. Roy lunged his jaw up and forward. His teeth snapped down on the man's ear, ripping through the center of its cartilage and tissue. Roy then sharply jerked his head to the side and backward, ripping the man's ear in half. Roy spit the lower half of the ear to the ground. Blood immediately began streaming down the side of the big man's face.

The giant shrieked into the air with the searing pain, his arms rising to the side of his head and severed ear lobe, and releasing Roy in the move.

Roy weaved back and forth, his vision blurry from lack of air. The giant dropped to his knees as a fourth Chinese man rushed in from the lot, joining them between the vans. He sprinted toward Roy.

After rapidly assessing the damage Roy had already done to his other three colleagues, the fourth man thrust a push knife with a T-bar handle into Roy's left side, piercing his kidney. Roy instantly bent sideways, moaning at the sudden severe pain. As Roy's arm instinctively dropped to his side holding the wound, the man swiftly withdrew the knife and thrust it upward. This time he shoved its razor-sharp edge into the left side of Roy's neck. The man repeatedly slid the blade sideways, jamming the edge where it sliced into and ruptured both his carotid artery and jugular vein. Blood gushed from the side his neck.

Roy staggered backward. His vision was going slowly dim. His sight vanishing, he collapsed to his knees, then thudded to the ground. Roy Phillips was dead.

The four Chinese assailants jumped up, piling into a van as the rest of the party left their table and ran to the parking lot. They climbed into both vans. A Chinese man slightly older than the others knelt by Roy and reached down to his rear pants pocket. He removed his wallet. Both vans then sped from the parking lot onto Main Street.

Back at their table, Sharon lifted her head, her eyes gazing into the distance. She had seen the Chinese men all suddenly leave their table. Her ears caught the distant wail of sirens — their yelping sounds were growing closer. Alarmed, she set the wine glass down and rose from the table.

Where was Roy? It wasn't like him to leave her alone like this for so long. Sharon began ambling tentatively toward the parking lot. Concern and fear washed across her face. An ambulance followed by two police cruisers screeched into the lot, their tires spitting out gravel as the vehicles skidded to a halt.

CHAPTER 2

U.S. Naval Submarine Base, Kings Bay
Georgia
Thursday evening, June 8th, 2300 hours

The air inside the U.S. Navy's 2nd Fleet communications center at Kings Bay, Georgia, was cool and crisp. The only light in the cavernous room was a radiant luminescence emanating from a myriad of computer monitors. The large clock on the wall showed that midnight was approaching. Growing weary after seven hours of doing nothing but staring into a monitor screen, Ensign Tom Ahearn's eyes suddenly widened.

The ensign abruptly shoved himself up to an erect position and pushed his swivel chair forward. He adjusted his headset and readied himself. There was an incoming transmission and more importantly, the message was arriving at a Flash precedence. That was not a normal occurrence these days in the 2nd Fleet comm center.

"This is Kings Bay Comm Center. Flash precedence request received. Accepted. Proceed with transmission," Ahearn said.

His hands rose to rub the beads of moisture that were beginning to blossom across his forehead.

"Kings Bay, this is SSN-Guardfish. We're sailing in our patrol area just off western Cuba in the Gulf of Mexico. We've been tracking sonar pings for nearly an hour now. We've identified two bogies attempting to intrude in the Gulf off the west coast of Cuba at approximately 22 degrees North, 88 degrees West and at a depth of 400 feet. Request authorization to engage."

"This is Kings Bay. Guardfish, do you have any profile data yet?"

"Guardfish to Kingsbay. Yes, that's affirmative. We've profiled both bogies. They're Chinese. Both are Shang Class nuclear boats. The Shang Class boats are armed with SLCMs, Sea-Launched Cruise Missiles. Do we have approval to engage?"

"This is Kings Bay. Hold on this transmission. We're contacting Operations and the Patrol Reconnaissance Force."

"Aye-aye, Kings Bay." Navy Commander Bob Kean, captain of the Guardfish, replied. He leaned back, easing off the mic. To him, the several minutes that would follow seemed excruciatingly long.

"This is Kings Bay, Guardfish. You are ordered to hold at your current location and depth. US Destroyers USS Lassen and USS Farragut are in your immediate vicinity. They're steaming to your coordinates. They will be on station in less than ten minutes. Rear Admiral Swinson, Operations, has approved engagement. However, since there are some international waters close by, authorization to engage has been delegated to Captain Zimmerman, of the USS Farragut. Captain Zimmerman will assess the situation and decide an operational "go" or "no go" decision. Acknowledge Guardfish."

"Guardfish acknowledges. Thank you. Kean out."

"Kings Bay out."

Minutes passed. Zimmerman soon came online. "Captain Kean, this is Captain Brad Zimmerman, USS Farragut. Do you have CATS, the Countermeasure Anti-Torpedoes, readily available? And if so, can you load in your forward tubes?"

"Aye-aye, Captain Brad. We must have read your mind. CATS are already loaded in forward tubes three and four. They're ready for launch."

"Super job, Bob. I like advance planning. With the CATS at our disposal to launch, there's only a very slim, marginal chance of damage to our vessels. Let's steam forward and press these bastards. Captain Bill McCoy, please swing the USS Lassen to the west of the Guardfish. I'll move to the east side of her. Captain Kean, if you haven't already, load torpedoes in your front tubes one and two, then open the tube doors. Their sonar will catch that, the doors opening. It should impress them that we're not screwing around."

"Aye-aye, Captain Zimmerman. Torpedoes are also already loaded. Doors to tubes one and two are opening. Can we push forward toward them at flank speed. That's to see if we can send some tingles up their spine?" Captain Kean asked.

"Indeed, sir. I like your recommendation. Engine rooms... full speed ahead," Zimmerman replied.

The three U.S. vessels propelled forward. Both of the Shang submarines immediately separated further and paused, ceasing their forward motion. After several minutes, the two Shang submarine captains wheeled their crafts 180° apart on opposite vectors, turning about, and headed back southward at full speed.

"Nice going, gentlemen. It appears they're beating feet. Tell you what, let's continue to steam ahead. Let's give them a moderate and steady chase until they make the move to steer their asses back south of Cuba. We will break off at that time. I'll transmit a report to Admiral Swinson at King's Bay. It was nice sailing with you guys. Have a great night, what's left of it. Zimmerman out."

The two Chinese Shang subs did exactly as Zimmerman thought they would, eventually disappearing south of Cuba. The three U.S. vessels turned about. They each eventually returned to their patrol areas in the Gulf of Mexico.

Inasmuch as this was the third confrontation with Chinese naval vessels in or near the Gulf in as many months, Admiral Swinson mentioned to Captain Zimmerman that he would up channel his report and brief the Chief of Naval Operations, the CNO. Further, he would ask that an ops summary concerning the continued Chinese probes be sent to the president.

CHAPTER 3

Langley Center, McLean
Northern Virginia
Friday, June 9th

It was nine o'clock in the morning and with his staff meeting concluded, Jack Barrett, the Director of Central Intelligence, the DCI as he was often called, was already on his fourth cup of coffee. He stood by the windows facing over the green forest to the headwaters of the Potomac, coffee in his right hand and a cane to steady himself in his left. His spinal surgery had been a resounding success, but his surgeon had advised him that he would probably be a bit unstable for a month or so. As his intercom jingled, he turned, ambling back to his desk.

"Yes, Barb?" he asked, pressing the intercom button.

"Sir, Dave McClure and Tony Robertson have arrived. They're in the lobby waiting to be escorted up to your office," Barb answered.

"Tell Security to bring them up, Barb," Jack replied.

"Yes, sir," Barb answered.

Jack settled into his chair and reached out to arrange the folders in front of him. His door opened as Barb let Dave and Tony walk into his office and then closed the door quietly.

"Have a seat, gentlemen. It's very good to see you both," Jack said.

"And we you, sir. We stayed informed on your condition in the hospital as long as we were able to. The word around the Agency was that your spine surgery was very successful," Dave replied, Tony nodding.

"It was indeed. That constant pain I was dealing with is completely gone. I just need to use this cane for a bit to ensure I don't lose my balance. And hey, you both look great. Tony, how's that arm of yours? I understand you were shot three times in it with significant nerve damage," Jack noted.

"It's fine, sir. Pretty much back to normal. The nerve tissue regenerated just as the doctors hoped it would. Thanks for asking, Mr. Barrett," Tony said.

"That's outstanding! I'm very happy for you. So, how are you both doing in general?"

"Thank you, Mr. Barrett. We're okay, just a tad weary, bored," Dave responded.

"And Omega? I understand that both of you were made offers to join up with them?" Jack asked.

"Well, sir, that's true. It's a relatively short story. I was made an offer, but after thinking about it and then discussing it with Karen, I declined their offer. Karen and I have a new baby girl due in eight weeks. I decided it was probably not a good time to get into something that would be even more all-consuming and dangerous. That's it in a nutshell," Dave said.

"I followed Dave's lead, sir. I declined as well," Tony said.

"Remarkable. I thought we'd lost both of you. I hadn't heard the final dispositions, but that's good news as far as I'm concerned," Jack replied.

"Sir?" Dave asked.

"What I mean is that right now I've decided that I'm going to make both of you an offer too. This moment. What I want to offer you is my removing the letters of admonishment in your personnel files and ordering them to be destroyed. I will reinstate each of you to your previous grade, position, and salary in the Special Activities Division. I offer all that if you'll agree to return. So, my question is, what say you?" Jack said.

"Sir, what about Mr. Novak? How is that going to work? He was pretty firm about what he was doing to us because we broke a primary rule," Dave asked.

"Leave that to me. That's my job, guys. I will talk at length with Pete. We'll discuss the mitigating circumstances that I saw surrounding the issue of your having gone rogue as well as the issue of you both receiving formal admonishments. I will discuss it with him in length until I have his agreement. Dave, Tony, I promise you that there will be no carry over, no consequences whatsoever. You will return to the Agency as if you'd just been off on some collateral assignment, duty, perhaps vacation. So, again, I ask, what do you two say?" Jack said.

Dave looked over at Tony. They made eye contact, and after a brief moment, both nodded. Dave turned his head back to Jack.

"Sir, that's quite an offer you're making us. Tony and I both say it's a deal."

"Excellent. Here are your operations support folders. They contain your identity documents and proximity access cards.

Security will activate them immediately. Your previous work-spaces, desks, and secure cabinets are still open...you can return to them at your will. Guys, I am very pleased to have you back on our team. You're both free to go. Take the rest of the day off. Just show up as usual Monday morning," Jack said, grinning broadly.

"Oh, wait," Jack intervened, "I have something else to relate to you. I'm afraid it's bad news...sad news. I received a call from FBI headquarters this morning. They received an urgent spot report from their legal attaché agent in Kingston, Jamaica."

"Jamaica?" Dave said.

"Yes. The report originally emanated from the Jamaican state police. Roy Phillips is dead. It was apparently an armed robbery in a parking lot that went bad in Ocho Rios where Roy and his wife, Sharon, were staying and having dinner one evening. Roy was stabbed multiple times in his kidney and neck. The robber or robbers took his wallet with credit cards and cash. I can tell you that despite the police report, we're going to take a hard look into the circumstances. I'm sorry to tell you this as I know you were both friends with Roy, especially you, Tony," Jack said.

"Oh no, not Roy! In my mind I can't imagine any situation where a single robber could take Roy down. Maybe even two robbers for that matter. Jeez, that's sad news," Tony exclaimed, his head dropping.

"I'm very sorry about the loss of Roy. As I said, we're going to investigate it, and make sure the robbery causal factor indicated by the police is credible. Roy was a good man and a valuable asset to the SAD and this Agency. No doubt, we'll miss him in the line-up. I suspect there will be more information developing as we continue to follow-up. I'll make sure you get access to it," Jack replied.

"Tony, I'm deeply sorry about Roy, but I do want to thank you and welcome you back. As I said, I'm very pleased to see you both. As for now, Tony, you're free to go. I have something I need to discuss with Dave alone. Take care," Jack said.

"Sir, thank you. I do admit that this all sounds very good. Thanks for the generous offer," Tony replied as he stood, walked to the door, and disappeared through it.

"Dave, What I wanted to mention to you is that after you return from Germany, I'd like you to go down to Jamaica, Ocho Rios. Nose around, reconnoiter a little. Talk to the police, the officers who responded to the crime scene. I want to ensure that law enforcement's logic of a robbery gone bad passes the silly test," Jack said.

"I'm going to Germany?" Dave asked.

"Yes, tonight. You have plenty of time today to talk to Karen, pack, and get to Andrews Air Force Base in Suitland, Maryland by four o'clock this afternoon." Jack opened a folder on his desk. "One of our jets will fly you over nonstop from Andrews AFB. Your pistol, mags, rounds, and holster will be in a diplomatic pouch, therefore there will be no need for you to go through customs. And you won't need a car. Your hotel is the Hotel Platzl just west of the Isar River that runs north-south through Munich. The hotel's a couple of blocks northwest of the *Alter Botanischer Garten*, the botanical gardens. Since the meeting is to take place Saturday night, you'll find that the location, *Spfandl Pilspub* on *Augustenstrasse*, is not far from the hotel. You'll meet at eight o'clock. It'll be easy to find...take a cab. And you will return nonstop on Sunday as well," Jack said.

"Meeting? What's the mission, Mr. Barrett?" Dave responded.

"Well, you've met with the BKA headquarters people in Wiesbaden on several occasions. They know you and trust you.

The BKA has a liaison officer to the *Bundesnachrichtendienst*, the BND, German federal intelligence service, headquartered in Berlin. His name is Gunther Dietzmann. Dietzmann is very worried about something and BKA headquarters appears to be in agreement with him. So, the request from BKA headquarters is for us to meet with him, try to understand his concern, and perhaps develop a course of action. As I said, the meeting with Dietzman is set for eight o'clock tomorrow night at the Spfandl Pilspub on Augustenstrasse. A photo of him is in the travel folder that Barb has for you. You'll have the whole day to get acclimated, the time change and such. The pub's on the west side of Munich past the Isar River.

"All right. Anything else?"

"As I mentioned, we've already made arrangements for you at the Hotel Platzl, not far away from the pub. Just maybe share a beer together and listen to what Dietzmann has to say. Report back to me. I'm fairly sure that I'll have Pete Novak attend our get together as well. He and I will then take it from there. Okay?" Jack said.

"Okay. One question—sir, may I ask how you were able to make all these arrangements so quickly and in advance of Tony and I meeting with you today?"

"Well, ah, I have to admit that I was fairly confident that you two might take me up on my offer to come back, return to the Agency. Call it intuition if you will,"

"And Jamaica?"

"I'd like to save the Roy Phillips and Jamaica issue for when you return from Munich. Barb has all your information for you, hotel reservations, a map, and other stuff," Jack concluded.

"Rules of engagement?"

21

"As always, it's the usual. I think I'll take this opportunity to bring you back to your training days. Question number one: what's the first commandment of intelligence, Dave? Remember?"

"Be offensive."

"That's one hundred percent correct. Good. Be offensive. Dave, your senses are fine-tuned—you know when something bad is coming your way. You've proved that repeatedly. I don't anticipate you having any issues on this trip. Still, in any armed confrontation, the man who hesitates and fires the second shot is often dying or he's already dead. If you sense something deadly is coming at you, shoot first. Fire the first bullet. First bullet."

"First bullet. Got it. Thanks, Mr. Barrett."

"Good. Go ahead and see Barb for your travel documents. Have a safe flight to Munich and see what our BKA friends are so hot about. Check your six while you're there and I'll see you when you return."

"Thanks, again, Mr. Barrett," Dave said, rising from his chair and reaching across Barrett's desk to shake Jack's hand. He headed for the exit door.

CHAPTER 4

Langley Center, McLean
Virginia
Friday afternoon, June 9th

Holding a CD with a classified SECRET wrapping around it in his left hand, Pete Novak knocked on Jack's door. Barb had already left for the day.

"Whoever's there, come on in," Jack exclaimed.

"Hi Jack, how's the back doing?" Pete asked as he entered Barrett's office. He walked toward Jack's desk and took a seat.

"I'm doing okay. My back is continually improving. I got through my third staff meeting this morning without growing twitchy. How was that FBI Foreign Counterintelligence conference?"

"Okay. Actually, nothing new. The fact is the FBI can't teach us anything that we don't already know, except maybe provide some information about domestic protest groups which lies totally on their turf. Still, they gave me a classified CD with the conference curriculum on it, so I needed to come by Langley and put it in my safe. I saw Barb's note on my desk that you wanted to see me. I don't know, there's a possibility that it might have some utility. I suppose the biggest benefit of conferences like this one is meeting a lot of senior people. That's always enjoyable."

"Good. I'm glad you got something worthwhile out of it," Jack said.

"Have I missed anything significant this past week? What did you want to see me about?" Pete asked.

"Internationally. Not really. Oh, except that I did receive a message from the Chief of Naval Operations, the CNO, first thing this morning about another confrontation in the Gulf of Mexico last night, this time with two Chinese cruise missile subs."

"Really? What happened?"

"Confronted by two US Navy destroyers and one of our own attack subs, as usual, the Chinese retreated. Obviously, they don't want to encourage a hostile engagement, but they still continue to probe. And I have some bad news about one of your folks in the SAD, Roy Phillips. Roy was killed in Jamaica in a robbery gone bad. That's what the Jamaican police believe occurred. We're going to go down there and take a look at the evidence ourselves. And well, King Charles had a cold this week and cancelled a visit to Parliament, but that's about it," Jack explained.

"My goodness, that's terrible about Roy Phillips. And the continued confrontations with Chinese vessels in the Gulf is curious, too. Anything else?"

"Yes, there is, and I'm glad you came by. Pete, please listen closely to what I have to say. I need to have your buy-in."

"All right? What?"

"This morning I had Dave McClure and Tony Robertson brought in to talk with me," Jack said.

24

"Wow. May I ask for what purpose?"

"Both of them received offers from Omega. For their own separate reasons, they ultimately declined the offers. So, I made an offer to them to return to the Agency. I'm having the admonishment letters you produced removed from their personal files and destroyed. I further offered to have each of them restored to their previous grade, position, and salary in the Special Activities Division."

"Damn, Jack! At the time that all occurred, you told me that you wouldn't countermand my decision! What the hell! I'll look ridiculous to everyone at Langley now! We have rules, some very important rules, and those two both violated a critical one! Dammit! I was then the Acting DCI!" Pete exclaimed, his voice rising.

"Take it easy, Pete. Don't shout at me. First of all—I didn't countermand your decision at the time, did I? Even though I pleaded with you to reconsider, I didn't countermand your decision. Number two—no, you aren't going to look ridiculous to anyone. The only people who will know the circumstances of this are you, I, Dave, and Tony. And you need to know that while they accepted my offer to return, they were both concerned about their future relationship with you. Finally, number three—yes, we do have rules, important rules. However, as senior leaders we need to consider any existing mitigating circumstances and take them into account in our decision making. I believe that's part of leadership...a critical part of good leadership. There were some very powerful mitigating circumstances in those men's actions, and I have decided to take that into account. Dave's wife's life was at stake, and further, Karen was pregnant with his child. That Russian, Vassily Krasnoff, whom our intelligence surmised had died after the Alaska operation, came back from the dead and kidnapped

Karen with the intent to kill her. So, Dave went after them. Pete, in my estimation, you should have considered that. But you didn't, and I let it ride at the time. Do you understand what I've just said?"

"Yes, but…"

"But what? No buts. I need to know that you are going to be able to work with those two men, to lead them, and do so in an unbiased fashion. Will you? Can you?"

"Or what?" Pete said, his face rigid.

"You know damn well that I have several options in that regard. At this point, however, I see no need to consider implementing them. I'm not going to threaten you, Pete. What I want is your understanding of my decision in this matter and what's more, your agreement to work in the future with these two men as you would with anyone. And yes, that would be symbolic of good leadership on your part! So, in that regard, what does the DCI's Deputy for Operations say? What's your answer?" Jack exclaimed.

Pete grew silent. He looked down at the floor for several seconds and then back up at Jack.

"The way you have explained it and laid it out, I will confirm that you have my buy-in as you initially put it. Jack, I guess I agree with you. I will admit that after those events, I myself did have second thoughts. I felt bad about how it all went down, most especially how it ended. In my heart, I didn't want to lose Dave and Tony, but I decided the rules would and should prevail. And yes, you're right, you didn't countermand my decision at the time. I suppose the bottom-line here is that I think we can move forward," Pete said in a meeker tone.

"Pete, that's something. Thank you," Jack said, reaching down to the bottom side drawer in his desk. He pulled out two crystal old-fashion glasses and a bottle of Red Breast 12-year-old Irish whiskey. He put a thumb's worth in each glass and handed one over the desk to Pete. Pete broke into a mild smile.

"Yes, that's something. I'd like us to make a toast to that," Jack said, raising his glass.

"Yes, sir. Thanks for taking the time and effort to fully explain your position. It would be difficult to take a stand against it the way you put it. A toast?" Pete said, rising to his feet, and raising his own glass.

"Then here's to us and the table dust, along with God, country, motherhood, and apple pie," Jack said, standing behind his desk with a broad grin on his face. Both men sipped at the whisky, both smiling at each other.

They reached across the desk and shook hands, then eased back in their chairs.

CHAPTER 5

Munich, Germany
Saturday morning, June 10th

The driver steered the beige Mercedes taxi deftly around the corner and drew up to the curb in front of the entrance to the Hotel Platzl. Dave reached over the seat and gave him a generous tip and received a broad smile in return. As he climbed out of the cab, Dave glanced upward…dark skies, cloudy, and a slight drizzle. Dreary. Germany often had days like this, just not so often down in Bavaria.

The flight from Washington, DC, had been a long one. They'd passed through some significant weather fronts while crossing over the Atlantic. The near constant jostling up and down in his seat while flying through the turbulence of the storms made it impossible to doze off. He was fatigued.

It was somewhat early in the morning in Munich at 08:30 AM. He'd caught a taxi outside the baggage claim area at the airport. Dave walked into the hotel and checked in at the lobby reception desk. The receptionist was a gal with red hair, blue-green eyes, freckles, and appeared to be in her mid-thirties.

She sized Dave up and, liking what she saw, gave him a mischievous smile. Dave smiled back, took his room proximity sweep card, and took the elevator up to his floor. He soon discovered the Agency had been unusually generous — they'd reserved a junior suite for him. Nice.

Once in the room, Dave shoved his suitcase through the small living area to the couch near the window. The window had a view down to the street filled with umbrellas that were bobbing up and down like popcorn in a popper. He collapsed on the king-size bed, pulled down the cover to lie on the pillow, and kicked off his shoes. He needed some rest. The meeting wasn't until eight o'clock tonight. Food could wait.

It was hunger that eventually woke him from his slumber. Glancing at his watch, he realized he'd slept over five hours. It was past two o'clock in the afternoon. Dave washed his face with warm water which made him feel refreshed. He took the elevator down to the lobby and walked into the hotel restaurant named: *Zum Wald von Bergen, To the Forest of the Mountains.*

Dave ordered a *Jägerschnitzel mit Spätzle*, a *Hunter's pork cutlet with noodles*, extra gravy, and washed it all down with a smooth *Spätlese* white wine from the Mosel Valley. He'd always considered the Mosel white wines to be a bit smoother than the tangier ones from the Rhine Valley. Everything was delicious. He decided to finish up with a slice of apple strudel and coffee.

Having charged the bill to the room and feeling stuffed, he left the restaurant and walked through the lobby. He exited out the doors and promptly noticed the dark clouds had faded and likewise, the drizzle had abated. The sidewalks were still damp, but the skies had transformed to just a light shade of gray.

ANDREW CERONI

Dave walked up one block, turned back again down toward the hotel, and strolled another block in the opposite direction. He returned to the lobby and decided to go back up to his room, relax, and perhaps study the folder Barb had given him that included a photo of Gunther Dietzmann. In the junior suite, he plopped on the bed, half the time watching the *Deutche tagesschau, German daily news*, on the wall-mounted tv, and the other half glancing through the folder.

At 7:30 PM, Dave donned his raincoat and left the hotel. Taxis were lined up in front and waiting. He took the first one. Barrett had said the Spfandl Pilspub was fairly close to the Platzl hotel, but Dave was still surprised that it ended up being an under ten-minute drive. After paying the driver, he walked into the pub and chose a table away from the windows but still in sight of the entrance.

There was a pleasant, orangish glow in the pub from muted overhead lighting. For the next ten minutes, Dave enjoyed sipping at a cool, golden pilsner beer. He hadn't had a German beer in years. He slipped his hand in his jacket to check his Beretta. It felt seated comfortably under his left arm in his slant-rig shoulder holster.

Dave looked up at eight o'clock on the button, as Dietzmann walked through the front door. Dave rose from his seat and walked toward him. The man had paused in the entranceway while his eyes scanned the tables of customers.

"*Guten abend, Herr Dietzmann. Good evening, Mr. Dietzmann*," Dave said in a low voice.

"*Guten Abend. Wie heissen sie? What's your name?*" Gunther replied.

"Dave McClure."

"David McClure?"

"*Ja, bin ich. Yes, it's me.*"

30

"Sehr gut. Es freut mich zu dir treffen, Herr McClure. Very good. Pleased to meet you, Mr. McClure."

"Also...am tisch, ja? So, at the table, okay?"

"Ja, gut. Yes, good." Gunther replied. Dave led the way back to his table in a corner area he had chosen. Gunther continued to glance around the room, nodded in approval, and sat across from Dave.

"Gunther, können wir auf Englisch sprechen. Gunther, can we speak in English?" Dave asked.

"Sure, that's okay with me. I have a strong fluency in English," Gunther said, glancing up as a waiter approached.

"Mein herr, was wollen sie zum trinken? Mister, what would you like to drink?" the waiter asked.

"Asbach Uralt, bitte."

"Danke, es wird sofort kommen. Thanks, it'll come right away," the waiter responded.

"Asbach Uralt? German brandy. A little strong, yes?" Dave said.

"Perhaps, Dave, but I think for what I'm going to relate to you, I need something stronger than beer."

"I see. Believe me, Gunther, I will be listening closely to what you have to say. Would you like something to eat," Dave replied.

"No, nothing to eat, thank you. My stomach couldn't hold it. I admit that I'm nervous. I have to be careful. This is dangerous for me. The fact is, I don't think even our Chancellor or any of our other cabinet ministers are aware of this. On the good side, however, I'm glad we came here to Munich to meet. It was only a short flight for me. This location is much more secure than anyplace in Berlin."

"I understand. Please know that you're safe with me. What you have to say will be held in utmost confidence. Let's

31

start with the generalities. What is this about? You're the BKA liaison officer to the BND, right?" Dave said in a firm voice.

The waiter approached and set the glass of Asbach Uralt on the table in front of Gunther.

"Thanks for that. Much appreciated," Gunther said, taking a sip of the brandy. He looked back at Dave, "And, yes, while working at the BND, I've developed some good friends within the headquarters. They're also concerned with what I'm about to tell you. And they're actually my source of the information, but neither they nor anyone else other than the BKA knows that you and I are meeting. So, I think what's important is that this information came to me from inside the BND and from BND agents. And again, it's very dangerous for me."

"All right. Who's involved?"

"My BND friends and I can't dare to up channel our concerns as it's also understood that the BND intelligence leadership has bought into this. They're aligned themselves with the overall strategy. And to answer your question, the crux of the matter is that's it concerns our Defense Minister, Andreas Bachmeier."

"Okay. Please continue…"

"Good. I think you and I first need to go a bit back into history to understand how this issue developed over time. Are you aware of the organization that was formed during the waning days of World War II, the Odessa? The Odessa network operated in Germany from early in 1944 up until the last days of the war and the ultimate fall of Berlin."

"Well, I've seen the movie, 'The Odessa Files,' if that's the context of what you're referring to. I'm also aware of Simon Wiesenthal's efforts hunting Nazis from his offices in Vienna, Austria, but that's pretty much it. We used to have an office in the Justice Department, the OSI, the Office of Special Investigations, that had the mission of hunting down Nazi war criminals living in the United States."

"Okay. I understand. Odessa was real. It existed and served many in the senior Nazi leadership ranks. There was another, somewhat smaller, but just as powerful organization, somewhat like Odessa. That was *Die Spinne, The Spider*. Die Spinne was also formed in 1944. It was instrumental in helping many senior level Nazi war criminals escape Germany and justice for various war crimes...to Argentina, Paraguay, Chile, Bolivia, and a few other locations like the Middle East."

"Die Spinne. The Spider? Interesting. All right, thanks."

"Our Defense Minister, Andreas Bachmeier's grandfather, Klaus Bachmeier, worked directly for Heinrich Himmler in the Schutzstaffel, Nazi Germany's SS, as a member of Himmler's immediate staff in Berlin. In the last days of the war, die Spinne was able to move Klaus safely out of Germany. He was taken first by aircraft to Malta, and then a day later, off the coast of Malta, he was met at sea by a U-Boat that took him into the southern Atlantic and finally to Argentina. Klaus' son, Andreas' father, Conrad Bachmeier, was raised in Argentina in the milieu of his father Klaus' continued rhetoric and support for Nazi ideals and objectives," Gunther said.

"I see."

"And just like his father, Conrad grew to be an avowed extreme rightwing fascist. Feeling it safe at the time, Conrad eventually immigrated back to Germany near Brandenburg where his own son, Andreas, got into politics and successfully so. And so, Andreas Bachmeier is now our defense minister. What's more, politically, that man is more than just extreme rightwing. He has two faces...the face he shows to the Chancellor in daily business and the face he shows to his closest friends in his private group. What I'm saying to you is that Andreas Bachmeier has served and is serving under a false identity as president of a clandestine, far-right organization known as the *Die Reichsdonnergruppe, The Reich's Thunder Group*. This group has some very high placed German politicians, corporate CEOs, and military leaders as members."

"Interesting, Gunther, please go on," Dave said.

"As you may be aware, Germany is involved in a comprehensive, massive remilitarization. Bachmeier has been and still is aggressively boosting defense spending on modern, state-of-the-art weapon systems. And he's using Russia's invasion of the Ukraine as the rationale for doing so. For armor—it's the new Leopard 2A7+ battle tank; for air force fighters—those are purchases of your own U.S. F-35A fighter jets and others; for naval vessels—it's guided missile frigates and submarines; and for the army—greatly upgraded infantry forces, both in numbers and weaponry. This build-up in all German military forces is enormous. Bachmeier has also constructed three new military bases around Berlin, ostensibly to protect Berlin from any invading forces that manage to cross our borders."

"Gunther, you said *ostensibly?*"

"Right. My BND friends and I don't believe the forces on those bases are intended to protect anything. Instead, they've been purposely structured and equipped for seizing things. Further, we've also learned that at some point in the future, Bachmeier has plans in place to move all his modernized armor, infantry, and air forces to locations within miles of the borders of Poland and the Czech Republic."

"Military base forces fashioned and equipped to seize? That's a curious assessment. If all this ramping up of forces is not being accomplished as a safeguard against Russian aggression, then what is it do you think that Bachmeier is really seeking in all of this?"

Gunther swallowed one last gulp from the remainder of his Asbach Uralt. His teeth clenched, gritting. His eyes glared into Dave's. He replied in a flat monotone.

"What Bachmeier wants, that is, after the arrest of the Chancellor at his Berlin Chancellery residence on Willy Brandt Avenue by Bundeswehr special forces, and that followed by an attack on constitutional organs, and the subsequent overthrow of the German government—is to install a Fourth Reich."

CHAPTER 6

Langley Center, McLean
Virginia
Monday morning, June 12th

Colorful rays of bright morning sunlight were streaming over the Potomac's headwaters and adjacent forests, and through the eastern windows of Jack Barrett's office. All three men, Jack Barrett, Pete Novak, and Dave McClure seemed to pause in unison to take a sip of their coffee. Gradually lifting his eyes from his cup, Jack's face rose with a skeptical look. He focused solely on Dave.

"That's quite a story, Dave. A Fourth Reich? Really? Everything that the Agency has gathered intelligence-wise over the last few months points to Germany's remilitarizing as being a direct result of Russia's invasion of Ukraine," Jack said.

"I understand, sir. However, I pose the question: should we, would we, want to risk ignoring the fact that Gunther Dietzmann along with his close friends in Berlin are in fact insiders at the Bundesnachrichtendienst? And further, that they're so concerned that they took the time to covertly communicate with us? Can we risk ignoring that?" Dave asked.

"No, I agree—fact is, we can't, and no, we shouldn't either. The information that Dietzmann gave you on Andreas Bachmeier's background, his father, Conrad, and his grandfather, Klaus, should be verifiable. That's a beginning, and I'm going to have our Analysis department delve into it immediately. We will also task some of our most sensitive sources, such as senior elites in the German government, regarding Andreas Bachmeier's political leanings, his standing relationship with the Chancellor, and his general mindset. We'll also have some Department of Defense assets discreetly begin to collect any information regarding the possibility of any existing German military plans to move armor, infantry, and air forces to locations near the Czech and Polish borders at some point in the future," Jack explained.

"That sounds great, sir," Dave said.

"When we have the results, all this data in hand, we'll have Analysis assemble a team to examine it and give us their assessment. It's just that, well, at the moment, Gunther Dietzman's story appears to be more than just a bit over the top. Pete, what's your impression on this?" Jack asked.

"I agree with you regarding the nature of Dietzmann's claim. Nevertheless, I also agree with the question that Dave has posed, that is, can we afford to ignore Dietzmann and his alleged intelligence information. That in my mind is an emphatic no, we shouldn't."

"Good. Thank you. Good discussion. Let's now set the tale of Germany's defense minister aside and talk briefly about subject number two for today: Jamaica. First, please know Dave that I regret sending you on back-to-back missions. I'm not crazy about doing that. However, you should also be aware that our objective in sending you to Ocho Rios is only to reconnoiter, to get a feeling regarding the Jamaican police concluding that the death of our Roy Phillips is attributed to a robbery attempt in a parking lot of Christopher's restaurant that went bad. I know it's not impossible, but given Roy's skill sets in hand-to-hand combat, it's not all that believable either," Jack said.

"I agree one hundred percent, Jack," Pete interjected.

"So, talk to the police, go to the site where the robbery took place, and churn all the data around in your mind. By the way, you'll be traveling, that is, registered at the car rental and at the hotel documented as Special Agent Neal Hawthorne, FBI. Accordingly, you'll have a passport, driver's license, FBI badge and credentials, and some pocket trash bearing that identity. Use that identification in talking with the police. And if you're queried by anyone else. Dave, does all this make sense to you? Is it logical?" Jack asked.

"Yes. I've got it, Mr. Barrett," Dave replied.

"Pete, anything to add?" Jack asked.

"No, not really. Still, to piggyback on what you said, Jack, I find it hard to believe that one robber could overcome and ultimately kill Roy. Even the presence of two robbers against him is a stretch. Roy was too highly skilled," Pete responded.

"I agree. On that note, I think I should take a few minutes to provide some additional information to you that comes from our embassy's initial talk with Sharon Phillips, but I don't know if it's relevant or connected in any way. I don't want to mislead you or have you focus on this info, Dave. At the time of the discussion, as you might imagine, Sharon was very distraught," Jack said.

"Yes, sir?" Dave replied.

"Right. Near the end of their dinner at Christopher's, Sharon said that Jack had become distracted by a group of men four tables away — ten to twelve men who appeared oriental, possibly Chinese. Coincidently, Kent Ormsby, the restaurant manager, had stopped by their table to visit with them. He related to Dave that the men claimed they were a Taiwanese tour group on an apparent extended trip to Ocho Rios. That and Ormsby said there were also some inconsistencies to their story. The bottom-line is that you should keep that in the back of your mind...the presence of a large group of Chinese on an extended stay in Jamaica. Who are they really and why are they there? Again, that's back burner information," Jack explained.

"That's interesting. Still, it could be significant," Pete said.

"I consider all things a possibility. We're not going to discount anything. And something else. I got a call over the weekend from Naval Intelligence at the request of the CNO, Chief of Naval Operations. There's been several confrontations in the Gulf of Mexico between our submarines and destroyers and Chinese cruise missile submarines attempting to enter the gulf. On each occasion, the Chinese ended up retreating, but nevertheless our subs had CATS loaded in their forward tubes, so we would have prevailed in any hostile engagement. The Chinese must know we have the CATS, and they wanted no part of a clash," Jack said.

"CATS?" Pete asked.

"Yes, Countermeasure Anti-Torpedoes — CATS. It's a torpedo-like, hard kill interceptor that once launched, homes in on a hostile torpedo and destroys it with its own explosive warhead. They're part of the Navy's Anti-Torpedo Torpedo Defense System...the Navy refers to that as the ATTDS.

"That's interesting," Pete said.

"I truly don't know if there's any connection between these naval confrontations in the Gulf and the possibility of

Communist Chinese being in Jamaica in more than just a couple in number. Remember though, that all this is back-burner information. Just keep it in mind, and refrain from focusing on it," Jack responded.

"Wow, that's interesting, Mr. Barrett. And in a way, I can see why the presence of so many Chinese men at that restaurant in Ocho Rios would raise Roy's curiosity enough to make him want to check things out," Dave said.

"Right. I agree. Remember though, don't let it distract you. Here's the plan…we're going to fly you on one of our own jets down to Montego Bay. Not commercial. One of our jets. Again, like Munich, you'll be able to pass into the airport without a customs inspection. Your pistol, mags, and rounds will be in a diplomatic pouch. There'll be a rental car for you at the airport. You'll drive over to Ocho Rios on the north coast road — it's not that far. And you'll be staying at the Moon Palace Resort on Main Street. It's a large resort. That's where Roy and Sharon were staying.

"Okay," Dave said.

"Dave, I'm thinking that you shouldn't need more than three nights or so to get a feel for what may have actually happened with Roy. Oh, and our jet will remain at the Montego Bay airport under appropriate security. When you're ready, they'll be there to bring you home," Jack said.

"Thank you, sir. I have a handle on the mission," Dave answered.

"Great. And remember before the Munich trip what I said to you about being offensive. Apparently, there are some bad actors down there, at least one, maybe more, whether criminal or otherwise. Use your intuition, your gut senses, and assume worst case in any confrontation. Don't cut anyone any slack. Lastly, if somehow, someway, while you're there, this incident smells of something more sinister, bigger, and perhaps with a focus and origin that's someplace not located in Ocho Rios, don't go it alone. Call us for back-up. I'm thinking about perhaps something that might be up in the mountains. By the way, the mountains south of Ocho Rios are called the Blue Mountains. I don't know, just don't get in way over your head. Ask for assistance first. Okay?"

"Yes, sir, thank you," Dave said.

"Pete, anything else you can think of?" Jack asked.

"Just that Dave, I want you to know I'm glad you and Tony came back to the Agency. What happened back then, both up in the Adirondack Mountains of New York and afterward here at Langley, as far as I'm concerned, it's all water under the bridge. I apologize for being overbearing and a bit too stern. Let's put all that in the past and keep it there. And I mean that sincerely," Pete said.

"Mr. Novak, I mean, Pete, that means a great deal. Thanks for saying it," Dave replied.

CHAPTER 7

Pumphrey Drive, Fairfax
Virginia
Monday evening, June 12th

Karen sat on one of the stools at the countertop, a frown stretching across her face. Her fingertips were thumping on the granite. She watched as Dave finished throwing water on his face at the sink. A towel now in hand, he turned to Karen.

"It's the job, honey. You know that assignments back-to-back are rare, but they can occur. It's the job," Dave pleaded.

"Well, I'm convinced now more than ever that you made the right decision in declining Omega's offer. I think if you'd gone with them. It would have had an unreal negative impact on our marriage, our life together. You recognize that we do have some significant events coming up, right?"

"The impending birth of our baby girl. Yes, I surely do."

"Yes, that, and me becoming a mother, and you a father. That will add a bunch of new responsibilities for both of us."

"I know, honey. We'll work it out as we go along."

"All right. It's just that, dammit, Dave, you just got back from Germany, and tomorrow you're heading to Jamaica. I'm truly sorry about Roy Phillips, but this is still a bit much. I don't like it," Karen said in a rising voice.

"I have to go, sweetheart. That's the bottom line. The Agency is not all that confident that the claim of the Ocho Rios police is credible, that Roy died as a result of a robbery gone bad. So, I'm going down just to talk to the police, visit the site of the murder, and examine the evidence. I'll then come back and brief Jack Barrett and Pete Novak on what I think. Nothing serious about this assignment. And it should just be a couple days."

"Okay. I just worry about you. And now more than ever with a baby on the way. Can you stay in touch?"

"Probably not. And you should understand that from your own experience in the NCIS, Karen."

"Okay, I do. Would you like me to drive you over to Andrews Air Force Base in Suitland?" Karen asked.

"No, you shouldn't. It doesn't cost anything to park near their air operations terminal," Dave replied.

"Will you be able to be armed down there?"

"Yes, and that's normal. Look, if things surrounding Roy's death seem to lead to a suspicion that something bigger, more ominous, is at play, I'll ask for assistance. Nothing to worry about in that regard. Honey, I love you more than anything else in the world. I'll be careful and I'll be back soon."

"A suspicion of something bigger, more ominous?' So, there is a possibility of a downside to this trip?"

"There always is that possibility. Karen, you must recognize that. Nevertheless, I'll be okay."

Karen rose from her stool and walked to Dave. She wrapped her arms around him and looked up into his face.

"And I love you too, Dave McClure. Come back safe," Karen said in a low voice. She leaned forward and kissed Dave.

"Can I help you with your packing?"

"Sure, honey, I would like that. Let's go upstairs," Dave said.

CHAPTER 8

Montego Bay, Jamaica
Tuesday afternoon, June 13th

On final approach into Montego Bay's Sangster International Airport, Dave stared out his cabin window, mesmerized by the magnificence of all the white sandy beaches, palm trees, and crystal-clear saltwater. Gorgeous. The airport itself appeared small for such a well-known tourist spot. It had just two parallel runways running east to west. The landing was smooth, no balloon bounces. Dave was grateful for that.

The rental vehicle at the Hertz airport desk ended up being a Toyota Highlander. The airport was right on Highway A1, the Northern Coastal Highway. After grabbing his Rimowa suitcase in the baggage claim area and loading it in the hatchback, he easily entered the ramp to the highway. Dave opened all the windows before heading out, driving east. The scent of the sea breezes flowing off the Caribbean was exhilarating.

"Karen, oh sweetheart, I wish you could see this. You, I, and Carolyn have to come down here in a couple years. I think we'll enjoy it immensely," Dave whispered to himself, smiling at the scenery.

It wasn't a long drive. Driving into town on Main Street in Ocho Rios, Dave cruised slowly down the thoroughfare. There were all sorts of colorful store fronts, shops, bistros, along with an accompanying abundance of shoppers. The Moon Palace Resort soon appeared on the left side, facing out to the Caribbean. It was grand, regal. Two large buildings stood opposite each other with one-level structures in-between that appeared to be terraced dining areas.

"Wow," Dave exclaimed to himself as he turned into the parking lot entrance, "Gorgeous!"

Walking into a spacious lobby toward the reception desk, he was surprised to see several short lines of people waiting to register. The Moon Palace Resort was apparently a very popular resort in Ocho Rios. The lines moved quickly, and he soon found himself talking to an attractive young black woman.

"Mr. Hawthorne, we welcome you to the Moon Palace. Your room is on the fourth floor. It's a corner room. It has a wrap-around balcony with sweeping views of the beaches and ocean. I think you'll enjoy it," she said.

"'Sounds great. I'm sure I will. Thank you," Dave replied.

It was just after three o'clock in the afternoon when, once in his room, Dave changed out of his travel clothes to a short sleeve, white polo shirt and tan shorts. He donned his white tennis shoes and headed back down to the lobby. He saw a young man who looked to be in a concierge uniform standing behind what was labeled an *Information Desk*. Dave approached him and the man perked up.

"Can I help you, sir?" the man asked.

"Yes. Can you tell me if a Mr. Kent Ormsby might be available? I'd like to speak with him. It won't take long," Dave said.

"Sure. May I ask what this is about?"

"I can't really discuss it outside of with Mr. Ormsby. Purely business. I'm Special Agent Neal Hawthorne, FBI," Dave pulled his badge and credentials from his pocket and briefly flashed them.

"Oh, I see. Kent is probably somewhere around the restaurant area. I'll bring him here to you, Mr. Hawthorne. Please have a seat in one of our leather easy chairs over by the cocktail table," the man replied, pointing to a small sitting area.

"Thank you."

Dave sat on a very comfortable leather chair and picked up a copy of a recent "*I Do Jamaica*" magazine off the cocktail table. He began browsing through its pages, amazed at how colorful and attractive they were.

"Special Agent Hawthorne?" a voice came from a male voice very near him.

Dave glanced up to see a tall man in island shirt and light beige slacks standing over him. He hadn't noticed the man approach him.

"Yes," Dave said and stood, "Are you Kent Ormsby?" Dave smiled.

"Yes, I am he. I'm pleased to meet you, ah, Special Agent Hawthorne. I understand you want to talk with me. By the way, how would you like me to address you?" Kent said.

"Just call me by my first name, Neal. The special agent thing is often overdone," Dave answered.

"Thank you for that, Neal. How can I assist you?"

"I'm here in Ocho Rios to examine the circumstances surrounding the death of Roy Phillips. Mr. Phillips and his wife, Sharon, were staying here at your hotel."

"Yes. What a terrible tragedy. Nothing like that has ever happened here, especially on Main Street or near our grounds," Kent said.

"Really? There's not much crime down here?" Dave asked.

"Not brutal, violent crimes of that nature. Pickpockets, shoplifters, yes, but murders are extremely rare."

"I see. Can you take me to the spot in the parking lot where the assault on Mr. Phillips took place?"

"Certainly. The yellow police crime scene banner tapes have been removed. That happened yesterday. Follow me please."

Dave followed Kent from the lobby to a side corridor and then out a side door from the hotel. Apparently, there were several parking lots. At first, they walked through the center of the lot and angled their way left, pausing near its edge.

"It's three o'clock in the afternoon, and as you can see, this lot is fairly empty. This is the lot people use to arrive for dining at our restaurant, that is, those who aren't currently guests at the hotel. Things don't pick up until dinner time here in this lot."

"I can understand that."

"Well, we're standing where it happened, Neal. This is where Mr. Phillips' body was found. Everything has been cleaned up since the police issued an approval to do so."

"Roy died right here. Damn," Dave said.

"You knew Mr. Phillips?" Kent asked.

"Yes, Mr. Phillips was also FBI, but he was on vacation down here in Jamaica, so he probably didn't bring his badge and credentials along with him," Dave replied.

"I see."

"Roy's wife, Sharon, said that you and Roy had discussed in a short chat about a table of presumably Taiwanese men in the dining area. Is that true?"

"Yes, I mentioned to Mr. Phillips that there were some inconsistencies in the story the group had once related to me. First, there had been an error in their billing during a prior visit and while I was trying to contact them to reconcile it, I called just about all the hotels in Ocho Rios. None of the hotels had a Taiwanese or Chinese tour group. Second, this group must have been on an extended stay and always came to dinner on the weekends in two vans with *Coral Island Tours* labels on the side panels. I was curious so I did some further checking and found that no such tourist agency even exists on Jamaica's north shore with that name."

"Those are very interesting observations. Thank you, Kent. Hmmm," Dave said.

"One more thing...this is, I think, both interesting and possibly important. My security personnel related to me that as they roamed the parking lots, they noticed the tires on those vans were caked with mud. Mud that had a reddish tinge—almost certainly from bauxite, aluminum ore. Bauxite mines in Jamaica are generally up in or near the Blue Mountains south of here, so that's where I assumed they were coming from. That is, where they're staying. As I explained to Mr. Phillips, Jamaican bauxite puts a reddish tint to the soil. Also, everything I've just told you, I also related to the police," Kent said.

"Kent, thank you very much for sharing all this. On that note, do you happen to know who in the police department might be in charge of the investigation?"

"Yes. Detective Lt. Harold Winston. The police department is actually very close to here...just a couple blocks due south on DaCosta Drive. Harold is a good man with a good reputation. As an aside, he likes to go by "Harry." He occasionally brings his family here for dinner," Kent responded.

"The police department...is it within walking distance or do I need to drive?" Dave asked.

"Oh, walking distance for sure. It's just several blocks away. Neal, I saw Mr. Phillips' body. It was gruesome. He had been stabbed multiple times in the side of his body and neck. That's not the viciousness that one thinks of when one contemplates a robbery. Whoever did this, I would very much like to see him or them brought to justice," Kent said.

"I appreciate that very much, Kent. Rest assured that we will be doing everything in our power to see that happens. Thank you, and I'm very pleased to have met you," Dave said. He stuck out his hand. After shaking hands, Dave and Kent nodded to each other and parted company. Dave turned toward the entrance to the lot and checked his watch—not quite four o'clock.

"Well, there's no time like the present, Sherlock. I might as well see if Detective Winston is still on duty today," Dave muttered to himself, walking out of the parking lot in the direction of the police station.

The avenues got a lot less busy after leaving the area of the main drag. The air was warm, thick, and humid. He could feel the fabric of his polo shirt clinging to the perspiration on his chest and back. He wriggled his torso to shake the feeling. After an under fifteen-minute stroll, Dave turned left on DaCosta Drive, and directly ahead, there it stood, the building housing the Ocho Rios Police Department. Holding onto the metal railing, he walked up the four concrete steps and then eased though the glass doors.

"Good afternoon, sir, how may I help you?" a uniformed woman behind the counter said with a Jamaican accent.

"If he's still here, I'd like to speak with Detective Lt. Harold Winston, please," Dave answered.

"And your business with Detective Winston is what?"

"I'm Special Agent Neal Hawthorne, FBI. My business, Miss, is with Detective Lt. Harold Winston and only him," Dave said in a firm but monotone voice. He pulled out his credentials case and badge and flashed them.

"I see. I'll call him and see if he's free," the uniformed woman said.

After a few minutes of low tone telephone conversation, the woman looked up at Dave. "Come through the gate, sir. It's not locked. I'll take you back to Detective Winston's office," she said.

Dave pushed the wooden gate open and followed the uniformed woman down the hallway. Halfway down the corridor, she knocked and opened a door on her right.

"Detective Winston, this is Special Agent Hawthorne," she said, letting Dave in the office and then quietly closing the door behind him.

"Well now, we don't have many visits from the United States FBI, so I'm pleased to meet you. Is it Neal?" Harold asked, rising from his chair and walking to the front of his desk.

"Yes, Detective, Neal is just fine," Dave replied.

"Then I'm Harry to you. What's on your mind this afternoon?" Harry asked.

"Roy Phillips."

"Oh. And your interest is what?"

"Phillips was also FBI, but he was on vacation outside the states, so he didn't carry his badge and credentials down here

51

with him. I've been sent to talk to the police here about the conclusion that a robbery gone bad was the causal factor. I trust you can understand that," Dave said.

"Yes, I do. I just wanted to know the FBI's interest. Have you spoken with Kent Ormsby at Christopher's restaurant?"

"I have. Kent sent me to you."

"I see. Kent's a good man."

"He is indeed. He said the same thing about you, Harry," Dave said.

"You're wondering about the robbery aspect. The report indicates we believe that was the causal factor for his death. And is it credible?" Harry said, leaning back to sit on the edge of his desk.

"Correct."

"The fact is, Neal, that I don't believe it myself, but I have no other prima facie evidence to go on. I have nothing else to pursue." Harry said.

"And any connection with the alleged Taiwanese or Chinese tour group that was at the restaurant that night?"

"So, Kent shared that with you. Right. The fact remains that I have no evidence that would specifically connect them to the murder of Roy Phillips. Nothing. I know what Kent must have told you about them not staying at any hotel here in Ocho Rios and about the false name of the tour company. We're examining that on its own merit. Nevertheless, neither of those things are crimes per se. At this point, I can't put action to any suspicion that I might have further on that. I don't see any judicial grounds in this case."

"Thank you, Harry, thanks for being so forthright with me. What do you personally suspect is going on with this Taiwanese Chinese tour group that's apparently on an extended stay here in Jamaica?"

"All right. Number one, they're not a tour group. I feel confident of that. Number two, they must be residing somewhere up in the Blue Mountains, and perhaps doing something not at all related to bauxite mining," Harry said.

"Interesting. Why do you say that?"

"Jamaica is an independent country and has been since 1962. However, we're still a member of the British Commonwealth of Nations, although I suspect that may change soon. From what I've been able to gather, our Governor General and the Parliament authorized China to lease an already existing site up in the Blue Mountains for bauxite mining. In addition, I've heard also that the Chinese are free to export the bauxite they mine, aluminum ore, back to China free of any tariffs. Apparently though, it appears that's not happening."

"Really? What concerns you, Harry?"

"We police here in town of Ocho Rios don't get up into the Blue Mountains except maybe occasionally on our own free time. We do that occasionally for hiking and such. However, some sheriff's deputies do roam that area on daily patrols. I know a few of them as friends and several have shared with me that lots of heavy equipment, trucks, have been going and are still going into the mining site, but so far, after months and months of some sort of operation taking place there, no bauxite is coming out for export. No ore that's been mined is moving down from the mining site to the port of St. Ann's Bay for loading on freighters. None. Still, I have had to remind myself that it's not remotely within my jurisdiction to investigate why that may be," Harry said.

"Wow. I see. Thanks for that, Harry. Can you tell me how I might be able to get up to near that bauxite mine site the Chinese are leasing from here?" Dave asked.

53

"Neal, first of all, I would caution you against that. The Blue Mountains got their name from the constant mist enveloping them. The mountains are shrouded in mist that gives things a blueish tinge. The timberland is basically a craggy, sloping jungle-like rainforest that smothers the hillsides. It's a wet, damp environment. In our rainy season, August through October, mini waterfalls develop and there are occasional landslides. This is June, so you're okay in that regard. You would travel around Hollywell Park which is over 4,000 feet in altitude. That's quite an ascent when you consider you'll be coming up from sea level," Harry said.

"Wow. In a way, though, it sounds beautiful," Dave answered.

"It is truly gorgeous in the daytime. The landscape however, it's quite rough. Perhaps more importantly, you should know that it's also been related to me that in addition to all the equipment going into the site, chain-link fences with razor ribbon attached on top have been apparently erected along with armed guards. Sheriff's deputies have reported that to me. I have to expect that our Governor General and Parliament are aware of this, but nevertheless, whether they are or not, I have to accept that they exist as a condition of the international lease they gave China."

"Okay."

"Now, to your question about how to get there: if you drive west out of Ocho Rios, you will soon see that a branch of Highway A3 splits off to your left and heads up into the interior. There are a multitude of forest roads off A3, but the one immediately after Moneague Lake to the left, east, is the one to follow. You would stick with that winding sometimes asphalt, sometimes dirt, road to Guys Hill and Castleton. You can avoid all these intermediate routes, however, if you drive first along the north coast to Annotto Bay, that's east of here on the Coastal Highway, and then take another branch of A3 into the interior. That route is more direct. However, after traveling through and past the Hollywell Forest and finally to Springhill, the roads become very rough mountain roads. It can be a bone-rattling ride. The Chinese mining site is between Springhill and Wakefield. Wakefield is a bit further south," Harry explained.

"Thanks, Harry. As soon as I get back to my room, I'll write it all down," Dave said.

"No need, I'll do that for you now, before you leave," Harry replied.

"You are a super guy. I have to admit that," Dave said, as Harry returned to his chair and pulled out a lined sheet of paper.

"Again, please remember that I don't recommend your going there. It could be dangerous. Your colleague, Roy Phillips, may have actually become a bit too curious in that parking lot, but as I explained, I have no evidence to prove that. Let me write these directions down for you," Harry said as he dropped into his chair.

The last thoughts through Dave's mind as Harry jotted down the directions was that he needed to go to the Montego Bay airport and call Langley first thing in the morning. He had noticed phone booths located there with commercial outside lines. Dave felt this was necessary in the unlikely but still possible event that his cell phone could have somehow been compromised.

He had to assume worst case. He needed to see this alleged bauxite mining site, but he also knew he would prefer some armed backup along with him to do so.

CHAPTER 9

Montego Bay, Jamaica
Wednesday morning, June 14th

Dave rose early at 6:00 AM. He ambled from his bed to the shower, toweled afterward, then climbed into a burgundy polo, tan chinos, and brown loafers. He packed his pistol, mags, and ammo in his locked suitcase in the hotel room. He didn't see any need for them. He stuffed his passport and driver's license with his badge and credentials into a rear pants pocket. After taking the elevators to the first floor, he grabbed coffee and breakfast crepes with slices of bananas and strawberries at the Café Bistro off the lobby.

Some minutes later, he climbed into his Toyota Highlander. The morning drive west to the Montego Bay airport was beautiful, the sand, ocean, and sky all filling up with the sun's light and coming alive once again. Other than occasional glances toward the Caribbean, Dave was too preoccupied with his thoughts to become engaged with the views. Instead, he went over in his mind what he would say to Jack Barrett.

He finally pulled into the airport's parking lot and chose a spot near the *Arrivals* doors. He ambled into the area of the baggage claim. It was here that he'd seen the phone booths. The baggage area was nearly empty. Not more than two or three people meandering about. The baggage handling conveyors were silent, unmoving.

Dave noticed his footsteps had a hollow, echoing sound to them as he walked across the tiled floor. Apparently, no jets came into Montego Bay this early in the day, not even from Great Britain. Dave had heard that a lot of Brits came down here on vacation, but evidently, there were no arrivals this early in the morning. He chose the last booth in a line of eight and dialed the number for Langley main.

"Langley Center, how may I help you today," a female voice responded.

"Dave McClure for Jack Barrett, please," Dave replied.

"Good morning, Mr. McClure. I'll put you through."

After two rings, Jack Barrett picked up his phone.

"Barrett," Jack exclaimed.

"Mr. Barrett, this is Dave McClure."

"Hi Dave, good to hear from you. Do you have something for us already?"

"I think so, sir, yes."

"Well, you couldn't have picked a better time to call. Pete Novak is sitting here in front of me. We were just finishing up discussing some of the takes from this morning's staff meeting. I'll put us on speaker. Are you using your mobile phone?"

"No, sir. I drove back to the Montego Bay airport. I'm in one of a bunch of commercial phone booths."

"Great thinking on that. You're on speaker. Please continue," Jack said.

"Sir, I've spoken with Kent Ormsby, the restaurant manager at Christopher's, and after that also with Detective Lt. Harold Winston of the Ocho Rios Police Department. Detective Winston is in charge of the investigation into Roy Phillips' murder. The bottom line is that Winston himself doesn't find it credible that Roy Phillips' death was the result of a robbery gone bad, but he indicated that he doesn't have any evidence to pursue it further. And in both my discussions with Ormsby and Winston, things keep circling back to this Chinese tour group which both Ormsby and Winston said looks more and more like they aren't really a tour group at all."

"Go on," Jack said.

"They can't locate the group staying anywhere in Ocho Rios and in fact the tour company logo on their vans is a name that doesn't even exist for any company on the north shore. Winston confided that he suspects Roy might have become too curious about the group, too inquisitive, and whatever his presence instigated, the Chinese ultimately saw him as a threat."

"'Sounds like a reasonable assessment," Jack said.

"Winston also related that he's received curious reports from deputy sheriffs who roam their patrol areas up in the mountains. The Chinese government has apparently leased a bauxite mine site up there in the Blue Mountains from the Jamaican government, but it doesn't appear that any bauxite mining is taking place at all. Winston cautioned me against going up there alone. He stated that other than the presence of jungle-like mountainous terrain, the mountains are immersed in mist, and the site is surrounded by chain link fences with razor ribbon placed on top. And there's a noted presence of armed security guards," Dave said.

"Armed security guards and chain fences with razor ribbon? I agree with you—that doesn't sound like something that would be installed surrounding a bauxite mine. Pete, anything?" Jack said.

"I agree. Jack, it sounds like it might be wise for us to make a journey up into those mountains, locate this alleged mining site, and take a good look," Pete said.

"Right. Dave, you gathered some good intel. Great work. Go ahead and return to Ocho Rios and stay put at the hotel. Unwind. I'll be sending Tony Robertson down to join you. Tony will be bringing with him two Colt M4 Assault Carbines with acoustic silencers, you know, just in case things get dicey. He'll also bring two of those multi-spectral camouflage suits that you used up in Maine a couple years ago. If you recall, those suits can actually bend light and have a Kevlar lining to boot. They collect all the natural ambient light that's present in time and place as well as light in the infrared, thermal spectrum as well. Those high-tech suits make you just about invisible. And they can elude night vision optics just as well," Jack explained.

"I remember those from the Maine operation up in Bar Harbor. Remarkable technology," Dave replied.

He'll also bring a special camera for you to use that operates in low light and even in total darkness. Use that to take photos of whatever you find worthy in your observations. Okay?" Jack said.

"That all sounds great, Mr. Barrett. Time frame?"

"Tony should be arriving there sometime tomorrow afternoon on one of our Air Division jets as you did. He should be calling you on your mobile to let you know when his flight will arrive. That will give you time to drive there and pick him up. We'll have him registered at the Moon Palace along with you too."

"Okay, sir."

"Dave, the mission...I just want you two to go up there to reconnoiter, to see if you can get a handle on about what's going on there. From what Detective Winston told you combined with what's been reported to us from Naval intelligence about continued confrontations in the Gulf of Mexico with Chinese submarines, there's a possibility we could have serious trouble brewing in the gulf. It's no secret to anyone that China has been flexing its military muscle lately. And as such, it could be a bit dangerous near that site up in those mountains. Nevertheless, I think it's time to make those bastards consider taking a few steps back," Jack said.

"I understand, sir. We'll exercise due caution," Dave replied.

"In that case and if at all possible, do all you can to try to avoid a fire fight. Those Kevlar-lined suits should protect you. On the other hand, however, always remember that you're authorized to take whatever action you decide you need to in order to protect yourselves," Pete chimed in.

"Message received, Mr. Novak. And thanks," Dave said.

"Pete, anything else come to mind?" Jack asked.

"No, I think we're good to go with this as we've just planned. We'll see if Dave and Tony might have an opportunity to determine what, and if anything nefarious, is taking place in Jamaica's Blue Mountains," Pete answered.

"Right. Dave, take care. We'll be waiting to hear from you. Afterward, you'll be returning to Langley with any photos you take for our tech folks to analyze. Excellent work thus far, Agent McClure," Jack said.

"Thank you, sir."

"Barrett out."

CHAPTER 10

Moon Palace Resort, Ocho Rios
Jamaica
Late Wednesday afternoon, June 14th

D ave sat comfortably reclined on a chaise lounge at the
rear of the hotel's covered terrace area. He faced out to
the sunlit blue Caribbean Sea. Killing time. Several young
kids were running along the beach chasing sand crabs
while their parents watched and sipped what looked to be
Margaritas. Dave chuckled at the sight. He set his glass on
the side table next to him. After a light sip, it was still holding just a tad less than a thumb of Redbreast Irish whiskey
with two cubes. His mobile phone rang. He pulled it from
his belt holster.

"Hello," Dave said.

"Dave, this is Tony."

"Hey buddy, it's good to hear your voice. Do you have
any idea when're you coming in?"

"Yes, noontime, twelve o'clock tomorrow, Thursday."

"That's an early flight."

"Well, you know, the Agency pilots don't have to follow the commercial routes. It's a lot faster that way. Dave, Pete Novak said we'll need to wait until this coming Friday evening to go operational. He said something about having to follow the vans into the mountains from Christopher's restaurant, or something like that. He got a country-brief brought over to him from the State Department. He said it looks like it's all jungle-like terrain up there in the Blue Mountains. He said you'd brief me up on everything I need to know when I get to Ocho Rios," Tony replied.

"That's correct. That's how Detective Harry Winston described those mountains to me. And they're blanketed in mist. That's how they got their name. The heavy mist that cloaks them — the Blue Mountains. Basically, it's sort of a sloped rain forest. So yeah, it would be best for us to try to follow the vans. We'll use only our fog lights on the Highlander for the mountain roads. That's if the Chinese come to the restaurant this coming Friday night. I'm hoping they do. They've been steady regulars so far. Good. In any case, I'll be there to meet you at the airport. No customs, right?"

"That's right. Mr. Barrett said I'll breeze through, and everything we need will be in diplomatic pouches."

"Great. We'll play beach bums for that afternoon!" Dave laughed, "See you then, Tony. By the way, how's the arm?" Dave asked.

"My surgeons and neurologist said I'm one hundred percent. I think that's why Barrett and Novak are sending me."

"That's super. Don't drink on the plane, Tony!" Dave said.

"Really? Don't drink on the plane? Some friend you are. It's an Agency aircraft, Dave, so I doubt they'll have any liquor, but it really depends on the pilot and crew you get. Some of them always have a little booze secreted in a cache somewhere on the aircraft. I'm sure you've heard stories like I have about those Air America pilots in Southeast Asia...there were always cases of liquor onboard. Anyway, if they do, hey, I'm having at least two vodka gimlets on the way down! After all, it is Montego Bay that I'm flying into, isn't it?" Tony answered.

"I guess there's no stopping you from doing that. All right, just take it easy. By the way, Tony, is there any other identity documentation you have that I need to be aware of?" Dave snickered.

"No. I'm travelling as me, Anthony Joseph Robertson. I think Barrett and Novak are of the mindset that as long as you're documented as an FBI agent, we should be okay and able to avoid any issues."

"I agree with them. Good. See you tomorrow, Buddy. You'll love Ocho Rios...it's gorgeous. Have a good flight down," Dave responded.

Tony clicked off and the line went silent.

Dave had been sitting for almost an hour on a metal bench in the air-conditioned baggage claim area of the Montego Bay airport when the baggage conveyers suddenly came alive and began moving. It was twelve o'clock noon. That was his cue. He walked across the baggage claim area toward the doors leading to the hangar where international government air-craft usually arrived and parked for debarkation. He showed his identification to the two security guards, and they immediately opened the doors for him.

Dave spotted it immediately...another Agency plane with no markings had just pulled up next to his own jet that was still parked in the hangar. Dave walked to its wingtip and paused as a gantry was being rolled up to the hatch. Tony was the first to step out the hatch. His hair was disheveled, his face pale. Dave's face wrinkled with concern. He walked to the gantry and then assisted Tony in walking down the last two steps.

"Tony, what's the matter. You look like twenty miles of bad road. Are you okay?" Dave asked.

"I'll be okay. I just need some rest. I had three or four shots of vodka, I don't know. I was feeling good and tried to doze off a bit, but I started having visions. Surreal, paranormal visions from the past. And damn, I found I couldn't relax or get a short nap. You were right about the booze. I should have laid off it. So, I'm a bit of a mess and in need of some rest." Tony replied.

"Visions?"

"Yeah, of that guy up in the Adirondack Mountains who we both got glimpses of. The guy who wasn't supposed to be there. For some reason, being on a plane and flying again along with the vodka, well, dammit, for some reason, it all rushed back to me. I couldn't shake it. It was nerve-wracking."

"You mean the guy whose face was painted half black and half red. The guy with the Mohawk haircut—Sheauga?" Dave asked.

"Shit. You even remember his name?" Tony exclaimed.

"It was him. Okay. Yes, Sheauga. The old Indian at the outfitter shop, Gyantwaka, told me all about him."

"Jeez, Dave. How do you remember that stuff?"

"Gyantwaka himself was one hundred percent Onondaga Iroquois. I don't know, but I myself haven't thought about it since then. I was able to somehow block it out for a long time. I needed to. And I admit it was spooky. A bit unreal."

"A bit unreal? Hell, it was unbelievable. Haunting. Well, I needed to get that out of my mind also. But on the way down here, it all came back for some reason. Damn."

"Tony, just take a chair over there and I'll go get your bags. How many, two?" Dave asked.

"Yeah, two, including the diplomatic pouch with the equipment. Maybe with Jamaica's island scenery and ocean air, I'll be able to shake this stuff off during the drive to Ocho Rios. I'll be okay, Dave. I just need a Mai Tai and some rest," Tony said.

"Rest, yes. The Mai Tai can wait. All right. All that's coming up. They're bringing your bags to us. Good. Let's get those and hit the road. Sound good?" Dave replied.

"Indeed, sir. I can't wait to see the views and the beaches." Tony said.

"We're off then."

The drive back to Ocho Rios and the Moon Palace hotel was uneventful. Tony was glued to the open windows, taking deep breaths of Caribbean Sea air, and gazing at the flowery foliage, palm trees, and beaches. He turned to Dave.

"I'm dying to change into shorts and a tee shirt and hit the beach. Maybe with a Mai Tai nearby."

"We'll have the time to do that this afternoon, so you have something to look forward to in the enjoyment arena. Afterward, we'll shower and have a grilled lobster dinner or something like that. It's tomorrow that we'll need to prep. Tony, you're sounding better, peppier," Dave answered.

"I feel it, too. This highway along the Jamaican north coast is awesome. Beautiful. I can't wait. Yeah, that old Sheauga memory of mine must've decided to take me along on a virtual hike back to New York and the Adirondacks!" Tony exclaimed.

"It's water under the bridge now. We'll be at the hotel in about ten minutes. I think you'll love your room," Dave said.

A weight had been lifted off Tony's back. He brushed his hair back and reclined in his seat. Smiling, he continued to enjoy the view out the windows.

CHAPTER 11

Moon Palace Resort, Ocho Rios
Jamaica
Thursday, June 15th

Thursday afternoon was filled mostly with beach time and a singular Mai Tai. Dave limited Tony to just one. Dave had a thumb of Redbreast Irish whiskey with two cubes. The two agreed that dinner at the hotel would be fine. As it went, they both had the grilled lobster and grinned while consuming it. Later, the evening in Dave's room was spent with Dave spinning Tony up. They both set their alarms for 06:30 AM to allow for an early breakfast and enough time for going over their equipment thoroughly.

On Friday morning, after breakfast at about nine o'clock, the two left the hotel to gas up the Highlander. On the way to the gas station and back, Tony's attention was still captured by all the colorful sights of the store fronts, bistros, and restaurants.

"Ocho Rios sure is a beautiful place," Tony said.

"Yeah, it is. A couple years from now, I'm going to bring Karen and little Carolyn down here. I think they'll love it," Dave replied.

"You're already envisioning life with a little girl, aren't you?" Tony asked.

"I suppose I am," Dave answered with a slight giggle.

"Nothing wrong with that, Buddy. Congratulations. I can't wait to see the little gal either."

"And you're going to be Uncle Tony."

"Uncle Tony? Wow! I'm going to love that. Thanks. *Uncle Tony*—jeez! That means I'll be part of the family!" Tony exclaimed.

"You already are."

They parked the Highlander in front of the hotel and went up to Tony's room to begin stripping down, cleaning, and loading their Colt M4 Assault Carbines and pistols as well as Dave's Beretta 92fs and Tony's Sig Sauer 229 Equinox. Tony was on the edge of his bed and Dave sat across from him on the couch. Between them, on the cocktail table, they sipped from ice teas and munched on an order of nachos with salsa that had been delivered to the room. It took about an hour and a half for all the firearms.

"Done. Good. Now all we have left is to unfold these multi-spectral camouflage suits. I hope they work as advertised," Tony said.

"They do. I used one on an op up in Maine years ago. They really make you just about invisible. I was shot up there one night—right in the middle of my chest. The Kevlar lining saved my life," Dave replied.

"That's certainly good to hear. When do we take off?"

"We'll head over to Christopher's about 5:30 p.m. Don't forget to put your hiking shoes in the Highlander, too. And hopefully, those Chinese guys will show up tonight."

"Right. I'm ready for this. It'll be the first op I've been on since my arm healed up. I'm actually looking forward to it, misty rain forest or not."

"I wouldn't be too eager, Tony, but you know that. Fact is, I'm ready to go, too. Let's carry all this stuff down and pack it into the Highlander. Then we have to come back up to the room or maybe go out on the terrace and chill for an hour or so," Dave said

The two meandered to the elevator, took it down to the lobby and then ambled out to the terrace. They declined any alcoholic drinks and ordered two iced teas. They watched as the sun was waning across the beach. People gradually meandered away, heading for their rooms and dinner.

"Time's up, Tony. Let's head upstairs, wash up, and meet back down here in ten minutes. We're off to Christopher's restaurant," Dave said.

"Will do, sir," Tony responded.

The drive was short. Both Dave and Tony noticed the air was cooling as evening approached. It was half past five o'clock when the two men walked into the restaurant. They chose a table near the waters of Harmosa Cove and ordered shrimp cocktails and crab-stuffed lobster tails. Kent Ormsby visited with other incoming customers and ambled over to Dave and Tony's table.

"Neal, good evening. Thanks for returning to Christopher's for dinner. I see you've brought company," Kent said.

"Thanks, Kent. This is Tony Robertson, one of my colleagues in the Bureau," Dave answered.

"Another agent. Well now, it seems apparent that you are indeed taking Roy Phillips' death very seriously. I like that. And appropriately so, I would add. By the way, I just received a call from my security folks…the Chinese group has arrived once again, as expected. Every weekend they come here. They'll be walking in soon from the parking lot, so I'll leave you two to your duties. God speed," Kent said.

"Thanks, Kent," Dave replied.

"Things are shaping up nicely, compadre," Dave said, glancing at Tony.

"Si, mi amigo," Tony responded as at least twelve Chinese men took two tables pushed together at the other end of the dining area, sat, and immediately began chatting.

"We're going to pay early, then wait until they leave, and pull out of the parking lot. We'll be playing catch up for a bit, but once we enter the mountains, we're going to keep a good distance back from the vans anyway," Dave said.

"Roger that." Dave and Tony enjoyed the dinner. It was scrumptious. And to avoid creating any suspicion, during the course of the meal the two avoided any glance toward the Chinese.

Dusk transformed to night. Strings of small white lights lit up around the dining area casting a mild glow onto the seated diners. At about eight-thirty after an exceptionally long dinner, it appeared that the Chinese group had paid their bill and were now just rising from their chairs to leave. Dave had paid their own check twenty minutes earlier.

"Game time. Let's give them a couple minutes, then head to the parking lot for the Highlander. We'll arm up while we're cruising on our way up the road," Dave said.

"Right."

The vans took a left out from Christopher's onto Main Street and headed east through town. At the slower town speeds, Dave was able to wriggle into his shoulder holster and Tony to clip on his belt paddle holster. The vans exited the town limits onto the north Coastal Highway. Dave followed at a discreet distance, assuming the Chinese were headed for Annotto Bay and the branch of the A3 highway that Detective Harry Winston had mentioned. About a half hour later, Dave saw his assumption was correct. At the intersection in Annotto Bay, the vans took a right turn on A3 ascending into the mountains.

Entering the mountainous, rainforest-like jungle, it was as though blinds had closed in the sky overhead. The several canopies of trees all around them turned everything outside of the windows into the blackest night. Roadside lamps were present but few and far between. Dave switched off his headlights and clicked on only the fog lights to keep them safely on the road surface. He could barely see the taillights of the vans, but that was a good thing. The Highlander's distant fog lights would hardly be noticeable to the Chinese drivers that far ahead of them.

As they rolled along, they passed through the dimly lit villages of Broadgate and Devon Pen. Later, entering the larger village of Castleton, the vans took a left turn onto the Hollywell Park Road. Detective Winston was indeed correct when he described this as one of the 'very rough mountain roads that would be a bone-rattling ride.' Dave and Harry took jarring bounces up and down as the Highlander shuddered along the pothole-ridden, furrowed dirt and rock road. It was back wrenching and mind-numbing, a jolting ride as the SUV vibrated left and right on the still ascending mountain road.

Over an hour later, they exited the park, ultimately cruising through the tiny village of Wakefield. Dave slowed down as the vans went left, turning north at the intersection with Highway B1.

"That's what Winston told me—the bauxite mine site was between Wakefield and Springhill. We must be very close,"

Dave said as they also took the left turn onto B1. We'll let them get a little further ahead."

Roughly ten minutes later, Tony turned to Dave and pointed up to the top middle of the windshield.

"Dave, look up. Straight ahead. You can see some bits of sky over the road. It's lit up. There must be some bright lights ahead, just off to the right. Maybe…"

"Right. The Chinese bauxite mine. I'll do a U-turn up here and park off the road on the other side. We may have to peel out of here fast. We'll slip on those multi-spectral camouflage suits and work our way through the jungle over there. Be careful—it looks like it's still rocky and craggy under the ground foliage."

"Got it. Bring our M4s?"

"Yes, and let's twist the silencers on our pistols. Do have your mini-Maglite? I think we're gonna need them in the thick forest," Dave said, jerking the Highlander as far off the road and into the jungle as he could.

Dave and Tony crossed the road, tentatively winding their way around trees and brush into the bushy thick jungle. Both could feel the jagged edges of the rocky turf beneath the soles of their boots.

"Man, this is rough ground," Tony muttered.

"It is for sure. As you can sense it, we're still climbing upslope. I think it'll be better for us to get above the site and take photos downward," Dave answered.

In their clamber uphill, as they came within twenty yards of it, they saw a perimeter steel chain link fence lit up by overhead lights. They dropped to all fours. Two guards with rifles slung over their shoulders passed between two large vehicles in the compound. They soon disappeared from sight.

"Damn, those guys were wearing military uniforms with a red star on their caps. Bauxite mining, my ass. Jamaica's filled to the brim with bauxite. Who the hell would come to steal any of it? So why the heavy security?"

"Let's continue around this way and staying this distance from the fence. In a few minutes, we'll be where we need to be for photos."

They both could feel the moisture trickling down the rocks under them, slowly soaking their shirts. It gave their chests an added chill.

Dave froze, placing his hand on Tony's shoulders to alert him. He could hear twigs snapping and the branches of brush being pushed back, cracking. Someone was approaching and was now very close. The Chinese must have security patrols outside the fence line as well. Dave and Tony eased down on their stomachs, lying flat as possible on the rocky soil.

They both heard what sounded like the metallic clicks of a round being chambered. A safety being clicked off. The guard was coming directly toward them. He may have sensed their presence. The guard's eyes scanned the undergrowth. Not good, however, all the Chinese sentry could see was foliage, but foliage that was shifting, moving? The multi-spectral camouflage suits were doing their job nicely. Was there an animal in the underbrush? The guard was just several feet away. He slowly raised his rifle, leveling it to his hip.

Dave suddenly lunged both of his legs forward and sweeping them to his left, striking the guard in both of his ankles. Dave swept the guards legs out from under him. The Chinese man's hands abruptly left his rifle to stretch out and break his fall. He thumped to the ground just feet from Dave and instantly reached for his rifle.

Dave fired his Beretta twice. Both acoustically dampened rounds thudded into the man's forehead, plunging through his brain. His mouth gaped open wide as though to shout. Spurts of blood and pieces of bone erupted from the two head wounds. The sentry's head went limp as his eyes rolled upward in their sockets.

"First bullet," Dave whispered.

"What?" Tony murmured back.

"Nothing. Look at the red star embroidered on his cap. Damn...these guys are Communist Chinese military. Well, I guess this is as good a place as any. Let's move closer to the fence line and take some photos."

"Okay."

The two men inched forward.

"Jeez, this ground isn't just damp. I'm getting soaked. I'm cold," Tony whispered.

"Detective Winston did call this place a rainforest. Back in the Highlander, I'll turn up the heat and we'll warm up."

Ending his crawl forward, Dave pulled the special camera from his pocket and began snapping photos of rows of large, wheeled vehicles supporting long, rectangular metal boxes. Inside each of the elongated boxes there appeared to rest six to eight large tubes.

"Whaddya suppose they are?" Tony muttered.

"Could be sections of large conduit pipes for moving the bauxite from the mine."

"I guess that makes sense," Tony answered, whispering.

After taking more photo shots of the different kinds of vehicles, equipment, and uniformed people moving in the compound, Dave and Tony edged themselves backward away from the fence and lights. After twenty yards, they rose off their bellies to all fours. They came back upon the dead guard lying in the underbrush.

"What do we do with him?" Tony asked.

"We'll take him with us. You take my rifle and his rifle. I'll carry him. We'll dump him somewhere off a cliff near the far edge of the Hollywell Forest Park. It'll be somewhere that the Chinese won't think to find him, and they won't know what happened to him. Maybe he went AWOL." Dave said.

"I love it when you use your noodle, Dave. Do you think you can manage carrying him by yourself?"

"Yeah. I'll get some blood on me, so I'll have to bear with that, but I can manage. He's not that big a guy," Dave replied.

After going slow and stumbling a bit through the thick jungle, they reached the B1 Highway. Dave lifted the hatch-back and dumped the Chinese guard in the Highlander. He pulled the cargo cover over him. Instead of going back south to the park road, Dave turned the Highlander around and headed north on B1.

"Where are we going now?" Tony asked.

"I've studied the maps. This is a far better road than that Hollywell Forest Park Road. B1 comes out on the north Coastal Highway at Buff Bay, just east of Annotto Bay. We'll dump the Chinese guy after we pass Balcarres. That's about fifteen minutes from here," Dave explained.

"Good thinking. What's next then?"

"When we get back to the hotel, we'll pack up and check out in the morning. We'll drive to the Montego Bay airport and fly home. We need to get these photos to Novak and Barrett for the analysis techies to examine."

"Roger that. Mission accomplished. Return to base. Do you think I'll have time for a cup of coffee?"

"Maybe. Come on, no. Let's concentrate on getting the hell out of here as quickly as we can. Who knows? What if the Chinese by chance do find the guard's body with two 9mm bullet holes in his head? Then what? No, the jet is waiting for us. We'll be up and away out of Ocho Rios first thing in the morning."

"All right. Maybe they'll still have some vodka on the plane," Tony chuckled, glancing to Dave who smirked back at him.

"Once we're on the plane, I'll call Jack Barrett to see if he's okay with waiting until Monday to look at the photos, or if he wants to see us over the weekend," Dave said.

"Okay. We're off."

CHAPTER 12

Langley Center, McLean
Virginia
Monday, June 18th

Jack Barrett had told Dave during his call from the plane that coming to see him Monday morning would be fine. He'd cancel his staff meeting, have Pete Novak in his office, and see Dave and Tony at 07:30 AM. That gave Dave time to spend with Karen over the weekend.

Karen was glad to see Dave return in one piece, especially so, as he related to her about having to kill the Chinese sentry up in the Blue Mountains of Jamaica. She had a bundle of questions though, which he didn't yet have the information approval for and couldn't answer her concerns.

At 07:30 AM on Monday morning, Dave and Tony ascended in the lobby elevator at Langley. They glanced at each other with deadpan eyes, not knowing what to expect, particularly with Novak present. Barbara greeted them with a smile, knocked, and opened Jack's door a crack. He beckoned her in.

"Good morning, gentlemen. Please have a seat. Dave, please give me that camera you have, and I'll plug the wire from my USB port into it. The monitor screen is behind me. I don't consider any of these photos to be classified…not yet," Jack said.

Dave handed over the camera. Jack plugged it in, then moved to one of the leather seats in front of his desk. Pete sat to the side of Jack. On the 72" screen, images of oriental men abruptly appeared in Chinese Communist military uniforms walking through a brightly lit nighttime compound.

"My, my, what have we here? Chinese military troops in Jamaica protecting a bauxite mine? A bit strange, don't you think, Pete?" Jack asked.

"I agree, Jack. I wonder what the hell's going on. Dave, you said you shot and killed a guard outside the fence with two acoustically silenced rounds?" Pete asked.

"That's right, sir. Tony and I were on the ground on our stomachs and crawling toward the chain link fence line when this sentry came upon us. I heard him chamber a round and click off the safety on his assault rifle. He raised his rifle to his hip and was about to open fire. With my own legs jolting forward, I swept his legs out from under him. He stretched out his arm from the rifle to break his fall, but immediately reached back for the weapon. I immediately put two silenced rounds into his head," Dave replied.

"Sounds like excellent reflexes on your part. Way to go, Dave. And you said that you dumped his body down a ravine on the way driving back. A ravine that was off a pretty good distance from the site itself?" Pete said.

"Yes, sir. I doubt they could ever recover it," Dave responded.

"Superb work, Dave," Jack said, smiling, "Yes, once again, inspired work. And you fired the first bullet. That's why you're both still here with us."

"Thank you, sir," Dave said, glancing at Tony.

"These are dark shots but still well enough defined. I think they're going to be discernable enough," Pete said.

"Yeah, Chinese military uniforms. I'll be damned. That detective you spoke with was spot-on. I suspect this site isn't about bauxite mining at all. And with guards both inside and outside the perimeter, eh? Damn. And there's those large vehicle-mounted rectangular boxes each with a large tube laid out inside. You think they might be conduit pipes for bauxite coming from the mine, Dave?" Jack exclaimed.

"That was just a WAG, sir. I really don't have a clue as to what they really are," Dave answered.

"Jack, could you have Barbara call Dan Alconbury and ask him to come up here. He's in Analysis. I've seen something like this before," Pete said.

"All right. What's his focus, his area of expertise, Pete? Why do we need him?" Jack asked.

"Missiles. All kinds. I have a hunch. A bad hunch," Pete responded.

"Missiles? Damn. You think..." Jack said, picking up his phone. He asked Barb to get Dan Alconbury up to his office.

It took a little more than five minutes, but soon Barb opened the door and let Dan enter the office.

"Dan, have a seat and look at the photo above me. It was taken a couple days ago in the Blue Mountains of Jamaica by Dave McClure here. Do you think you see anything that might bear on your area of expertise? Anything there that strikes you?" Jack asked.

"Sonofabitch. Shit, you said these things are in Jamaica?" Dan asked.

"Yes, and Chinese military personnel were seen all over that compound," Pete said.

"Mr. Barrett, I was hoping that one day I might have an opportunity to see these. Those are Hong Niao cruise missiles. Chinese Land Attack Cruise Missile launchers, LACMs, but these here are bigger than any I've seen photos of, at least compared to the size of the personnel walking by them. Damn, and this is in Jamaica?" Dan said.

"Cruise missiles? Shit is right. You said Hong Niao or something like that?" Jack asked with a questioning look.

"Yes, sir. The Hong Niao, HN as they're referred to in China's missile series. I'm familiar with the HN-1A, HN-1B and even the HN-5B series. However, these babies must be the new, state-of-the-art HN-6B missiles that I've read intelligence reports about. I thought they were in the prototype stage, just coming out of research and development, but the Chinese must be way ahead of that, past initial operational test and evaluation. If these are the HN-6Bs, they're supersonic, satellite guided, and nuclear capable. They carry advanced, long-range topographical data as back-up in their onboard computers. As you may know, sir, cruise missiles travel at very low altitude, following the nap-of-the-earth topography, and are extremely difficult to detect, track, and destroy while they're in flight," Dan went on to explain.

"Dammit! In Jamaica? Do you have any idea of what their range is, Dan?" Pete asked, his voice rising.

"Yes, sir, in this area the HN-6Bs, my best guess is it's about 2,000 plus kilometers. That's between 1,200 to 1,300 miles. They can strike Washington, DC from Jamaica. Like I said, these look like the new long-range HN-6Bs and they're externally guided to their targets by Chinese satellite platforms."

"Shit. Double shit. Jack, what do we do now? Ideas?" Pete said, his eyes open wide in wonder.

80

"No question about it—this goes to the President. We need his determination. Hong Niao, HN-6B cruise missiles in Jamaica? I consider it urgent. And we'll go there today if I can get an afternoon slot to see him. You'll come with me, Pete, if I do get a time. I'll emphasize the urgency.

"Right," Pete said.

"Dave, leave the camera. I'll put those photos you took on a USB flash drive and take them with me to The White House. And also, Dave, Tony, you two bad asses have once again done a superb job for the Agency and the nation. I'll ensure you get back-briefed on what the President decides. Pete, I'm going to have Barb call the White House as soon as we break up here. And Dan, man, did you nail it. Excellent call on this," Jack exclaimed.

Everyone rose from their seats. Dave, Tony, and Dan turned and walked to the door. Pete stood, staring at Jack, and slowly shaking his head, his face wrinkled with concern.

That afternoon, at exactly 1:50 PM, Monday, the 18th, Jack Barrett's armored black limo turned off Pennsylvania Avenue and was waved through the front gate of The White House. The limo eased up along the side entrance and came to a stop. Pete had a little difficulty undoing his seatbelt, but eventually it clicked free. Barrett spun around to him.

"Nerves?" Jack asked.

"A little I suppose. This is big, Jack. Really big," Pete replied to which Jack nodded.

Jack and Pete rose out of the limo's back seat and traipsed up the stairs into the west entrance of The White House where they were met by several Secret Service agents.

"Mr. Barrett," the lead agent said in greeting.

"Gentlemen," Jack replied.

A steward dressed in a tuxedo also met them and guided them down the wide, red-carpeted corridor. Minutes later, the steward opened the door allowing Jack and Pete to enter the Oval Office. The Secret Service agents remained outside in the hallway. The President glanced up from his desk, closed a folder, and rose from his chair. He wore a dark navy suit, white shirt, and burgundy necktie.

"Hello, Jack, Pete. It's great to see you again, but hey, this had better be good because I passed up on drinks and hors d'oeuvres with my secretary of defense and secretary of state at the Republican Club. Please, have a seat, and go ahead, fire away. What do you have for me?" the President asked.

Jack Barrett gave the President the flash drive. A large screen descended from the ceiling to the President's right as he plugged in the drive, rose, and took a seat next to Jack. Jack explained everything that Dave and Tony experienced while investigating the death of operations officer Roy Phillips in Ocho Rios, Jamaica. He then explained Dan Alconbury's analytical determination of the photos that Dave took that what they were viewing were batteries of Chinese Hong Niao, HN-6B, cruise missiles — missiles that were supersonic, satellite guided, and nuclear capable. Missiles that were serviced by Chinese military personnel at the site in the Blue Mountains under heavy security. And further, that these large cruise missiles had a range of 2,000 plus kilometers, 1,200 to 1,300 miles...long enough to reach and strike Washington, DC from their site in Jamaica.

"Damn. I told you that this had better be good, Jack, but hey, I think you went over the top on it! Truly, I didn't expect something like this. And so, what does the President think?

Other than informing me of the situation, that's what you came here hoping for, right?" the President said, rising from his seat. He walked toward the windows, glanced out, and ambled back with his head down and his hand on his chin. He settled into the chair behind his desk and stared at Jack, Pete, and down at his desk.

"Shades of 1962, Mr. President?" Jack asked tentatively.

"Actually, no. I agree that one might think that initially. I don't see it that way. Not really. There's a great deal of actions that need to be taken on our part, but I don't think that in reality it's parallel to the Cuban Missile Crisis. Let me gather my thoughts here. First of all, this is today, not at the height of the Cold War in 1962. Second, Jamaica isn't Communist Cuba. Not close. Jamaica is a nation very friendly to the United States. I doubt that the Governor General of Jamaica even knows what's going on at this bauxite mine site. Second, China isn't the Soviet Union either and Xi Jinping isn't Nikita Khrushchev. Third and last, I'm not President Jack Kennedy who felt the need to expose the situation and negotiate. No. We're not going to leak even one iota of this to the media. I will personally see to it that any person who leaks any of this will be tried, convicted, and hanged for treasonous acts against the nation. No, I'm not going to pursue negotiations. We're going to give China a chance to back off and save face on the world stage, and I think they'll jump at the opportunity," the President exclaimed.

"Sir?" Jack questioned.

"Jack, you, Pete, and your folks will do the planning, but this is the crux of it as I envision it. We're going to take that base, bauxite mine, whatever the hell you want to call it...take it down. And take it down hard. You will determine how best to do that but please with a minimum to no loss of life on our side. I could care less about those fucking Chinese military troops and excuse my French, please. Pick a place, a port, a harbor, on Jamaica's coast, north or south, where you think it will be easiest to transport the cruise missiles after we remove them from the site. I'll have two US Navy guided missile cruisers rendezvous there with you. Those navy frigates have the equipment on board to onload and offload cruise missiles. All the other vehicles, heavy equipment, and such, will be turned over to the Jamaica Defense Force, the JDF, to utilize as they so determine. If I recall, their headquarters is in Kingston, Jamaica, so our embassy there can coordinate that part of the operation. The JDF can tear that site down, fencing, lighting, everything. I feel confident that China's going to lose that lease. One of my staff will give that task to State Department to jump on. Make sense?" the President asked.

"Yes, sir, it does. And the Chinese military personnel, those alive and any dead?" Jack asked.

"I'll have the Defense Secretary order TRANSCOM, U.S. Transportation Command, at Scott Air Force Base, Illinois, to move the Chinese prisoners and any dead from the Kingston airport back to Beijing. I doubt China will have any objections to that. Finally, your forces will depart on those Navy cruisers on the north shore upon mission completion."

"What if there's an overall Chinese outrage at what we do and the resulting bloodshed?" Pete asked.

"Right. Well, first and foremost, we'll be giving China a chance to save face in the international arena. Nobody other than the United States government and China will know about this. Xi isn't going to like it, but he'll be in a tight box and he'll know that he needs to choose the right option."

"That makes sense," Pete said.

"I suspect the Jamaican government will be very pissed at what the Chinese used that bauxite mining site for. We'll also caution the Jamaica government to keep it mum, no media involvement. And not to be missed, this will be a statement of resolve from the United States followed by a personal statement from me to President Xi that if they overreact at our gracious offer, I will install cruise missiles complete with nuclear warheads not only on the island of Taiwan but also on the four major Japanese islands of Honshu. Hokkaido, Kyushu, and Shikoku. And further, that they will be cruise missiles with extremely short flight times to their Chinese targets," the President declared.

"Wow. That's quite a stand, an extremely firm position, Mr. President," Jack said.

"I am convinced that it's time to give the Chinese a lesson in power. And it's time for China to join the world of nations in peaceful interaction, in a way of international harmony," the President stated in a firm voice.

"Congratulations on your position, Mr. President. This nation dearly needs something like this. And the timeframe, sir?" Pete said.

"This coming Thursday evening. Two and a half days from now. We don't need elaborate plans. We need adequate yet effective plans that we're confident will succeed. As you said, Jack, this is big. So, I'd like a meeting in this office Wednesday afternoon on how it will go down. You may want to task the NRO for some overhead coverage of the site, how it's structured," the President said.

"Indeed, sir. I will do so," Jack replied. The three men rose from their seats and shook hands.

"Godspeed, patriots," the President said as Jack and Pete left the Oval Office.

CHAPTER 13

St. Ann's Bay
North Coast, Jamaica
Thursday evening, June 21st

At seven-thirty in the evening, the huge hulks of two steel gray U.S. Navy cruisers, USS Normandy and USS Gettysburg, dropped anchors in the harbor off St. Ann's Bay. They would move closer to the piers later that night. One hour passed and at the onset of darkness, the USS Oregon, a black colored nuclear attack submarine, surfaced in the port at Buff Bay on the north coast of Jamaica. At the same time, the USS South Dakota, another attack submarine, surfaced near the port at Annotto Bay also on the north coast. And lastly, at eight o'clock, the USS Virginia, an attack submarine, would surface at the edge of the port of Harbour View, east of Kingston on the south coast.

At eight-fifteen sharp, the CIA's SAD Special Ops teams would disembark the submarines on rafts to their respective landfalls. The submarines would then depart, submerging into the Caribbean Sea with a mission accomplished, and would return to their patrol areas in the south Atlantic. After sinking their rafts, the teams would await troop transport trucks on loan from the JDF that would take the three teams inland, ascending into the Blue Mountains. The op, nick-named *Operation Steel Crab*, had begun to gel.

Dave McClure and Tony Robertson arrived with their twenty-four-man Alpha team aboard the USS Oregon at Buff Bay. As would the other two teams, Bravo and Charlie Teams, Dave and Tony would quickly, but quietly, travel ashore with their team under the cloak of darkness. They would move as swiftly as possible to their truck conveyances…then, tally up and hop aboard.

Many of the men were carrying new spec ops Sig Sauer SAW M250 full auto rifles, and some had the new Sig Sauer M5 assault rifle. Both are chambered in 6.8 mm and wired with the M157 fire control system that puts rounds on target more rapidly and accurately than ever before. The teams bore very heavy firepower with high rates of fire. As Novak had directed and spec ops personnel had once named this kind of op, this was to be an *assholes and elbows* operation. No hesita-tion, no holding back.

After seizing the site at the conclusion of the operation, the three teams would all eventually leave Jamaica aboard the two guided missile cruisers at St. Ann's Bay. Four US Navy de-stroyers would join the cruisers at sea off the coast of Jamaica and escort them on their way back to Norfolk, Virginia.

Inclusive with Dave and Tony's team was a twelve-man team of Oriental-appearing men who originally emanated from the Philippines, Thailand, and Japan. They were dressed in olive green Chinese military uniforms with red stars on their caps. The only difference in uniform motif was they also bore a large, luminescent white skull embroidered above their left shirt pockets, this for recognition. Their job was to enter the compound first, before all the teams, approach and then seize the command center in the middle of the compound. They would fire a red flare overhead when the command center was secured. This task was critical in that it would prevent the Chinese from communicating with their Beijing headquarters and launching the missiles at any point during the attack.

As the raft he was sitting in shuddered through swells, Tony abruptly yanked his neck to his left, avoiding a spray of seawater from the bow of the raft. He glanced at Dave, grimacing. Dave smiled back, glancing up at the starry night sky. He inhaled a lungful of sea air.

"This damn seawater's not so warm after the sun goes down, is it?" Tony muttered, frowning.

"No, I guess it isn't, but it's bracing, and that helps to keep me alert while I scan along the shore," Dave replied to which Tony nodded in agreement.

The shoreline was rapidly approaching. In minutes, the men pulled up on a sand beach. Once all equipment was offloaded, several of the team members pushed the two large rafts out in the water, slit the sides with their knives, and placed weights in them. Both rafts began immediately to sink beneath the water's surface.

The Alpha team members scurried across the dark beach and climbed into the backs of the two olive-colored transport trucks. Dave and Tony took seats next to each other on a bench in the first truck. They glanced up to see a heavy canvas cover over them. The men jolted backward in their seats several minutes later as the trucks lurched forward.

"We're on our way. You said these trucks will take us within about one to two miles of the site. That right? And then we trek the rest of the way through the jungle?" Tony said in a low voice as the trucks rumbled up the road.

"That's right. Charlie team's gonna have the roughest route coming up from the south. The jungle terrain to the south of the compound is much steeper and rockier. It has lots of jagged rock ravines. That's what the maps showed anyway. Once we're in position, we'll probably have to wait a bit for them to catch up to us," Dave replied. Their bodies shook sideways as the truck swerved through the turn onto the B1 Highway and began ascending into the mountains.

"Well, somebody always gets the shit end of the stick, Dave. You know that. I'm glad it wasn't our team," Tony replied.

"Oh, I don't know. Those guys here with us in the Chinese uniforms are going to have to enter the compound before any of us, walk right through the center of the camp to the command center, and look totally nonchalant about it. No, I think they have that end of the stick."

"Yeah, you might be right on that," Tony answered.

Alpha team leader, Steve Tedesco, stood up from his bench. He began to speak in a tone loud enough to be heard above the truck's rattling rumble.

"All right, guys, as you've been previously briefed, this will be the drill—we're executing a three-pronged attack on the Chinese cruise missile compound. Alpha and Bravo teams will move north at two different angles to the compound and Charlie team will be approaching from the south. After we leave the trucks, the drivers will continue to drive north a bit, pull over, and park. They'll sit there waiting for us. That's for our final extraction. Clear?"

Heads nodded.

"So, once off the trucks, all of us in Alpha team will walk east into the jungle about a hundred yards and then we'll turn

90 due south. Single file. I'll be taking the lead. That route should eventually take us to the furthest east end of the compound where we'll cut through the chain link fence. Our guys with the Chinese uniforms and white luminescent skulls on their shirts will ingress, entering the site, and proceeding to the command center. They'll fire a red flare when they've secured the command center. Okay so far?" Steve asked to which everyone nodded affirmative.

"Good. Again, single file through the uphill jungle. Don't spread out until we're in sight of the fence line. I want total silence on this trek, no talking, whispering, coughing, nothing whatsoever. Go ahead now and ram a round into your breeches...leave your safeties on until we're in position near our cuts in the fence line. Before we charge through the hole in the fence, I want each of you to throw a flash bang as far as you can over the fence toward the center of the compound. Clear?"

"Yes, sir," the men said in hushed voices, nodding their heads.

"Also, as you're aware, what we're all toting is now state-of-the-art and, in some cases, prototype, weaponry. If firefights develop, the Chinese will be badly outgunned. Bad for them, that is. Make sure your tactical vests are tightly fastened. They can save your life. After we've secured the site, trucks with Jamaican JDF forces will be arriving to take custody of any Chinese prisoners along with however many dead bodies in body bags and transport them to the Kingston airport. From there, USTRANSOM airlifters will take them temporarily to Richmond and ultimately on to Beijing. That's not our concern. The heavy vehicles in the compound carrying the cruise missile launchers will be following close behind our trucks to St. Ann's Bay. Once there, they'll be onloaded to two of our waiting guided missile cruisers. After the onloading of the missiles, then we'll be boarding those cruisers as well. Questions?"

All heads shook left and right.

"Then God bless you all. Guys, remember, no hesitation on this one. If you receive fire or observe any Chinese about to fire, take them down. Go full auto. You each should have more than enough mags. Stay safe and keep your finger near the trigger. Let's go kick some Chinese ass and fry their egg-rolls for them!" Steve said as snickering chuckles erupted throughout the truck.

The ride became more jarring as the trucks ascended to 4,000 feet between the Hollywell Forest Park and the edge of the Blue Mountains. The thick, sturdy treads on the large tires bounced in and out of dirt ruts and potholes. The damp chill of the rainforest increased as the trucks were soon enshrouded in thick mists of nighttime in the Blue Mountains. The men glanced around at each other with nervous eyes.

After another fifteen minutes of riding in the back of the trucks, Steve Tedesco rose once again in his seat. His right hand reached up to grasp an overhead bar supporting the canvas top to steady himself.

"We're near the drop off point, men. We offload six minutes from now. This foggy mist outside will be much thicker now as we continue our ascent. Once we enter the jungle, it'll be black as hell. Feel free to use your mini-Maglite...just keep them pointed down at the ground in front of you. Be careful of your footing. The terrain will be filled with rough, furrowed ground and jagged rocks. I don't want to have to deal with injuries before we even get to the target. Take a moment now to tighten up your gear. We'll group at the side of the road, and I'll take the lead into the forest," Steve said.

As the trucks came to a shuddering halt, skidding to a stop, the men lurched sideways on their benches. Tailgates were suddenly yanked open, and the men hopped one by one to the road's dirt surface and walked to the edge of the forest. As the trucks pulled away, the men grouped together on the side of the mountain road.

"As we approach the fence line, George Fulton and Rick Bergman will move up and cut the fence for our makeshift Chinese team to ingress. We'll wait for their red flare for us to move in through the fence. Remember, before you move forward, each of you toss a flash bang up and over the fence into the courtyard of the compound. No grenades or shooting near the missile launchers. They may have nuke warheads," Steve Tedesco said in a low murmur. He waved his arm forward and entered the forest. Everyone followed single file.

The jungle-like rainforest was damp, chilly, and its foliage wet with dripping water from the heavy mists. Every leafy branch they brushed against dribbled a wet spot on their shirts and pants. Being under several canopies of trees and on a moonless night, a total blackness enveloped them. The men began to light their mini-Maglites at the ground immediately in front of them.

Alpha team began carefully plodding forward over the stony ground. Despite the cool air, as they trudged ahead beads of sweat soon blossomed on their foreheads in the humid air. Their black uniforms were gradually becoming soaked both from both the humidity and the heavy, soggy mist.

"Man, this is dark as I've ever experienced. I can't see more than five feet in front of me. It's like being in the deepest cave," Tony whispered.

"It sure is. There're three canopies of tree branches above us blocking out the sky. It reminds me of the dense forest in the Aberdare Mountains in Kenya — but that's another story," Dave murmured, moving up behind Tony, "And don't worry, it's me. I'm just moving up closer behind you."

Steve Tedesco raised his arm, bringing the column to a halt. All could see the glow in the sky up ahead from the site's bright lighting. The line of men paused in place.

"Okay, we're good, but spread out a bit now as we approach the fence, and stay close, shoulder to shoulder. Drop to a low crouch as you go. We'll go down on our stomachs about twenty yards from the fence and crawl forward. Let's rock and roll!" Steve muttered in a low voice.

The fence was soon cut by Alpha team, and the Chinese look-alike squad climbed through. They were soon out of sight. Steve and his team lay prone by the chain link fence, their SAW M250 and M5 rifles at the ready. Bravo team led by Andy Wickman notified Steve that they too were in place. All that remained was for Charlie team to report.

Minutes ticked by. They heard muffled shots coming from inside the compound, most likely near or in the command center. The sounds appeared to come from varied calibers. Paul Enatsu, Charlie team's lead, confirmed they were now in place and the fence was being cut for their ingress.

The first few minutes blew by rapidly. A bright red flare suddenly skyrocketed up from the center of the camp, its light radiating in the night sky over the compound.

"We have a go! All right, men! Throw your flash bangs over the fence now!"

Seconds later, there were thunderous explosions of light and sound from the flash bangs. "Let's go! Spring through that fence, men!" Steve said.

All three teams instantaneously shouted at the top of their lungs while dashing through the fence line, drowning out all other sound. The boisterous yell into the night air from three directions along with the deafening detonations and light blasts of the flash bangs were close to paralyzing the Chinese troops inside the site. Those passing through the compound were instantaneously dazed by the thunderous roar…what the hell was happening?

Frozen in place, the Chinese blinked their eyes futilely, blinded for seconds by the brilliant explosions of the flash bangs. The ones who raised their rifles to firing positions were mowed down instantly by a loud staccato of gunfire bursting from SAW M250 fully automatic rifles. Riddled with bullets, those troops abruptly collapsed, thudding down to the dirt in groups of four to five at a time.

Coming from the south, Charlie team met the least resistance. Since the Chinese were aware of how difficult the terrain was to their south, they never anticipated an assault from that direction, and so had then lightened the security patrols along that fence line.

Charlie team actually found themselves able to penetrate the center of the compound first of all three teams, firing at Chinese rushing toward the command center. Once again, the incredible firepower of the SAW M250s cut down the throngs of Chinese soldiers sprinting toward them. The Chinese were desperately hoping to launch their missiles before the compound fell, but the enormous rates of fire pounded into and ripped their bodies apart. The rattle of automatic gunfire spread throughout the site.

One Chinese sentry had moved stealthily around a cruise missile launcher and raised his assault rifle directly at Tony. Tony missed it. His eyes were glued to the center of the compound. Dave spotted the sentry immediately, dropped to a kneeling position and fired a burst of rounds up and into the center of the man's chest. Tony swiveled just in time to see the man's body thumping to the ground. He looked at Dave and nodded.

The teams continued to move forward, steadily approaching from the fence lines to the center of the compound from their three approach angles. The remaining Chinese troops, finally sensing it was futile to continue to resist, began tossing their rifles and pistols to the ground. One singular Chinese military man pushed his way through the surrendering troops. He strode in front of them to the center of the compound.

"I am Colonel Cheng. What you American pigs have done here is an outrage! I will ensure that each and every one of you is prosecuted in international court! Drop your weapons now and I will spare your lives!" Cheng shouted as a look of defiance washed across his face.

"Colonel, if you don't drop your pistol now and surrender, you will join your fallen comrades in a pool of your own blood! Drop it now or I will give the command to fire. There won't be enough of you left to send back to Beijing in a box!" Steve Tedesco yelled back at Colonel Cheng, stepping forward and leveling his M5's muzzle at the Colonel's chest.

With a look of defeat, Colonel Cheng's eyes dropped. His arms fell limply by his side. He reached to loosen his pistol belt, letting it drop to the ground. He then backed up to the line of Chinese behind him who would soon be prisoners.

"Smart move, Colonel Cheng! All right, Charlie team… the Jamaican Defense Force trucks will soon arrive. So, begin to search the compound for any stragglers and escort them here. Alpha and Bravo teams…move up and start pulling the Chinese troops' arms behind their backs and place plastic zip handcuffs on them. Remove the weapons of the dead after putting them in body bags that will be stacked for us on the trucks. Move everything here to the center of the compound. Those who have been designated as drivers from all three teams will begin to climb in and start the engines of the missile launch vehicles. Let's go, Gentlemen, move quickly," Steve barked.

Time clicked away in a flurry of activity. Three hours later at St. Ann's Bay harbor, Dave, Tony, and the rest of Alpha team looked on from a pier as the cruise missiles were removed from their tubes and loaded onto the two U.S. Navy guided missile cruisers, the USS Normandy and the USS Gettysburg. Steve Tedesco walked toward them.

"Dave, Tony, you, and the men of Alpha team performed superbly. And get this—there were no fatalities on our side! That's huge! There were some gunshot wounds, about ten of them, but none of them life threatening. Those men will be treated in the medical dispensaries on the cruisers," Steve said.

"And the Chinese?" Dave asked.

"Two TRANSCOM airlifters have loaded all the Chinese prisoners who will be taken temporarily to Richmond until arrangements are made to fly them on to Beijing. There are quite a few young troops, and I wouldn't be surprised if a couple of them ask for asylum. Body bags are going to a morgue in Richmond also for subsequent transportation to Beijing. I understand from the JDF that Colonel Cheng tried to commit suicide with a pocketknife he somehow still had on him. He was treated for a slash wound to his left wrist. Cheng's probably not going to have a heartwarming welcome back in Beijing. Overall, I would say this has been a stellar success. Well done!" Steve exclaimed.

"That's a feather in your cap, Steve. It was well planned and executed. Congratulations. And the bauxite mining site?" Dave said.

"I imagine the JDF will begin disassembling and moving the equipment out to their own warehouses and dismantling the compound as soon as tomorrow. Fencing, lighting…it will all go. It won't take long for the jungle to overgrow into that site. This is a fait accompli," Steve answered.

"Do you have a handle on the fatality numbers for the Chinese?" Tony asked.

"Yes…39 dead, 36 survivors. Of the 36, there are 12 wounded, although not severely," Steve replied.

"Man, that's really a lopsided victory and a sloppy defense. Thank God," Tony said.

"Indeed. The missiles are almost all onloaded. The teams will start boarding the cruisers within the hour. The Captain of the USS Normandy said that once they're underway, there will be hot meals for everyone on both ships," Steve added.

"Where're we headed?" Dave asked.

"Norfolk, Virginia. We'll be transported by bus from there up to Washington, DC. Andy Wickman, Paul Enatsu, and I need to contact Jack Barrett and Pete Novak as soon as we're in town. That's to give them a brief overview on how the op went down," Steve said.

"Well, say hi for Tony and I. 'Sounds like a plan, Steve. Again, very well done on your part. This was a well led op," Dave said.

"Thanks again, Dave. Coming from you two badasses, that means something. I suppose we should make sure we have all our gear and are ready to board the cruisers when they give the word. The ships' captains are eager to move out and clear the harbor," Steve said as he walked toward another group of Alpha team members.

Dave and Tony glanced at one another.

"And before I forget, Dave, thanks for taking down that

Chinese guy who had his sights on me. Really, thanks. I was too focused on the center of the compound," Tony said.

"You'd have done the same for me. It's the past, but you're welcome."

The two men shrugged, picked up their M5 rifles lying at their feet, and ambled closer to the ships.

CHAPTER 14

Langley Center, McLean
Virginia
Monday, June 25th

Just after lunch together and as deep in conversation as they
now were, Jack Barrett and Pete Novak looked up from
their seats as Barbara knocked on Jack's door. Jack glanced at
Pete and Pete nodded back.

"Yes? Is it you, Barb? Please, come in," Jack said.

"Mr. Barrett, it's Dave McClure and Tony Robertson. They
said they had a one o'clock meeting scheduled with you,"
Barb said, poking her head in the door.

"That's correct, Barb. Time got away from us," Jack said
looking again to Pete.

"Go ahead. It's okay," Pete said and once again nodded.

"Please, have them come in," Jack said.

"Good morning, gentlemen," Jack said as Dave and Tony
walked through the door, "Please, have a seat."

"Tired?" Pete asked to which both Dave and Tony nodded.

"That's to be expected. That was one helluva operation down in Jamaica that you two participated in. What that means is we want to say a very strong 'well done' to both of you," Jack said.

"Thank you, sir. Any word yet on the Chinese reaction, sir, or is it too early?" Dave asked.

"Yes, there is. I'll give you the whole nine yards. As a matter of fact, after visiting the State Department, the Chinese ambassador was in my office at eight-thirty this morning. He left, went back his embassy to contact Beijing, and then got back to me. Xi Jinping has in no uncertain terms accepted our offer to avoid holding any negotiations, therefore keeping this issue out of the media. It's obvious he wants to save face, both internationally and among his own Chinese citizenry," Jack said.

"That's a big one," Tony remarked.

"It is for sure. After all, we should remember that Xi is certainly up to his ass in addressing the severe economic issues in China amid calls for him to step down. Not that that will ever happen. Arrangements are being made as we speak for TRANSCOM to fly the Chinese prisoners and their dead in body bags back home. The National Security Advisor advised me that the President took a personal call yesterday, Sunday, from Xi. It turns out that Xi was a bit upset."

"I would imagine so," Dave said.

"Right. The White House says the President, bless his heart, got pretty damn stern with Xi and told XI that if he persisted in his so-called outrage, what specifically, he the President, would install on the island of Taiwan and the Japanese islands. That was the end of discussion. Xi folded. The Chinese are accepting our terms, we're happy, and the Jamaican Defense Force is happy. As an aside, Xi also confirmed that he would

issue immediate orders for his submarines that have attempted intrusions into the Gulf of Mexico to return to their patrol
areas in the Pacific Rim," Jack explained.

"About Jamaica? Is the government there okay with everything that went down in their Blue Mountains?" Tony asked.

"Good question. It turns out that a great deal of the equipment boxes the JDF took from the site contained modern
weaponry. And to boot, State Department sent me a report
that the Jamaican Governor General himself offered an apolo-
gy for what happened with the lease he had let to the Chinese
on the bauxite mining site. He said they should have maintained a much higher level of due diligence," Jack replied.

"Wow. It sounds like a clean sweep," Dave said.

"I think it was. So again, well done. Dave, I have something else I want to ask you. Any more questions regarding
Jamaica?" Jack asked. Dave and Tony shook their heads.

"This next subject is about Gunther Dietzmann, and your
meeting with him in Munich," Jack said.

"Yes, sir?" Dave asked.

"In your talk with him, did Dietzmann share the names of
any of his sources in the BND?" Jack asked.

"No, sir. He said they were all personal friends based on
his frequent liaison interactions with them. He also said this
matter was a dangerous situation for all of them. Do we have
a problem in our analysis and collection efforts?" Dave asked.

"No, it's not that. We're still actively collecting and analyz-
ing...and now even more so. It's worse than that. Bad news,"
Jack responded.

"Sir?"

"Gunther Dietzmann is dead. Police found his body in the
early morning hours this past Saturday floating face down in
the Spree River in Berlin. Dietzmann was strangled to death.

The autopsy over the weekend indicates his neck had been cut severely deep. Our station chief at the embassy in Berlin added the word is that it's been determined Dietzmann was strangled with a wire, a garrote. And man, that's a horrible way to die, poor guy," Jack explained.

"Oh, no. That is really sad. Gunther was a nice guy, too. He was scared to death, Mr. Barrett, very scared. He said he was glad we chose Munich to meet because Berlin would have been far too dangerous," Dave said.

"And obviously, he had cause to believe it was," Jack replied.

"What now, Mr. Barrett?" Dave asked.

"Gunther Dietzmann's assassination obviously elevates our concern that what he related to you, even though it seems a bit wild, over the top — may actually be true. We contacted the Simon Wiesenthal Center in Los Angeles, and their researchers were able to verify for us from their documentation that apparently, the grandfather to Andreas Bachmeier, Klaus Bachmeier, did actually work directly for Heinrich Himmler in the SS, the Schutzstaffel, during World War II. They also were able to confirm from their records that the organization, *die Spinne, the Spider*, did successfully evacuate Klaus in 1945 from Berlin to somewhere in South America as they did so for many others. They didn't have any information to indicate that the final destination was Argentina. They said they don't know much at all about Andreas' father, Konrad, or Conrad as we now know him, and went so far as to say anything they provided on Conrad would only be speculation on their part," Jack said.

"My goodness, then there may be some truth to all this — that is, what Gunther told me," Dave replied.

"Right. A Fourth Reich? Jeez. No, we're taking it seriously. And like I said, even more so now with the news on

Dietzmann's death. We're energizing and tasking our sources. And Analysis is examining the results of their collections. We definitely want to know, need to know, if Bachmeier and the German military have plans at any time in the near future to move troops and armor close to the borders of Poland and the Czech Republic. That's despite what's going on with Russia, Belarus, and the Ukraine."

"Damn," Dave uttered.

"Right. If the BND or the German Ministry of Defense was keeping an eye on Gunther and his friends as well as putting a surveillance on them, then it's possible they went to Munich as well. Munich is the BND's old stomping grounds, that is, before they moved their headquarters from Grünwald in Bavaria to Berlin. And if so, Dave, then they may have a take on you as well. We'll have to keep that in mind as we move forward. That's where we are at this point. And you're up to speed on this issue too, Tony," Jack said.

Jack continued, "Oh, before you guys leave, I think I'll go ahead and mention what is at this point a purely tangential issue. Although this will almost surely take you back in your memories. Pete, I'm sorry…I meant to spin you up on this FBI report today. I just never got around to it. Sorry. Dave, Tony, do you remember the German terrorist, Franz Altmann, and his *die Rote Sturm Bewegung, RSB, the Red Storm Movement*? He's the one you killed in a hand-to-hand combat confrontation in Colorado Springs."

"That's okay. I'm all ears, Jack," Pete replied, smiling.

"You mean the Franz Altmann who was in New York City's Staten Island and later in Colorado Springs? I had a high-speed car chase with that bastard. After I executed a pit maneuver and rolled his vehicle, he climbed out and came at me. I had no choice. I had to kill him," Dave asked.

"That's the man. I'm not questioning your action in that op, not at all. This concerns a report we received from the FBI headquarters here in Washington, DC. It originated from their field office in Cheyenne, Wyoming. Specifically, it's about the area that is mountainous and heavily forested just west of Cheyenne. You may know that we have a strategic ICBM missile base there just to the north of Cheyenne, F.E. Warren Air Force Base. They control over 150 Minuteman III nuclear missiles," Jack said.

"Yes, sir, I'm aware of that. I'm originally from Colorado Springs. I've driven through Cheyenne on more than a couple occasions and even visited the base there once," Dave answered.

"Good. The report originally came from a couple of citizens, a man and his wife, who were hiking on a sloped trail above one of several valleys south of Otto Road. Otto Road itself is just a little south of the east-west interstate I-80. The hikers had a pair of binoculars and a digital camera with them for any opportunities to take photos of scenery and wildlife. They observed a line of men in black, tactical gear walking through the valley below. Through their binoculars, they noted that the men appeared to have military grade assault rifles slung over their shoulders. The hikers felt it was possible that it could be a police or federal agency exercise. Thus, they weren't too concerned at first, but they watched and listened as the men joked around and broke out singing some kind of a marching tune. Obviously, the men weren't aware at all that they were being observed," Jack said.

"It does sound as though it was possible that it was some kind of exercise, Jack. Don't you think so?" Pete asked.

"At first as I read through the report, sure, I did. However, that is, until the hiking couple realized all the men were singing in German. At that point, they then began taking photos with their camera of each of the men strutting along and singing until they passed from sight. Their camera had a 110 mm telephoto lens—that's not a real long telephoto lens, but then they didn't envision any need for a longer one during a hike out there," Jack replied.

"All of the men were in black tactical gear and singing in German? I see. This could be interesting," Pete replied.

"I agree. The FBI office in Cheyenne sent the citizens' digital photos along with an agent report to headquarters. The FBI in turn, based on the content of the report, forwarded the photos and the report itself as a courtesy to the *BundesKriminalAmt, BKA, Federal Criminal Office*, in Wiesbaden, Germany. After their initial technical analysis of the photos, the BKA routed them over to their *Terroristen Gruppe, Terror Investigative Group*. What finally occurred was the BKA got back to the FBI with a comment that while the photos were a bit grainy, the photo of the man leading at the front of the single file column did appear to have facial features very similar to someone they've been familiar with for quite some time, a German national, Sigmund Degler," Jack said.

"And Degler is who?" Pete asked.

"Sigmund Degler is the number two man in Germany's terror group, the Red Storm Movement. He answers only to their leader, Seigfried Weber," Jack said.

"Damn!" Tony remarked.

"Damn indeed, Tony. And accordingly, with the possibility of a foreign terror group, especially this Red Storm Movement, on US soil once again, we're very interested. By the way, given both your performances in New York City and later in Colorado Springs, the FBI said they would once again appreciate your assistance in this current matter. If that takes place, it would be as a tag-along role, in no way at the lead. Not now, in no way immediate, but if things of concern continue to develop out there in the Cheyenne area. That's the Bureau's call. What say you two to the FBI's invitation? And you, Pete?" Jack responded.

"I'd be okay with it, that is, as you noted, in a support role. Even though that didn't mean much last time," Pete said with a slight chuckle.

"I would find it interesting, Mr. Barrett, Mr. Novak. If it comes to that, you can count me in," Dave answered.

"Me, too," Tony said.

"Great. I thought so," Jack said as he grabbed his cane leaning against his desk and rose from his chair. Pete, Dave, and Tony rose with him.

"Pete, join me here in my office, tomorrow morning, nine o'clock. I want to discuss this Bachmeier thing a little further," Jack said.

"I'll be here," Novak said, nodding.

"Dave, Tony, you guys take it easy. I'll see you around the campus," Jack said.

"Yes, sir," Dave and Tony replied in unison.

PART II

The only reason a warrior is alive is to fight,
and the only reason a warrior fights is to win.

Miyamoto Musashi
A Book of Five Rings

CHAPTER 15

Laramie County, Wyoming
North of Granite Canyon
Tuesday, June 26th

" This coffee is so bad...it tastes like shit," Fritz Kitzler muttered, frowning, and kicking at the coals with a boot.

"Fuck you! Then make your own fucking coffee! I suppose your sleeping bag was a little too lumpy too, eh, asshole?" Einhardt Müller replied.

"Knock it off, you two. Stop your bickering or I'll send both your asses back to Munich where you can explain your behavior to Herr Weber. You want that?" Sigmund barked as the two men melted to silence.

Sigmund glanced up at the tall pines. Rays of the sun were beginning to seep through. He smiled at the sight and took a long sip of coffee from his own cup.

"Yechhhh! Fritz is right! Only this shit is really worse than just any shit! It is worse than elephant shit!" Sigmund uttered in a loud moan.

"Herr Degler, I've never tasted elephant shit myself!" Jakob Koehler exclaimed, chuckling.

The whole camp broke out in laughter, even Fritz and Einhardt who glanced up and grinned at Sigmund. The rest of the men moved up closer to the fire, still laughing their butts off.

"You haven't tasted elephant shit? I seriously doubt that Jakob!" Sigmund said, nodding approvingly at Jakob.

The camp once again erupted in howling laughs. Both Sigmund and Jakob knew the men needed to relieve some of the nervous anticipation. And the fact was they all needed to shake off the stress. This was the opportunity.

"Anyway, it's the ground coffee beans. They're dog turds. Fritz, Einhardt, nobody could make good coffee from this crap! We'll make sure we get some better coffee grounds in town today. Don't worry. Just go ahead and drink your juice or bottled water for now," He growled in a loud voice.

The men finished the rest of their breakfasts of scrambled eggs, bacon, and warmed bread. Oskar Durchdenwald glanced up to Sigmund and set down his empty plate on stones around the firepit.

"Sigmund, we've been here for three days now, hiking, sleeping in tents here in the forest, and eating from around a campfire. I would like to ask you, what's your take at this moment?" Oskar asked.

"Oskar, look, we all signed up to this, didn't we? And primarily so to avenge the murder of our comrade, Franz Altmann, and his team. We need to remember our commitment. That being said, I think Franz made some mistakes in his target selection process. They ended up paying dearly for it. We're not going to make that mistake. For now, I want us to continue to go dressed in civilian clothes at varied times after midnight, during the early morning hours, along the north-west edge of Roundtop Road outside the base. Test the perimeter fence line and see if we can determine when the shift change takes place among the security forces patrols. I think that's enough for us to do for now. We're in no rush. We want to nail this big time," Sigmund explained.

"Thank you. All right. Do you think our explosives will be powerful enough?" Oskar asked.

"To blow off a portion of the hatch on a Minuteman III silo? Yes. I am convinced of that. It will provide us with enough of an opening to throw the other explosive packages with their ten-minute timers down the silo. Those explosives combined with the fuel in the missile will result in a tremendous detonation and fire. We will get the hell out of there as quickly as possible. I have been assured the resulting violent blast will be enough to fracture the missile's nose cone and its nuclear warhead. The resulting nuclear contamination will quickly spread over the base and then over northern Cheyenne. Given what the prevailing winds might be at that time, maybe even up to the northern suburbs of Laramie. The wind here mostly comes from the northwest. We should be okay going back west into the mountains. That will be mission accomplished for us and we will head home having fulfilled our objective."

"Every time you explain what's going to take place, it gives me chills," Horst Bierlein said.

"I can understand that Horst but take a moment and try to imagine what it's going to give to *die Amerikaner schweine, the American pigs*! This will make Franz Altmann's spirit smile down upon us. It will be a nuclear disaster of an immense proportion in Cheyenne," Sigmund exclaimed.

Horst nodded to Sigmund in agreement as cheers erupted around the campfire. Men began nodding and laughing with their team members. Sigmund was satisfied that the ice had been broken and a focus on the mission restored.

Sigmund Degler walked away from Jakob, his number two, and the ten other men around the campfire with a slight smile creasing his face. Jakob Koehler soon followed. They shook hands. Together, the two men stood at the edge of the tree line staring in wonder at the beauty of the valley below them.

"We need this, Jakob. Successfully attacking and destroying an American strategic ICBM silo will make the Red Storm Movement feared throughout the world. Seigfried Weber will be beyond himself, delighted, and we will have handed the organization a great triumph. This mission is both doable and critical for us."

"I agree."

"And finally, it will begin to move us ahead in getting the regime change we want so badly in our homeland of Germany. And hell, the Americans? They will rue the day they blew Franz's remains all over a field in north Colorado Springs. Assholes. There wasn't enough of him left to send back to Germany for burial. They are going to pay dearly for that," Sigmund said.

"I agree. It will do that. What do you think? Maybe we should take the team into town for dinner tonight? You know, lighten things up, a little treat," Jakob replied.

"Good idea. We will. Then, we will go back to business."

CHAPTER 16

Pumphrey Drive, Fairfax
Virginia
Wednesday evening, June 27th

"She's pushing at my stomach wall," Karen said, holding her tummy. She was standing next to Dave in front of their living room front window.

"Well, she wants out. She wants to join us and look at the world around her. It doesn't hurt, does it," Dave replied.

"No, not at all. It's just, well, I realize that I have a little person inside me. You know, they say a newborn baby already knows the voices of his or her mother and father and is very relaxed when near them after birth," Karen said.

"Really? Wow. That's interesting. So, Carolyn will already feel safe and comfortable around us and hearing our voices."

"Yes. That's what the literature says. Dave, this is going to be so fantastic. Our little girl. Our Carolyn. I am so looking forward to this."

"I am too, sweetheart."

"Anything breaking at the office?"

"Nothing urgent. Some analysis is going on concerning a matter in Germany. And there's been an FBI report about something going on out near Cheyenne, Wyoming. That's FBI turf. Other than that, it appears everything right now is business as usual."

"You just came back from Munich. Does this 'matter in Germany' have to do with that trip?" Karen asked.

"It does, yes, but it's nothing but analysis work now," Dave replied.

"Okay. When I think back, I'm glad you passed up on that offer from Omega, but it still seems you can be yanked away so quickly on an op and at the drop of a dime. I do worry often about that. I wish we could have, you know, a more normal life, especially with the baby coming." Karen said in a low voice.

"A normal life? What's that? Sweetheart, I know working for the Agency is different, but I still think that's an odd comment coming from a former NCIS agent. From someone like you who's familiar with the lifestyle of agents in our business. Do you mean some normal life like what's in that Sheena Easton song, 'Morning Train' — *My baby takes the morning train; He works from nine to five and then; He takes another home again; To find me waitin' for him...?* That was 40-50 years ago. I don't know anyone who lives that kind of life anymore. Really, honey, that's really strange coming from you. Tell me honestly, sweetheart, are you unhappy?" Dave asked.

"No, I'm not unhappy. I love you to death, Dave. And yes, my NCIS special agent background should give me a more of an understanding and acceptance for what you do. I think it may stem from the pregnancy and the expectations I'm experiencing for the baby. A woman's physiology changes during pregnancy. That's probably it. I'm sorry I have these misgivings. It must be the thoughts surrounding a new little one in our lives," Karen said.

"I do understand, and I promise I will keep that concern in my frontal lobes," Dave answered.

"At this moment, I sure could use a kiss and a hug. And a little bit of forgiveness," Karen said.

"There's nothing to forgive. You are the love of my life, and you always will be. If something's ever bothering you, I don't want you to hold it in. Just open up and tell me," Dave answered.

Dave walked to Karen, took her in his arms, kissed her, and held her, "Jeez, I can't get too close to you with that bump in your belly," Dave said.

They both laughed. As Dave drew away, Karen wiped the wetness growing in her eyes and smiled.

"New subject, honey. What shall we have for dinner?" she asked.

"Let's go out to eat. How about that great Lebanese restaurant up Ox Road in Vienna?"

"Deal! Give me a minute and I'll go change," Karen said, smiling.

Dave eased himself down on the sofa, while countless thoughts began to fill his mind.

CHAPTER 17

F. E. Warren Air Force Base
Cheyenne, Wyoming
Early Thursday morning, June 28th

Airman Al Tagliani extended his thin neck around the corner edge of the concrete bunker. His brow wrinkled.

"See them?" Tagliani asked.

"Yeah. A couple of people taking a late-night walk on Roundtop Road. They're dressed in civilian clothes you can see every day all around the base. That happens, doesn't it, Al? This is what you radioed me about?" Staff Sergeant Ted Denton asked.

"Sarge, it's now two o'clock in the morning. There's two men there, not a couple, not a man and a woman. And last night I also saw two men, not the same ones as these two, and that was at one o'clock in the morning. They were also walking along Roundtop Road near this same stretch of fence line. This is the most remote section of the missile field out here and at these hours, I don't think it's just a couple taking a late evening stroll," Tagliani said.

"All right. What are you getting at, Al?"

"Watch the closest guy, nearest the edge of the road. He's moving toward the fence, just like the man last night. He'll grip the middle strand. I think they're testing the wire. This ain't a chain link fence. Out here, the fence turns to spaced out, heavy, singular runs of steel wire. We never did get the electric or microwave fencing at this base."

"There was a time when that fence middle strand was electrified, but they did away with that. Okay, I'll stay a bit. I'm watching him. Ah, there he goes. Shit, you're right, he's yanking at the middle wire. I wonder what the hell that was all about. We have signs posted on that fence every fifty yards or so that you can't miss and read, *Use of Deadly Force Authorized*. What the hell do they think they're doing?" Denton responded.

"I don't know. I haven't seen them try to enter the fence line. They're just walking along it at this strange early morning hour and seem to be testing it. Weird."

"All right. Good observation on your part, Al. I'll put it in our shift report and recommend a copy goes over to the OSI. Who knows, maybe the agents there will want to conduct a surveillance out here some night," SSgt Denton said.

"AFOSI? Wow. Okay, thanks, Sarge," Tagliani replied.

Two days later, Saturday, at three o'clock in the morning, and 100 yards into the meadow west of both Roundtop Road and the air force base fence line, the two special agents crouched low for cover. Even in late June, the night air in southern Wyoming had a considerable chill to it. While hunkering down in the tall grass and feeling some gooseflesh rising from a nippy breeze, Special Agent Rich Coleman shook his shoulders. He continued to press the night vision binoculars to his eyes.

Rich glanced over at his partner, Special Agent Eric Schofield, who was wondering what Coleman was able to see.

"It looks like Major Lundquist was right in sending us out here, Eric. The men are out there…two of them walking on the edge of the road near the fence, just like Security Forces reported. I agree, it's curious. This is the second time tonight that we've had a good look at these guys. We saw those two other men doing the same damn walk earlier at one o'clock. Then they turned into this meadow and walked back up into that tree line north of us and disappeared. I wonder what the hell is going on." Rich said.

"Should we take a short jaunt over there and intercept them. Walk up to them and maybe ask a few questions?" Eric asked.

"No. They don't appear to be trying to enter the missile field. The major said just to observe," Rich answered.

"Okay. Then should we take off now?"

"Yeah, mission accomplished. We'll brief Major Lundquist in the morning."

"Okay. Hey, before we take off, let me take a look through the binoculars."

"Sure, here you go," Rich said.

"Thanks," Eric said, taking the binoculars in his hands and raising them, "Who the hell are those guys?"

CHAPTER 18

F. E. Warren Air Force Base
Cheyenne, Wyoming
Early Thursday morning, July 5th

Eight Security Forces personnel from the air force base, six AFOSI special agents from the local base detachment, and six FBI special agents from the Bureau's Cheyenne office stood loosely grouped behind a concrete bunker in F. E. Warren's missile field at one o'clock in the morning. Dave McClure and Tony Robertson were also there, standing next to the cluster of men. Minutes passed until wrist watches read one-thirty in dark morning hours.

Each member of the assemblage had an assault rifle draped over his shoulder and a semi auto pistol strapped to his web belt. The men sniffed at the breezy, Wyoming chilly night air, their memories of the recent July 4th weekend cookouts with their families dissipating. Dave McClure slowly crouched low and peered around the edge of the bunker.

"Well, whaddya know…there they are. They're here. It's a bit early for them to appear tonight, and it's not just the usual two of them approaching. There's a whole cluster of them in black tactical gear rambling down in single file from the tree line. There at least ten or more of them. They're pacing themselves slowly and quietly down through the meadow toward Roundtop Road. And it looks like they all have rifles slung over their shoulders. I think we're about to find out what this is all about," Dave said.

"Does it look like that's their destination, the road?" Bob Wickman, the FBI team lead, asked.

"Hard to tell at this point. But with that many of them, I'd venture to say that may be doubtful, Bob. I think they're headed for the fence line. They could be intending to approach that furthest silo out in the missile field. About six of them appear to have large back packs...just a guess, but worst case is they might contain explosives. Any explosion inside a silo combined with the rocket fuel, well, the resulting spread of radiation would be a God-awful disaster," Dave answered.

"Right. Okay, who's got a pair of night vision binoculars available?" Bob asked, looking at the faces of his team members.

Special Agent Cleve Barton handed him the binoculars that had been strung around his neck.

"Thanks, Cleve," Bob said.

"Are we certain this is the optimal time, Sigmund?" the German terrorist Jakob Koehler asked.

"There's no such thing as being certain in this type of operation, Jakob. Our reconnaissance patrols have continually confirmed that this was the hour with the least perimeter patrols around those missile fields. We're going with that. Let's pick up the pace a bit, but quietly," Sigmund said.

"Okay, thanks," Jakob answered.

"Dammit. It looks like you nailed it, Dave. They're crossing the road and heading for the fence line. A guy who has now moved up to the front of the line has a large set of wire cutters in his hand," Bob said.

"Yeah, they're going for the fence," Dave replied.

"All right, we've got about a foot of grass on this side of the fence too. It may be enough to cover us. Dave, Tony, you come with us to the other side of the bunker. AFOSI and Security forces, drop down on your bellies, click the safeties off your rifles, and begin moving through the grass toward that last silo. We'll do the same thing from the other side of the bunker. Stay low and crawl forward as quietly as you can. No firing until after I've told those bastards to halt in place and drop their weapons. Let's go party, gentlemen," Bob said as they began shuffling away from behind the bunker.

The FBI, AFOSI, and Security Forces personnel left the protection of the concrete bunker and crept forward through the grass on their stomachs. The safeties on their assault rifles had been clicked off. Special Agent Bob Wickman watched as the man in the lead on Roundtop Road cut through the middle wire.

One after another, all the men in black garb stooped down and entered through the fence line. 'The use of deadly force was now authorized,' Bob thought to himself as he rose to kneeling position.

"You men halt! Stop! Halt where you are! You have entered a US Air Force Base fence line where the use of deadly force is authorized! I order you to drop your weapons! Drop them now—or we will open fire!" Bob yelled at the top of his lungs and then rapidly dropped down to lying on his stomach. He raised the rifle to his shoulder.

"Abort! Abort! It's a trap! Get the hell out of here! Go back out through the fence and up to the trees!" Sigmund Degler shrieked, "Fire at the grass in front of that bunker as you're leaving!"

The Red Storm team opened fire first. A clatter of automatic gunfire filled the night air over the missile field. FBI agent Steve Bentley straightaway took a bullet in the center of his forehead. Blood spurted out over his face. He instantly collapsed into the grass.

Tony Robertson took aim at the German shooter who had just shot Bentley. Tony rose to his feet. He fired a burst that stitched up Armand Ostermeyer's torso with 9mm rounds. Blood dribbled from Ostermeyer's chest and abdomen as he stumbled backward from the impacts and fell to the grass.

"Tony, get down!" Bob Wickman shouted.

Sigmund Degler saw Ostermeyer peppered with rounds and fall to his death. Now on the other side of the fence and moving through the meadow, Sigmund halted in place. He raised his rifle to his shoulder and took careful aim. The sights at the end of the barrel were precisely trained on Tony's form. Sigmund emptied his magazine at Tony's chest and fired. A continuous spurt of rounds exploded into Tony's chest, plunging through his body.

Tony's knees buckled. A look of stark horror swept across his face. His rifle dropped from his hands as he grabbed desperately at his ribcage and fell to the ground. Happy to have found his mark, Sigmund turned and bolted for the tree line.

Dave, his eyes open wide in shock, saw Tony collapse. He let go of his rifle, leaped to his feet, and ran to Tony's side. His shrieks into the night air soon turned to sobs. Tony was unmoving. His eyes were opened wide. Dave pulled Tony's head up, drawing him to his chest.

"No! No! No! Tony! Don't do this...please, don't die! Don't...no!" Dave wailed, cradling Tony's limp, lifeless form, "Tony...!" Dave exclaimed, rocking back and forth on the grass with Tony in his arms. Tears welled in his eyes.

FBI agents Bob Wickman and Cleve Barton were the first to run to Dave's side. Bob reached down and gently held Dave's right shoulder.

"Dave, I am so sorry. You can't help him—look at his chest...it's a mess. Tony's gone. I'm sorry. Please, ease him down so my men can lift him up and carry him with us," Bob said in a soft voice as he softly tugged at Dave's shoulder.

"Tony! He was my best friend...my buddy! And now you tell me he's gone, dead," Dave moaned, "Oh....no!"

"He is gone, Dave. It appears he may have taken at least four bullets dead center to his chest. A heart shot, for sure. We can't help him. Please, let him go, let go, Dave," Bob said in monotone.

"Tell me, did you see the shooter? Was that Degler?" Dave said with a sob, staring at the meadow and the trees beyond it.

"I think it was him, yes," Bob said.

Four FBI agents leaned over and lifted Tony from Dave's arms, carrying him away. Dave sat motionless on the ground, his head bent downward and shaking slowly back and forth. His sobs were growing further apart and quieter. AFOSI agents had moved up by the site's perimeter and examined the cut wire to determine how best to repair it.

"Tony...my friend..." Dave mumbled as he slowly pushed himself to his feet. To steady him, Bob put his hands under Dave's left shoulder and lifted.

"We need to go after those sonsofbitches…kill every fuck-ing one of them," Dave muttered, tentative as he staggered forward.

"We will, Dave, just not tonight. They'd have the advan-tages of the darkness and the trees in the woods. They could cut every one of us down. No, we'll head out after them to-morrow. I'm going to ask for two teams of FBI agents and some SWAT members from the Cheyenne police department."

"Okay," Dave muttered.

"We'll get them and that's not conjecture on my part. We'll run their asses down in the mountains," Bob said, still sup-porting Dave's shoulder. Dave's walking grew steadier. Bob gradually released him but continued to walk alongside him.

"Thanks, Bob. I just can't believe it. Tony was the best friend, the best partner that one could have. Jeez. I saw the asshole who shot him—Sigmund Degler! I'm going to cut that bastard's heart right out of his chest! That German sonofa-bitch is a walking dead man!"

"Calm down. You'll get that chance. I promise you, you'll get that chance, Dave," Bob replied.

"I'll have to call Pete Novak and Jack Barrett. Tony's name will be engraved in the marble Honor Wall. I suppose given that he was once a green beret and the circumstances of his death, his funeral may take place at Arlington," Dave said, his voice growing clearer, stronger.

"Okay. Look, you're getting way ahead of yourself. You need to calm yourself. Maybe silently pray that the Lord will take Tony into his arms. Prayer can help. Still, if you want to and think it's necessary, you can use our secure phones to call Novak and Barrett.

"Okay. Thanks. It's just that…oh, my God."

"I understand. Try to get yourself together now. We'll be

starting out early tomorrow morning, and you'll be right with us. Those Red Storm bastards are going to be running like hell. They know damn well that we'll be coming after them and fast. Dave, I do understand your sadness and your anger in this. We'll get them."

"Thanks, Bob. I doubt I'll be able to sleep much tonight. I'll call my wife Karen in the morning. Virginia is two hours later from here. She liked Tony a great deal, too. He was going to be Uncle Tony to our new baby girl."

"He can still be Uncle Tony. Your stories will make her aware of him. Come on, let's get off this missile field."

Dave and Bob walked silently together across the field to the SUVs. Dave raised his hands to wipe the wetness from his eyes and the tracks of tears from his cheeks. His face grew stern.

"Tony…" Dave whispered to himself, his head drooping, his shoe scuffing at the dirt.

CHAPTER 19

F. E. Warren Air Force Base
Cheyenne, Wyoming
Friday morning, July 6th

It was early in the day. The sky on the eastern horizon was just beginning to turn gray. Dave McClure leaned against the hood of one of the FBI's black Tahoe SUVs, his hand on his cell phone holster. Knowing he had to call Langley and brief Pete Novak about Tony Robertson's violent death, he struggled once again to regain his composure and gather his thoughts.

"Central Intelligence Agency. How may I help you?" a young male voice answered.

"Pete Novak, please. This is Dave McClure."

"I'll route the call, sir."

"Novak," Pete answered.

"Sir, it's Dave McClure. I need to brief you on Tony…"

Pete cut him off. "Dave, I've had this FBI spot report on my desk less than five minutes. I couldn't get past the first few lines. It says Tony was shot to death," Pete said.

"Yes, sir. He and one other FBI agent, Steve Bentley."

"Are you okay, Dave?" Pete asked.

"To be honest, no, not really. I don't have a wound or anything. I just can't get past..." Dave replied.

"Tony was your best mate. I know that. You're hurting."

"I suppose I am. I have a hard time believing he's gone. And so fast. Just like that, Tony's gone," Dave said.

"The FBI report also notes that Special Agent Bob Wickman indicated that it was Sigmund Degler himself who shot Tony. That correct?"

"Yes. FBI teams are coming in this morning. We're going to track the Germans into the mountains. I'm going to catch that sonofabitch, kill him myself, and cut out his heart. I'll nail it to a tree," Dave responded.

"Dave, that's anger and depression speaking. Fact is, Degler would be better taken alive. That's my guidance to you. And you're a tag-along. So, in no way should you be upfront," Pete said.

"I know."

"When are you taking off?"

"The first FBI team is already here. They came in a Sprinter van. The second team is in route. It shouldn't be long. Does the FBI report say anything else useful?" Dave said.

"Not really. Like I said, I couldn't get past the first few lines. I need finish reading it and then brief Jack Barrett. Dave, I mean this, you stay safe. With Tony's passing, it's gonna be bad here on the campus. I don't want it doubly bad."

"Thanks, Pete. I'll give you a call to back-brief you once all of this is over."

"Stay safe. God bless you. Novak out," Pete said. The line clicked off.

Dave moved to the side of the van and eased down to sit on the runner's step up. He rubbed his forehead. This was hard, mentally. It was almost like reliving Tony's death again. He had to call Karen. He dialed the home landline and on the third ring, she picked up, recognizing the number of Dave's cell.

"Dave? Hi, Sweetheart. This is an odd time of the day for you to call. Is everything okay?"

"No, it isn't honey. Bad news, really bad news."

"What? Are you okay?" Karen asked.

"Yes, I'm fine. Karen, Tony's dead. He was shot to death last night," Dave said.

"Oh God, no. Tony? Sweetheart, I am so sorry. I know what the man meant to you. He was your best friend and your partner. And he was going to be Uncle Tony after Carolyn is born," Karen said.

"Yeah, Tony was thrilled at the prospect of playing with little Carolyn and being called Uncle Tony."

"You must feel terrible. Really down."

"I do. It's something that I'm going to have to find a way to deal with it. That's all. I loved that guy. There really is no other option. It'll take some time. I think that going into the mountains today with the teams of FBI agents might help in that regard. It's me along with two FBI teams."

"Going into the mountains? That sounds dangerous. Dave, please be careful. I want you back home and, in my arms," Karen said.

"I'll be fine. Like Pete Novak instructed me on the phone, this is the FBI's party. I'm just a tag-along. I can't be up front. I have to go, honey, the second FBI van is pulling in. I'll be home to hug and kiss you," Dave said.

"All right. Good-bye, Sweetheart," Karen answered as Dave clicked off.

CHAPTER 20

Roundtop Road
West Cheyenne, Wyoming
Friday morning, July 6th

After passing through the yet unrepaired perimeter fence with Special Agent Bob Wickman leading, Dave McClure and the two FBI teams gathered together on Roundtop Road. Bob Wickman walked to the center of the group.

"Gentlemen, good morning. To begin with, I want to confirm to you that we lost our own Steve Bentley and CIA agent Tony Robertson last night. I've asked the Lord to bless their souls and to heal the hearts of their families and our own hearts at their loss. God bless them. They were heroes," Bob said, the men all lowering their heads and nodding.

Bob continued, "Also, the BundeskriminalAmt, BKA, in Germany sent us a digital photo file of known Red Storm terrorists. The man that Tony Robertson shot and killed before he himself died was a man named Armand Ostermeyer. Ostermeyer was known to have participated in several bombings in Germany and France resulting in a loss of lives. Tony

Robertson ensured for us that Armand wouldn't be doing any more bombing. So, now, we're going to trek into the mountains west of here and track the rest of those bastards down. As General George Patton once said, 'May the Lord have mercy on our enemies, because I won't,'" Bob smiled as the men all nodded in approval.

"Don't get me wrong, though. This is not a revenge trip. We're going to hunt those sonsofbitches down and bring their asses to justice. That's our mission. In the Bible, in Hebrews 10:30, it is written: 'Vengeance is mine; I will repay, says the Lord.' Having said that, I don't want any of you to put yourself at risk in any way, shape, or form. If you're fired upon or determine you're about to be fired upon, shoot 'em and bring 'em down!" Bob exclaimed.

"Thank you. All right. Initially, Alpha team under Terry Ford will take the lead along with Dave McClure and I. Bravo team under Brad Nelson will follow. In the afternoon, Alpha and Bravo teams will switch positions. And no talking or other noise making. We need to stay stealthy. Everybody get all this?" Bob asked to which a bunch of 'yes, sirs' and nodding heads responded.

"Good. Well, let's go track those sonsofbitches down," Bob finished.

After crossing over the sunlit grassy meadow, they entered the thickly treed incline of the pine forest. It was murkier and darker under all the tightly grouped trees. However, ground cover and bushes were minimal due to the acidity of the soil brought about by the abundance of brown pine needles. The trail itself was all rocks and dirt, very little grass or weeds.

As the sun rose, the air warmed. After a couple hours of hiking and breaking into a light sweat, Dave admitted to himself that although Wyoming nights were chilly, hours of trekking through the woods in July would soon have anyone perspiring. Trudging uphill just behind Terry Ford, Dave turned to Bob Wickman.

"Do you think there's a chance of catching up to them today?" Dave asked.

"I don't think so. Not today. They've got a good head start. Then again, it's possible they don't know yet that they're being pursued, so they might be moving at a light pace. We won't have any fires tonight. We'll be dining on the FBI's exquisite version of K-Rations," Bob answered.

"Sounds yummy," Dave replied to which Bob broke out in a laugh.

"Oh, they're real yummy," Bob said, chuckling.

The men trekked through the morning. The ascent wasn't all that steep, but it was constant. By noontime, many of the team members were panting for air and sweating. Bob turned, looked down the trail at them, and raised his hands in a 'T' — Time Out.

"Let's take a break for lunch, guys. Drink your water, hydrate, and refresh yourselves. Let's take at least a half hour. Does that sound like enough time?" Bob asked.

The men all grunted, nodding their heads. They moved to the sides of the trail where they plopped down and slipped the packs off their shoulders.

"Dave, we're having the same delectable repast for lunch as we are for dinner. FBI K-rations. They're in your pack. Have a seat and enjoy. By the way, the beef jerky in the K-rations is actually pretty damn good," Bob said.

"Hey, I'm hungry. I'd enjoy anything now, even your K-rations and water," Dave replied as he moved to the edge of the trail. He squatted down, wiping some sweat from around his neck, and opening his pack.

"Guys, when we take off, Bravo team under Brad Nelson will be taking the lead throughout this afternoon. Alpha team will follow. Rest up. I have a feeling it will be a long afternoon, but I also suspect we're gaining ground on these German terrorists," Bob announced. He stepped over to the edge of the trail and eased down next to Dave.

"Really think we're gaining?" Dave asked.

"Yes, I do. I think it's possible we may sight and catch up with them tomorrow."

"You're an optimist, Bob. I like that. Myself, I try to take it as it comes, no matter how good or how bad," Dave said.

"I've noticed that about you. Enjoy lunch."

After twenty-minutes, Bob checked his watch and rose to his feet.

"Let's begin to tie things up, men. We take off again in ten minutes," Bob said, his voice firm. Minutes passed. Bob stood, slid his pack over his shoulders, and bent down to pick up his rifle. Dave followed suit.

"All right. Let's go. Keep your eyes scanning the woods, left and right, and keep your ears open. For the balance of the afternoon, I'd like us to be trekking at a bit faster clip. It won't be long now. We'll catch those German terrorists. They're going to pay dearly for killing Steve Bentley and Tony Robertson as well as intruding on one of our air force bases. They're overdue for justice, but it's gaining on them," Bob said in a hushed voice.

The afternoon seemed long. While the grade of the trail appeared to lessen somewhat, even nearly leveling off, the air continued to grow hot and sticky. As they slowly gained in altitude, the teams found themselves swatting away the bites of black flies. Dave pulled his collar up around his neck. Despite the sweat and now the swarms of biting flies, he found the beauty of the Wyoming forest was nearly overwhelming. Absolutely beautiful, he thought.

The increase in their elevation brought groves of Aspen appearing on each side of the trail, their leaves fluttering in the slight breeze. The two teams of agents were amazed at the splendor of the woods as they passed through. Their faces filled with smiles even as flickers, woodpeckers, magpies, finches, and other birds ignored the group of hikers, zipping from tree to tree in search of insects. Chipmunks and squirrels scurried along the leaves and pine needles on the forest floor, seeking acorns, nuts, and other attractive things to munch on.

As late afternoon approached, light began to slowly fade among the trees. The sun was setting behind the more distant, higher mountains. As it did so, the air grew cooler, and the flies gradually disappeared. The woods eventually became dusky, beams of sunlight no longer streaming through tree branches. Bob swiveled about and once again raised his hands in a 'T' — Time Out.

"All right, men. We've covered enough ground for today. Thank you for keeping up with the faster pace. Go ahead and pick a place with enough room to settle down. Eat dinner and drink enough water to hydrate. This was a long afternoon, lots of sweating. There are thermal blankets in your packs. They're large enough to lay on the ground under you and then wrap around you. Use your packs for pillows."

Grunts of relief emanated down the line of men. They stepped to the side of the trail and plopped on the ground.

"By the way, if you haven't noticed, the tracks from our Red Storm terrorists have grown a lot fresher. They'll no doubt bed down for the night too. What that means is we may very well see some action tomorrow. So, eat and cuddle up in your blankets. Get some rest...we all may need it tomorrow. I'm sending a sentry on the trail uphill from us and one downhill from us. Nighty-night, guys," Bob said. There were chuckles from the men settling in and bedding down for the evening.

As the teams settled down, Dave picked a spot, pulled out the package of K-rations, and laid out his thermal blanket. He edged down on it and wrapped it around him. He felt the blankets were a nice idea. After pulling up his canteen from his web belt, he began to chew on a strip of beef jerky. Bob was right...the jerky wasn't bad at all. Actually, pretty good.

Lying against his pack, thoughts began to barrel through his mind about what may come the next day. Tomorrow may very well be the day of reckoning for Sigmund Degler and his group of Red Storm terrorists. And as Tony's killer...Dave hoped he would get the opportunity to face off with Sigmund himself. Working on munching crackers with the jerky, he pushed himself more erect against the pack.

His eyes scanned up and down the trail. It was growing dark, near black in the woods now. Dave glimpsed upward. There were gaps in the tall pines where he could see patches of a black sky sprinkled with millions of pinpoint orbs of light. The sight was somehow restful.

Finishing with a K-rations energy bar, he reached back to stuff the wrapping from the package in a pocket of the backpack. He pulled up the blanket and slowly forced his eyes closed. There was a slight chirping sound...probably some birds settling down in the trees for the night. That too felt sort of pleasant. Dave smiled.

CHAPTER 21

Mountains west of Cheyenne
Wyoming
Saturday morning, July 9th

Dave rose to a sitting position with his thermal blanket wrapped around him. It was early morning in the Wyoming mountain woods. The woods had transformed from its nighttime black to a morning's dark gray. The air was cool, aromatic with a pine aroma. Peering into the woods, he could see there was a slight mist that appeared to float just above the ground. It had an eerie look to it.

Birds began chirping in the trees by the hundreds. The forest was awakening in anticipation of a new day. He pushed the blanket off him and stood up, stretching his legs and arms. He stepped into the center of the trail.

"You're an early riser," Bob Wickman whispered, his eyes barely open, squinting.

"Not usually. Something woke me. I think it was those hundreds of birds chirping above us in the trees," Dave answered.

"Yeah, they are loud, aren't they? Again, this morning, we'll all have to settle for water or cold tea. No fires. We don't want to put any smoke or the odor of burning wood in the air. There are a couple bottles of tea in your pack."

"Cold tea? Well, that still sounds a hell of a lot better at this hour than just cold water. I'll munch on an energy bar from one of my super-duper FBI K-ration packages," Dave murmured, sitting down on the blanket once again and rummaging through his pack for a bottle of tea and an energy bar.

"We'll get started in about an hour. I don't want to wake the men now. It looks like there's a low ground fog out in the woods today. It'll impair our vision, so it'll be better to let that dissipate before we take off. I think I'll have some tea too," Bob said, sitting upright.

The two men sat next to each other wrapped in their thermal blankets. Dave munched on an energy bar, washing it down with tea. Bob chewed on a piece of beef jerky with crackers. They glanced around the woods but couldn't see much due to the early hour and the mist that hung just above the ground.

"I have a strong feeling that we'll see some action today. I can feel it in my blood. Make sure you have a round loaded in the breech," Bob said.

"Thanks. I usually do, but I'll check. Don't you think they'll be outgunned?"

"Yeah, but we could still lose somebody, and I want to try to avoid that," Bob said.

"Then tell the guys to shoot first. If they see a firefight coming, fire the first bullet. Remember, these are German terrorists, Bob. We owe them absofreakinglutely nothing. Nothing," Dave said.

"Interesting insight. I may do that. Thanks," Bob said with a slight smile.

"I'm gonna walk up and down the trail a bit. Try to get all the stiffness out of my bones."

"Okay, just don't go too far. I think I'll get up and stretch myself."

Dave meandered up the trail, staying within eyesight of Bob. He inhaled the pine forest air, then turned and began walking back down the trail. The cool morning air was invigorating, enhanced by the aroma of all the damp pine needles on the ground. He walked to the end of the line of men who were now beginning to stir in their thermal blankets at the side of the trail. He stopped back at his own sleeping spot.

"Feel good?" Bob asked.

"Yeah, it did. These woods are gorgeous. I wish we were here under different circumstances," Dave answered.

"I know. Me, too. But it's who we are, and this is our mission. And we're about to pursue it again," Bob said.

"I'm going to remind myself of that several times today. Thanks, Bob," Dave answered, smiling.

"Somehow I doubt that Dave McClure needs any reminding about mission priorities," Bob replied, snickering.

The light in the forest slowly but steadily brightened. The sun was now over the horizon of the mountains further off. Soon, beams of sunlight would be streaming through the high limbs, branches, and leaves.

Bob shoved himself to his feet and glanced up and down the trail. Men were sipping tea or water and munching on breakfast bars and beef jerky.

"Men, we'll move out of here in twenty minutes or so. Police your areas for any trash, wrappers, and stuff, and put anything you find back into your packs. Check your weapons.

Ensure you have a round in the breech. I have a strong hunch that we're going to catch up to the Germans today and see some action. Terry Ford and Alpha team will lead off for the morning. Thanks."

As Bob had announced they would, the teams moved out twenty minutes later—single file, trekking up the trail. The air began to transition from a cool early morning to a warmer midmorning. Bob maintained a good pace. He was serious about catching up to the Germans.

Dave was walking to the right of Bob and Terry, his eyes constantly scanning the forest, his rifle now hugged across his chest. The steepness of the trail's grade had lessened a great deal. They appeared to be approaching the first crest of the mountain.

After a little over an hour of hiking, an area to his right caught Dave's eyes. He paused, his head tilting to further examine the sight. Leaves and stems were broken. Ground clutter had been flattened. It looked as though something had squeezed through here. It may have been a wheeled vehicle.

"See something, Dave? All the primary tracks go up the trail. That's where our group has gone," Bob said.

"Yeah. You're right. Probably nothing," Dave answered.

They hadn't progressed more than a half hour from the spot where Dave had paused, when Bob raised his hand in the air and spun around, signaling the men to halt. He then flattened his hand down and patted the air. They all dropped to a crouch. Quiet. There were sounds coming from up the trail—like engines cranking, attempting to turn over, but not starting.

"Could be ATVs. I thought it might be a possibility that they could have some. They may be all out of gas," Bob said.

"ATV? Hmm, I wonder," Dave muttered to himself.

138

He lifted himself up and moved over in a crouch to the side of the trail. Turning around, he then hustled back down the trail. He soon came to the stretch where he had paused earlier. It could be an ATV that had squeezed off the trail here.

Dave stepped into the woods and followed the weaving of the tracks. They twisted around the large trees but leveled a few saplings. This was something large...yeah, it could be an ATV. Dave continued following the tracks. He suddenly dropped to his knees at the sound — the cranking of an engine. Not far ahead. He faintly heard men's voices. No doubt about it, they were speaking in German.

Dave quietly slipped the rifle off his shoulder. He unsnapped the retainer strap in his holster and drew the pistol. He clicked off the safety and cocked the hammer, then rose to a crouch. He stepped tentatively forward, his eyes searching.

He saw them. Two Germans in black tactical garb standing on the same side of an ATV, its hood open. They were leaning over examining the engine.

Dave walked forward, his pistol in a two-hand grip. As he stepped closer, he began to sing an old German tune in a low melodic voice.

"In München steht ein Hofbräuhaus, eins, zwei, g'suffa! Alles gut hier, meine herren?In Munich there stands a Hofbräuhaus, One, two, chug it! Everything okay here, gentlemen?

Startled, the men rapidly spun around. Seeing Dave with his pistol drawn, they reached for their holsters.

"Lassen ihre waffen fallen oder sie sind tot! Drop your weapons or you're dead!" Dave shouted.

"Amerikanisches Schwein! American pig!" The one on the right blurted out.

"Nein! Nicht! Sie sind tot! No! You're dead!" Dave exclaimed.

Both men grabbed the grips of their pistols and yanked them from their holsters. Dave instantly opened fire. In just seconds, with a two-hands grip, he swept his muzzle from right to left and fired three rounds plunging into the center of each man's chest at blistering speed. The two men staggered backward and went limp, their pistols sliding into their laps. The head on the man on the right slipped sideways, thumping against the large rear wheel. The head of the man on the left thudded down on a metal step-up.

Dave kept the barrel of his pistol aligned on the men, sweeping it slowly between them. They were motionless, sputters of blood seeping down their shirts. He abruptly dropped into a crouch, his eyes skimming the woods for the possibility of a third man who would be another threat. There was nothing.

Dave gradually rose, clicked the safety on, and holstered the pistol. He approached the dead men. They were both middle-aged, probably in their forties.

Dave slumped to the ground, sitting a few feet from the ATV, and shaking his head. He pulled out his water bottle and took a long sip. He could hear the pounding of boots on the ground behind him, approaching from the main trail. Bob Wickman was at the lead as the FBI agents entered the little clearing. Bob's eyes swept from the ATV with the Germans sprawled on parts of it and then to Dave. Terry Ford and some agents gathered around him.

"Dave, are you okay?" Bob asked.

"Yeah. I'm just giving the adrenaline a chance to run out of me, but I'm fine," Dave answered.

"So, you did see something when we passed that spot, didn't you. Very observant on your part, fella. I wonder if these two broke off from their main group to go AWOL. You know, maybe thinking that any pursuers would follow the larger group," Bob said.

"I'm not sure if we'll ever know the answer to that one, Bob," Dave said as he rose to his feet.

"These two were apparently both facing you, so I suppose you gave them a chance to surrender, right?"

"I did. Yes," Dave answered, as Bob stood facing the ATV.

"Both of these men appear to have been shot three times dead center in their chests. Their pistols are loose, so they had drawn their weapons. I say, that was some superior combat shooting on your part, Dave. But look, you really shouldn't break off like that and go it alone. You could have been the one shot and killed," Bob said.

"I spoke to them in German. I told them not to draw their weapons, but they did. My pistol was already drawn, and I was in a two-hand shooting stance. I couldn't miss at that close range. I had no choice," Dave answered.

"I see. Okay. I'm just glad you're all right. Not a scratch on you," Bob said, turning to the group.

"A couple of you men drag these dead guys up to the trail and lay them there somewhere. There'll be a recovery of their bodies later. It's certain that the Germans know we're after them now. They had to have heard those shots. We'll need to be more careful as we move forward. Let's get back on the trail and continue the hunt. We'll take a two minute breathing break, but guys, we're close. Very close," Bob exclaimed.

Bob, Terry, Dave, and the agents turned and walked back to the main trail, weaving around the trees, and staying behind the men ahead of them who were dragging the bodies.

The teams trekked back up the trail, anticipation on their faces now having seen several dead German terrorists close up. The sun had moved directly overhead, and the air warmed significantly. After little more than an hour of trudging uphill, sweat was once again building up on their faces, necks, and backs. Bob Wickman paused turning back to the group.

"We'll take a quick break here for lunch and rest. We'll pick up the pace after that. If we can end this today, capture these terrorists, and bring them to justice, then let's do it. Brad Nelson and Team Bravo will take the lead for the afternoon. Break!" Bob exclaimed, as the men moved to the side of the trail.

Dave and Bob slipped off their packs and plopped down once again next to each other. Dave pulled out beef jerky, crackers, and tea. They glanced at each other while chewing on their food.

"I heard that you and your wife are going to have a baby. That right?" Bob asked.

"Yeah, and it's close now time wise. I want to be there. That's too important to miss," Dave answered.

"I'll pray for you to make it. It is important. You'll get back there and be there for them, Dave," Bob said.

"Thanks. I appreciate that. It is weighing somewhat on my mind."

The men finished their food and cleaned up. They stood once again and slipped on their packs. Brad Nelson and Bravo team walked forward of the group to again take the lead. Bob, Brad, Dave, and the FBI teams began tramping ahead on the now almost level ground. Dave moved to the left of Bob and Brad. After marching past the row of out-of-gas ATVs, Dave glanced over at Bob.

"Seems like we're close to the peak of this low mountain. What's on the other side, Bob?" Dave asked.

"There's a slight descent to a stream and meadow. Much higher mountains are beyond that though, south, and west of Laramie. I'd really like to avoid that mountain range, if at all possible. We're prepared, but not so well prepared for the wilderness that's in those mountains," Bob said.

"I see. Sounds like my trip to Alaska. I trekked into the Chugach Mountains and then into the Wrangell-St. Elias Wilderness. The Wrangell-St. Elias is larger than the country of Switzerland. It was extremely rugged."

"Right."

The FBI group had hiked for another two hours. Black flies returned but not in the hordes the teams had previously experienced. An abrupt barrage of automatic gunfire filled the air. There were at least three Germans well ahead of them firing from behind a large fallen log. Aiming slightly downhill, their first bursts had gone high, the rounds zipping just above the FBI agents' heads. No one was hit.

"Down! Take cover and return fire!" Bob shouted out.

The men dropped down and clambered behind the trunks of trees. Slipping off their packs, they returned fire with their M5 full auto assault rifles.

Dave glanced to his left. There was nothing there but a low, rocky ravine. Interesting. Perhaps it could keep him below ground level and in good cover, he thought. He slipped off his rifle, then his backpack. He glanced back to his right. Everyone was focused uphill and firing. Dave crawled to his left from his spot and along the depression of the ravine. His chest and legs scraped over rocks and dead tree branches. Slow going.

When he'd finally reached an area that he gauged to be about thirty yards away from his group, he made a right turn and continued forward on the mild slope. He was perspiring heavily. The rocks and branches had torn some small holes in his shirt and pants, but he could see beds of pine needles covering the ground ahead. The terrain would improve as he ascended.

He kept slithering ahead. It wasn't long before he realized that he'd come parallel with the Germans shooting from behind the fallen log. There appeared to be three of them and they were still firing full auto at the FBI agents. He decided it would be best to continue about twenty yards further up behind them.

He was careful to stay as low as he could. As he went, the beds of damp pine needles cushioned him. They were easier to crawl over and, in some cases, even slide across. When he reached what he thought was twenty yards, he paused. He checked his pistol, fully loaded mag, and one in the breech. He turned to his right to crawl directly behind the Germans.

It didn't take long. In a few minutes of skulking forward, the sounds of his scraping on rocky ground was again repressed by the constant staccato of automatic gunfire filling the air. He took a quick glance. He was directly behind them. He slipped his pistol from his holster, clicked off the safety, and cocked the hammer.

Dave slowly rose to his feet. His arms stretched out before him, he held his pistol in a two-hand grip. Beads of sweat trickled down his face and neck. He was concerned at first about the rounds coming upward from the FBI group, but none appeared to impacting near him. When he was just twenty feet away from the Germans and the large log, he paused.

"*Ah, wir haben ein truthahn schiessen! Ah, we're having a turkey shoot,*" Dave said in a loud voice.

The three Germans swiveled their heads and shoulders abruptly about. Their eyes opened wide, looks of astonishment washing across their faces.

"*Legen Sie ihre waffen auf den boden! Jetzt! Put your weapons on the ground! Now!*" Dave barked out.

The German on the right grimaced. He began to rapidly jerk his rifle around. Dave knew that assault rifle was more deadly than any pistol, so that man was instantly nominated target number one. The other two swiftly went for their holsters.

Dave opened fire, pressing the trigger, and firing repeatedly, moving his barrel from right to left. In less than five seconds, he put two rounds pounding into each man's head. A spray of red blood, bone, brain matter, and other gore burst from their skulls into the air around them. Dave stepped backward. He again went into a combat crouch, his eyes skimming the woods 180 degrees from left to right. Other threats? He saw none.

Dave dropped to his knees and then collapsed backward against a tree trunk in a sitting position, staring at the carnage before him. He slowly shook his head as he holstered his pistol. The rattle of gunfire had suddenly stopped. A dead silence engulfed the forest. Dave strained his neck to see downhill over the log.

"All's clear up here, Special Agent Bob Wickman!" Dave yelled out.

There was quiet. Dave could hear a slight sound of muffled voices coming from down the trail.

"Dave McClure, is that you?" Bob yelled back.

"Yes, it's me, Bob! There were three of them up here, but they've gone to meet with Jesus!" Dave shouted. There was mumbling of laughs and chuckles from the agents crouching down the trail.

It turned quiet again. Dave pulled out his water and groped in one larger food pocket. A surprise. He pulled out a Hershey's chocolate almond bar. A treat. He could hear boots coming up the hill, so he unwrapped the chocolate bar and began chewing. It was so sweet with crunchy almonds. A slender smile etched across his face.

Bob appeared walking around one end of the large log and Brad around the other end. The teams of men followed. Bob and Brad stared at the three stone dead Germans and shook their heads. Special Agent Gene Kaminski walked to Dave and laid his M5 rifle and backpack to the side of him.

"Thank you. And you are," Dave said.

"Gene Kaminski. I saw you crawl away from us down there, but I didn't think I should try to stop you. So, my pleasure, Dave," Gene replied.

"Well, I'm pleased to meet you, Gene. Thanks for toting up my rifle and pack," Dave replied.

"Three more dead terrorists. All three shot twice in the head. Two taps each. And they were facing you, their two pistols and a rifle on the ground next to them. Dave, I...I don't know what to say," Bob said.

"Hey, I told these guys in German, in their own damn language, to put their weapons on the ground. If they'd done that, they would have saved themselves, but they took the chance and went for broke. I think that maybe along the road to becoming a hard-core terrorist, one might become too radicalized to even think straight. And once again, my pistol was already drawn, and I had a two-hand grip. They saw that. Still, they went for it. Foolish, stupid actions by three idiots," Dave replied.

"I agree with you. What do you think about them?" Bob asked.

"They've got to be stay-behinds. Their job was to slow us down and keep us from moving ahead on the mountain while Sigmund Degler and the rest of his team get back some of their lead on us. Perhaps maybe even escape,"

"I agree with that assessment. Since these bodies are on the main trail, we'll leave them here for a later recovery. And once again, that had to be quite an impressive display of combat shooting," Bill said.

"Thanks for that. But it really was a stupid move on their part. They paid for it and now they're dead," Dave answered.

"I think this has been enough for today. We'll have to tie it up tomorrow. As tired as they must be, Degler and the remains of his team won't get far. Half of them are already dead. Let's go up about fifty, sixty yards past the Germans and the log. We'll pick out our spots and bed down there. It's possible that their dead bodies could draw predators," Bob said.

"Sounds like a plan," Dave said, smiling.

"Let's get on it then," Bob replied, taking a last look at the bloodbath of the three dead Germans shot in their heads. He turned and walked up the trail. Dave, Brad, and the teams of men followed, shaking their heads at the Germans. Brad patted Dave on the back.

"I don't know how you do it, Agent McClure, but I'm sure glad you're on our side," Brad said, chuckling.

"Thanks, Brad," Dave said. The two shook hands and continued to walk up trail with Bob.

CHAPTER 22

Mountains west of Cheyenne
Wyoming
Sunday morning, July 10th

A hand reached over to give Dave McClure's right shoulder a gentle shake. Dave flicked his eyes open.

"Uh-huh," Dave muttered.

"It's Bob. It's an early start for us today, Dave. We're going to try to finish it, wrap it up," Bob said.

"Thanks for the nudge. I needed it. I was really in a deep sleep from the events yesterday."

"Well, for how you performed yesterday, you certainly deserved a good night's sleep. Let's see if we can finish off this hunt for those German terrorists today."

"Indeed, sir," Dave answered, rising to a sitting position, shaking off remains of his slumber.

The teams didn't spend long on breakfast. They were filled with an eagerness to get back on the trail and with a high pace enabling them to catch up with the Germans today and end the chase. Bring those assholes to justice. In less than twenty-five minutes, the group had packed up and was trekking up the trail which was beginning to level out. Bob, Terry, and Dave were in front, Alpha team just behind them, and Bravo team trailing. The men appeared invigorated to be trekking in the morning air and were moving at their fastest clip yet.

Two hours later, sunbeams began streaming through pine and aspen branches. Birds flitted about between them. The air was once again warming. Their quick stride had not lessened — the terrain was now easy to pass through.

Several bursts of automatic gunfire rattled through the air. Terry Ford took a round in his right thigh and immediately collapsed to one knee. Dan Rittenhouse behind Terry stumbled to his side, falling sideways as a round bashed him in his upper right chest. All the men lunged to the ground. Bob pulled Terry behind a tree for cover. Gene Kaminski skittered over and did the same with Dan.

"Shit! That was sudden. And they were far more accurate this time. I count three of them!" Bob exclaimed.

"I think you're right—I saw three too! It's level ground now...easier to sight in on us! Bob, bring all the men upward and spread them out. Those bastards will be quickly outgunned by our rate of fire. They'll be ducking more than shooting," Dave answered as he glanced off to his left.

"Good idea!" Bob responded, motioning with his left arm for the teams to move up and spread out.

Dave slipped off his rifle and pack. He rose to a crouch, fired a long string of rounds at the Germans, and began running to his left across the woods. Rifle sights followed him. Bullets hammered into trees, splintering bark as he ran.

"Dave! No! Don't!" Bob shouted.

"That sonofabitch, Degler, is not getting away! No way, Bob! Don't worry, I'll be okay!" Dave yelled out.

"I'm going to find that sonofabitch, gut him out like a twelve-point buck, and nail his liver to one of these pine trees," Dave muttered to himself.

As the shots aimed at him trailed off, Dave rose more erect and went into a full sprint. Soon near fifty yards away, he turned right. In minutes, he rapidly was dashing through the forest, zigzagging around trees, and smacking branches away as he went. The rattle of gunfire suppressed the noise he was making himself. He passed the Germans off to his right and kept going. Just above the three Germans, he began to circle around to bring him back to the trail.

Dave tore through the woods as fast as his legs would take him. Swiping away branches and leaves, he burst into the open, back on the trail, but well beyond the three Red Storm shooters. He swiveled and dashed off to his left running.

Jakob Koehler stepped out from the edge of the woods some twenty yards ahead of Dave. He began firing, his rushed shots going wide and low.

"Geh mir aus dem weg, Idiot! Get out of my way, idiot!" Dave yelled, his face frowning but turning quickly to anger.

Dave pulled his pistol from its holster and began firing continuously at Koehler. The German backed up to his rear, rounds smashing into the tree next to him, pummeling off pieces of bark. Dave adjusted his aim as he stomped forward.

Two rounds pierced Koehler's right thigh. Two more rounds followed, pounding into his lower abdomen. Another three rounds smashed into his chest. Finally, two rounds struck the base of his neck. Blood spurted from the multiple wounds. A stark look of horror washed across Koehler's face before his eyes suddenly rolled upward. Koehler fell backward, thudding to the ground. His head cracked against a tree trunk.

"Idiot!" Dave bellowed as he rushed past the man, keeping the barrel of his Beretta pointed at the German as he slowed to a jog. Koehler was motionless.

Sigmund Degler couldn't be too far ahead. Dave could now see the bright sunlight across the grass in the meadow beyond the edge of the forest. As he jogged ahead, he caught the gurgling sound of water. That had to be the stream that Bob mentioned yesterday. Dave soon approached the tree line. Glancing quickly in all directions, he could see there was a drop off embankment to the stream itself, and the meadow beyond.

Abruptly a gunshot exploded into the forest air. The round plunged into Dave's left shoulder. He winced at the sudden pain. He then saw Degler standing near the top of the embankment, not thirty yards away. Dave raised his pistol. Degler once again pulled his pistol's trigger, but there was no blast from the muzzle, just a sharp click of the hammer. The German's magazine was empty.

Dave attempted to return fire, but the Beretta also clicked empty. How the hell did that happen? In his eagerness to chase down Degler, after killing Koehler, he should have rammed in a fresh magazine.

Degler tossed his pistol to the ground and pulled a hunting knife from its sheath on his belt.

"I'm not going to rot in some prison, asshole. You're not taking me alive!" Degler barked, taking a step closer.

Dave dropped his pistol. He pulled his own SOG titanium knife from its sheath and thrust it forward from his hip.

"I have no intention of taking you alive, Sigmund. You have to answer for the death of the man you killed in that missile field, Tony Robertson," Dave replied in a growling voice, raising his knife.

Dave flipped the knife in his hand, the metal pommel of the grip now facing forward. The edge of the blade itself facing outward along his forearm.

"You must mean that dumb ass who stood up in the missile field after shooting Armand Ostermeyer. Such a stupid, dumb ass man, And I see you must know a little about knife fighting. It won't make any difference, pig," Degler said, laughing.

At that, Dave lunged forward, flying toward Degler. Almost on top of the German, he leaped as high into the air as his strength would allow him, both boots bashing into Degler's chest. The German fell backward, hit the ground hard, and tumbled down the embankment into the water of the stream. He rose quickly to his feet and lurched forward at Dave's approach.

Dave blocked a knife thrust. As he drew his arm back, his razor-sharp blade slashed across Degler's chest. The German winced, then moaned at the blow. Degler countered with another thrust, this time lower, aimed at Dave's abdomen. Dave blocked this move, his titanium blade slashing Degler's wrist as it drew back.

Dave instantly followed in raising his right leg to hip height, snapping it forward into Degler's left knee, cracking the kneecap and collapsing it. Dave immediately pulled his leg back to his hip and snapped it upward. This time his boot smacked into the German's left jawbone.

Degler fell again, rolled backward down the embankment, and splashed into the stream. He struggled to rise, but Dave was on him instantly, grabbing him by his neck.

Dave shoved Degler's head under the water. In a frenzy, Degler jammed his knife into Dave's left side, barely missing his kidney. Dave promptly rammed his own knife into the center of Degler's chest, just under the sternum. With all his strength, he then thrust it up into Degler's chest cavity, piercing the German's heart.

The knife slid from Degler's hand as his fingers slowly unfurled. Bubbles spewed upward in the water from his mouth and nose as clouds of red blood pumped outward from his chest mixing with the water of the stream.

Dave forced himself up as Degler's body abruptly began to drift downstream. Dave grabbed him by his collar, yanking him from the water and up onto the mud of the embankment. He plopped down at the edge of the stream, gasping for breath, shaking his head.

As his senses once again gathered about him, Dave moved closer to the stream and began washing the blood from his hands and SOG knife. He wiped the blade clean on a dry portion of his shirt, slipped it back in its sheath, and inched away from the stream.

"Damn. We got his ass, Tony, ole buddy," he mumbled to himself. He managed a slight smile, "We got him."

Dave noticed the forest had grown quiet. The clatter of gunfire had dissipated from the air. He didn't bother to turn around as he heard the sound of boots pounding along the trail toward him.

Bob Wickman stepped slowly up to him, placing his hand on Dave's shoulder. Bob glanced to Degler, then to Dave. He saw the blood gathering on Dave's shoulder and oozing from his side.

"Dave. You've been shot. And it looks like you've got a stab wound on your side," Bob said as Alpha and Bravo teams approached the stream.

"It's not bad, Bob. It just aches. I think the bullet went clear through my shoulder, but I don't really know," Dave said.

"It did. And that's a good sign. Who has the medical kit?" Bob exclaimed, turning around.

"I do, Bob," Randy Thorne replied.

"Good. Come up here, Randy. Patch up Dave's shoulder and his side. He's got a bullet wound and a stab wound. We'll get him fully attended to back at the air force base," Bob instructed.

Randy rushed forward and kneeled next to Dave. He opened the medical kit and began cleaning Dave's wounds.

Bob looked out at the sunny meadow beyond the stream, then walked away from the men and raised his satellite phone. In a few minutes, he ambled back to the group.

"Dave, we'll get you patched up as well as we can here, but F.E Warren AFB has medical support. They'll finish taking care of your wounds," Bob said.

"Thanks," Dave said, smiling and nodding back.

"Men, the Air Force is sending out four helicopters to that meadow over there that we're facing, just across the stream. For now, just settle down and take a break. Munch on those wonderful FBI K-rations. We'll leave this bastard Degler's body right here on the embankment, maybe pull him up a little from the stream. The recovery team will get him. Guys, I admit this was a tough one. And you all performed superbly. So, thanks, and congratulations on a job very well done," Bob exclaimed.

The men around him raised their fists in the air and nodded their heads. Everyone patted each other on the back. They sat down reaching for their water bottles and waiting for the instruction to move across the stream and into the field. Bob eased down on the ground next to Dave and placed his hand on his shoulder.

"You know, fella, I've been trying to figure you out for days now, and I think it's time I admit I'm stumped. You, that is, you yourself killed seven of a ten-man German terrorist team, and we got the other three. Jeez. Their bodies are back on the trail, too."

"And?"

"What I mean is that, Dave, on the one hand, you're the epitome of a badass...a badass of badasses. Yet on the other hand, you're a keenly intuitive and sensitive guy. I wonder if you might split down the middle psychologically someday. I want you to know, though, that the bottom-line is I'm very pleased to have met you and had you along with us on this op," Bob said in a low voice.

"Thanks, Bob. Same here. The reality is that it's not the first time I've heard that. Fact is, sometimes I wonder myself if I'll crack down the middle like an ancient Greek vase. However, so far, my separate, opposing personality traits seem to work things out together symbiotically," Dave said.

"Well, I do hope that someday we'll meet again. I'd like to continue to see how you're doing. This is going to be a huge blow to Germany's Red Storm terror movement. They'll be dealing with the loss of their number two man in command, Sigmund Degler, and their up-and-comer, Jakob Koehler."

"Huge blow to the Red Storm? That doesn't even begin to break my heart. Anyway, same to you. I'd like to see you again. In my estimation, you're one of the good guys, Bob."

Both men glanced upward as they heard the whirr of helicopter rotors approaching over the treetops.

"There they are. Coming to take us back to the base and then home. The Air Force guys have been great. What do you say you and I go home?" Bob asked, smiling.

"Sounds like a plan." Dave replied with a grin.

The two men reached over and shook hands. Bob then slipped his backpack over his should and picked up Dave's.

They slung the rifles over their shoulders. Bob reached down and eased Dave up by grabbing him around his waist. The two of them and the teams ambled across the stream and into the sunlit meadow as the helicopters settled in the grass, shutting down their engines and rotors.

CHAPTER 23

Arlington National Cemetery
Northern Virginia
Three days later, Wednesday morning, July 13th

Dave stood straight as a flagpole, bracing, his body rigid near the coffin in his black trench coat, black suit, white shirt, and black tie. His hands were balled into fists in the pockets of his trench coat. The air was damp and cool, very unlike most July mornings in Virginia. There was also a slight but steady drizzle from cloudy skies looming overhead.

The minister had begun the conclusion of his words and blessing over Tony. Dave reached up to pull his collar closer to his neck. He'd forgotten to bring an umbrella. Others standing around the coffin held their own well up over their heads.

Jack Barrett and Pete Novak stood together on the other side of the coffin. They noticed Dave, but were reluctant to approach him, assuming he might yet be wrapped in dark depression. At this moment, they felt it best not to force him to attempt to communicate.

A shadow from an umbrella swept over Dave's head. He glanced up, then to his left. He was surprised to see Bob Wickman standing next to him, holding an umbrella over both of them. They both smiled and nodded at each other.

The minister finished with making the sign of the cross and repeated the Lord's Prayer along with the voices of the crowd of mourners. People began to lean out to drop flowers on the coffin and then began dispersing. Dave dropped a rose with its stem on the coffin, as did Bob. They turned away and ambled toward the area where cars were parked.

"How is it that you're here in Washington DC, Bob?" Dave asked.

"I was called to the headquarters for an interview regarding the operation and its events in Wyoming. It's a standard practice for what we determine to be significant investigations and operations. How're you doing, Dave? Holding up okay?" Bob said, noticing Dave's eyes had filled with tears.

"I'll be okay...I'm just trying to come to terms," Dave said as he wiped a tear trickling down his face.

"Let's pause for just a moment. I'd like to share something with you."

"Okay."

"My grandfather was a Marine. He fought in the Pacific against the Japanese...Iwo Jima, Guadalcanal, other places. I knew him, loved him, but as a young fella, I really didn't know him as a man, his feelings, or his convictions. He had apparently related to my father how so many soldiers in Europe and the Pacific formed friendships and strong bonds during that helluva shit war. What was so grievously sad was that so many of those men never returned. Survivors who came home looked for meaning, ways to come to terms and accept the deaths of their buddies. After the war, my father eventually became a captain in the New York Police Department, the NYPD. Grandad shared with my father that he'd found two verses in the Bible that had comforted him and eased his grief—John 16:22 and Psalm 147:3. It was those passages along with the lyrics to a song that Bing Crosby recorded in 1944 and made a hit from, "I'll Be Seeing You" that he felt allowed him to move on in several occasions. It's a sad song, but I also find it uplifting," Bob explained.

"Okay."

"John 16:22 reads like this, *"So also with you: Now is your time of grief, but I will see you again and your hearts will rejoice, and no one will take away your joy, and no one will take your joy from you."* Psalm 147:3 is shorter and reads, *"He heals the brokenhearted and binds up their wounds."* Apparently, my father found those verses comforting in also subsequently dealing with violent deaths that occurred now and then in the department."

"John 16:22 and Psalm 147:3?" Dave said.

"Yes, those two verses and the lyrics to "I'll Be Seeing You." I have to say myself that those things have in some way helped me on occasion, too. I've lost a couple good friends in the Bureau. So, if you can, take the thought of those passages with you. Think about it. It may very well get you past all this," Bob said.

"Thanks, Bob. I'll do so. As I've said before, you're indeed one of the good guys," Dave replied.

They shook hands, embraced, then turned and walked to their separate cars. Sitting in his black Audi 6 sedan and before pressing the electronic ignition button, Dave reached up and wiped the tears from his eyes. A single sob escaped his lips.

>>> <<<

Hours later that same day, past 10:00 o'clock at night, and in the McClure home on Pumphrey Drive, Dave sat in his underwear on the couch in the family room. Karen had gone to bed an hour ago. On the cocktail table in front of him, a large Bible, NIV version, was opened to page 2,108 where the verse of John 16:22 lay in print before him. He'd tabbed that page as well as page 1,216 for Psalm 147:3. Lying next to the Bible was a page with the lyrics from the song "I'll Be Seeing You" that he had printed from his desktop computer. And next to those things was an Old-Fashioned glass filled with a thumb of Redbreast Irish 12-year-old whiskey. The whiskey was yet untouched.

Dave leaned back against the cushions of the couch. He'd read the verses and song lyrics more than just several times. The Bible passages did help. He felt they gave him a measure of clarity and acceptance. He glanced up to the ceiling.

"Thanks, Lord. Rest in peace, Tony. I love you, buddy. I will never forget you. And I promise you that through the stories of Karen and I, little Carolyn will come to know you as Uncle Tony," Dave whispered.

Dave reached over to take a first sip of whiskey, but he suddenly alerted. Karen's frantic voice unexpectedly echoed down the corridor from the master bedroom.

"Dave! David! Come here! Quickly, please!" Karen shouted.

Dave's hand recoiled from the glass of whiskey. He leaped up from the couch and ran down the hallway to their bedroom. The light was on in the bathroom. He pushed open the door and rushed inside.

"Dave, my water broke! The baby's coming! We need to get to the hospital fast! I can go throw a robe and slippers on. You get dressed." Karen exclaimed.

"Okay. I'll throw on jeans and a shirt. Loafers. We'll make it, sweetheart. Let's go. We'll make it."

"Where will we go?"

"Inova Alexandria Hospital. It's the best one and it's the closest one — right off Fairfax Boulevard."

"Okay. Great," Karen said as the two of them parted company.

They took Karen's 4Runner. It was larger and Dave knew it would be more comfortable for Karen. In less than twenty minutes, they pulled in front of the doors to the Emergency Room. Dave shut the engine down and helped Karen out of the SUV and through the glass doors. A MedTech rushed over and helped Karen into a wheelchair.

"Situation, sir?" the young man asked.

"My wife is pregnant. Her water broke. The baby is coming," Dave replied.

"All right. Have a seat here, sir. I'll take your wife to our surgery suites. The obstetrician may offer you to come and be present. We'll see."

The man pushed Karen in her wheelchair through another set of doors. Dave looked around and saw colored plastic chairs lined against the walls. He chose an orange one and eased himself down onto it. He wrung his hands, waiting. About ten minutes later, the MedTech reappeared, walking through the doors.

"Sir, are you David McClure?"

"Yes. Is everything okay?" Dave replied.

"Oh, yes. Please come with me, sir. Dr. Schwartz offered for you to be present. Dave rose and followed the young man. In the room adjacent to the surgery suite, Dave was donned with a gown, cap, and facemask, and then ushered into surgery.

"Good evening, Mr. McClure," Dr. Schwartz said

"Good evening, sir…Dr. Schwartz," Dave answered.

"None of that formal stuff. I'm Dr. Sam to my patients. Come closer," Dr. Sam said. Karen lay on the delivery bed. She smiled up at Dave.

"I've already administered a neural block for her. She'll be fine. Would you like to cut the cord?" Dr. Sam asked.

"Cut the cord?" Dave replied, his face a bit pale.

"Yes. That is, as long as you don't go and faint on me," Dr. Sam chuckled.

"I'll be fine, doctor. Thanks. You have no idea of the things I've seen," Dave said, becoming excited.

"And I don't think I want to know about the things you've seen. So, good. Come closer to me. Dad is going to cut the cord and bring this young child into the world. Nurse, give the surgical sheers to Mr. McClure. Help him adjust his holding them for a clean cut."

The nurse handed the sheers to Dave. At the birth, the doctor folded the chord and held it up. Dave cut it.

"Congratulations, Mr. McClure, you're the father of a healthy baby girl. Carolyn, I understand," Dr. Sam said as he placed the baby in Karen's waiting arms. A smile stretched across Karen's face.

"Thank you so much, doctor. This is a wonderful experience," Dave said.

"That's what I try to make of these events, David, a joyous occasion. We'll be moving Karen up to her room and baby Carolyn to the nursery. We'll have you paged up to Karen's room when we have her settled. So, please, wait outside for just a few moments," Dr. Sam said, smiling.

Roughly ten minutes later, Dave found himself sitting in a chair next to Karen's bed. She had drifted off to sleep. He remained for another ten minutes or so, then rose, leaned over her, and kissed her forehead. He stepped quietly from the room.

Once on the elevator, he stopped two floors from the main floor. The nursery. He was able to spot Carolyn immediately. She too was asleep though wriggling slowly about in the hospital basinet. He walked back into the elevator and took it down to the main floor.

Walking along a quiet corridor that would take him out to the parking lot, he paused to lean against a wall. His dear friend, Tony, had lost his life just days ago. His funeral was held only earlier just today. And then also, today a new life appears in the world, their little Carolyn. Dave glanced up to the ceiling.

"You do work in mysterious ways, don't You? Thanks, Lord, for your gifts and your blessings," Dave whispered.

Dave pushed off the wall and continued to meander down the silent corridor, out the glass doors, and into the Virginia night air. And he smiled as he did so.

PART III

Power always has to be kept in check because power exercised in secret, especially under the cloak of national security, is doubly dangerous.

U.S. Senator William Proxmire

CHAPTER 24

Langley Center, McLean
Virginia
Monday morning, July 18th

Jack Barrett eased back into the cushion of his leather swivel chair. He set his cane leaning against the wall next to him. Sitting in front of Jack's massive fortress of an executive desk in their own leather chairs were Dave McClure and Pete Novak. Jack took a sip of coffee before beginning.

"So, my first question has to be, how are you, Dave?" Jack asked.

"I'm fine, sir. Getting along," Dave answered.

"Congratulations on the birth of your new baby child. Is she doing well?" Jack queried.

"Yes, Mr. Barrett, Carolyn is doing fine," Dave replied. "She's changing our lives. Thank you for asking."

"I can imagine. How's that bullet wound in your shoulder and the stab wound in your side? Are they healing up well enough?"

"They are, sir. The healing is going well."

ANDREW CERONI

"Good. Finally, I caution myself to ask this, but how's your head doing? You lost your partner and friend, Tony Robertson? Tony's death brought this whole building into a state of shock followed by a mass mourning for his passing. Some time has passed, but not a lot. Are you finding that you're able to deal with it?" Jack asked.

"Yes, again, sir. After the funeral, an FBI Agent, Bob Wickman, shared with me some verses from Scripture and other things he said might help me. I've found them to be a comfort to me and have eased the grief that I was experiencing with Tony's passing. I met Bob when he was the lead for the two FBI teams on the hunt for those Red Storm terrorists in Wyoming," Dave answered.

"He sounds like a great guy. It was good of him to take the time to share with you. Dave, the FBI report I read indicates that you yourself killed seven of a ten-man German Red Storm Movement terror group, including their number two in command, Sigmund Degler himself. Is that accurate?" Jack asked.

"I did, Mr. Barrett. Please know that in each of those confrontations, I had no other real option."

"And I believe that. You had a gun fight resulting in a bullet wound in your shoulder and a knife fight that put a stab wound in your side just above your kidney. Yet once again, you prevailed. That had to have been a remarkable demonstration of some damn deadly combat skills. The bottom-line is that I want to thank you for a job extremely well done," Jack said.

"Thank you, sir."

"All right. Now, other than checking on your physical and mental health which I really wanted to and needed to do, there are other reasons I wanted to see you this morning. These are

168

things that I've given a great deal of thought to. I decided that along with Pete, I wanted to read you into them."

"Sir?"

"Don't be concerned. These things are in no way negative and are very good, in fact, almost splendid things. They're about events and changes that will be coming to this Agency at the end of this year. Pete is already aware of everything I plan to tell you," Jack said, glancing over at Pete who was smiling and nodded back.

"Yes, sir?"

"Dave, this coming January 1st, I'm going to retire from the Agency. I've given it a lot of deliberation and I've always come around to the same conclusion...it's time for me to leave. I've discussed this with some of my closest friends who have also retired from our sister intelligence agencies, NRO, NSA, DIA, and the like. In fact, I've already been invited to join a couple interagency intelligence groups of retirees that meet for lunch around the Metro Area," Jack said.

"My goodness," Dave said.

"I truly believe that I'm ready for the change and I'm even thinking about buying a new set of golf clubs. PINGs, the best. Those clubs should psych out any competition for the first few holes we play until they realize just how really terrible I am," Jack said, chuckling.

"Wow. Mr. Barrett, this is big. Please accept my congratulations and God bless you, sir," Dave replied.

"Thank you. The promotion board's deliberations for my replacement included Pete Novak, however the board was convinced that Pete was more critical to the Agency remaining as the DepOps than he would be in the director's position. Nevertheless, they expressed an extreme confidence that a directorship was in Pete's future. Pete, please accept my sincere thanks for the manner in which you handled the board's decision."

"Sir, I'm honored to have been considered. I'm also very pleased with their comments about what lies ahead for me," Pete said, still smiling.

"They didn't have to make those predictions, Pete, especially in writing, so congratulations on how they viewed you. I'm in complete agreement with them. You are absolutely indispensable in your role as the Deputy Director for Operations. At the moment, we don't see anyone onboard in the Agency who could fill your shoes," Jack said, turning back to Dave.

"Now, back to Dave. Dale Stratton who leads up Special Activities is going to replace me as the Director, the DCI. He's a super guy and an extremely bright fellow who's well known in the community," Jack continued.

"I know Mr. Stratton fairly well. A promotion to DCI will be absolutely super for him. Thanks for letting me know that," Dave replied.

"Dave, now, what I am extremely pleased to relay to you is that beyond the upcoming promotion to the Director's position, the next highest promotion in all of this shuffle that's imminent in the Agency will concern you, Dave McClure," Jack said.

"Sir?" Dave said.

"In that regard, I am absolutely delighted to advise you that effective January 1st, Dave, you will be promoted to the position of 'Principal Assistant for Special Activities to the DepOps.' The position of 'Principal Assistant' is a huge promotion. In accepting that promotion, you'll receive a 92% increase in salary, and you'll be awarded a 45% increase in vacation days. Dave, I offer you my heartfelt congratulations. How does this strike you? Questions so far?" Jack asked.

"Principal Assistant for Special Activities? Mr. Barrett, I...I'm overwhelmed. It's hard to believe this is happening," Dave said, his eyes wide.

"That's understandable. Again, my sincerest congratulations. In my estimation, the board made the right choice. Questions?"

"Well, may I ask, sir, what are those things you refer to, vacation days?" Dave replied.

Pete Novak buckled over and broke out in a raucous belly laugh, "Always the smartass!" Pete exclaimed, still giggling.

"No, Pete, I've always liked Dave's wit, his sense of humor. Sometimes that can be the all-important factor in reducing stress in a group," Jack said as Pete, still chuckling, nodded back.

"Dave, what this means is there will be no more gun battles for you. No more bullet wounds. No more knife fight clashes. No more stab wounds. And no more close-quarter, hand-to-hand combat, that is, unless you and Karen end up doing that at home!" Jack guffawed at his own humor.

Jack continued, "Seriously though, you will have a large plate of responsibility. You'll be responsible for all Agency special activities, including those of our land division, naval division, and air division. You will almost certainly be asked on occasion to engage in testifying before the House Permanent Select and Senate Select Committees on Intelligence as well as meeting personally over lunch with congressional leaders and senior managers in the intelligence community. How does that all sound?" Jack queried.

"Mr. Barrett, I wasn't kidding when I said I was overwhelmed by this. It's like a dream come true. Please accept my thanks to both you and Mr. Novak for your support. Really. I don't think this would have happened without that," Dave responded.

"You're welcome. Actually, however, the promotion board deliberated over several personnel files and your ultimate selection for principal assistant was unanimous. Bar none. As I said, this all occurs January 1st and we're now in July. There's plenty of time to consider the intricacies of what your new position will entail. Talk to Dale Stratton. Obviously, he's been informed and is aware of all these impending events. Dale's an unequivocal expert in special activities. And I might add, as are you. Also, make a couple trips to Nordstroms and buy some new, snappy suits over the coming months.

"I will do those things, sir. This is so exciting. Unbelievable."

"Maybe so, but it's the future reality for you. And by the way, you're free to discuss all this with Karen. I suspect she'll be ecstatic at the prospects of such a new structure in your lives together. You started a family. So now, continue to build the family. In conclusion, I want you to know that I'm absolutely thrilled about the prospects for your future as well as Mr. Peter J. Novak's here. After January 1st, it's going to be an exciting time for all of us. I have no doubt that I'll make a few visits to the campus to stay in touch. You're not going to completely lose me," Jack concluded.

"I'm certain you're correct, sir. I'm just completely overwhelmed. At this moment, I just have difficulty envisioning it," Dave said.

"Of course. That's to be expected. Gentlemen, I propose a power lunch today in the senior staff dining room at 11:30 AM. Dave, as the Principal Assistant to the DepOps, you will now have unrestricted access to the senior staff dining room. Leaders on Capitol Hill enjoy coming here on occasion to tour the facility and then finish with lunch in that room with views out to the headwaters of the Potomac. The soups, salads, and sandwiches are superb, to die for. And I've ordered a bottle of

Dom Perignon to be drawn from a Top Secret SCI vault that I have in the subbasement to toast to these coming events. Deal?"

Pete and Dave glanced at one another and returned a smile to Jack, "Deal!" they exclaimed.

"Super. Pete will escort you into the dining room today. It's protocol. And Dave, after today, I don't want to see you around the campus for a bit. Take this week and the next to fully recover. I would like you to come back as close to 100% as possible. At that time, you'll have a brief medical exam, a stamina check-up, and at some point, you'll need to fire a box or two of rounds at the range.

"Okay, sir, I'll remain scarce," Dave replied.

"Good. I have one last topic I want to discuss. Between now and January 1st, there is one more matter that has increased the Agency's apprehension. It's one that could represent an ominous cloud on Europe's horizon—and that's Germany. We have time to briefly discuss the issue. Are you still with me?" Jack asked, checking his watch.

Faces turned somewhat solemn. As Dave glimpsed over his shoulder, Pete nodded to him in his agreement to discuss the next subject Jack had just raised. They turned back to Jack in tandem.

"To say we're concerned is an understatement. We're very concerned, however, as yet the fact remains that we have little actionable intelligence to go on. Still, from what we validated concerning Defense Minister Andreas Bachmeier's background, his father, and his grandfather as well as Gunter Dietzmann's assassination in Berlin, we believe we're justified in our concern. I've briefed the President. He has approved our initial, low-key strategy," Jack said.

"And that is?" Dave asked.

"When you're ready, 100%, we're going to send you back to Berlin. You'll travel under your true name like you did when you met with Dietzmann in Munich," Jack said.

"The mission, sir?"

"Stay one week. We want you to just be there. Be casual. Be seen. Of course, the BND will quickly come to know you're back in country. The idea, legend, is that you're taking time off for R&R and decided to visit Berlin. So, explore, sightsee... art galleries, museums, botanical gardens. We think it's possible that something may come out of the woodwork... perhaps approach you," Jack explained.

"I see. I understand," Dave said.

"For this trip, we're making reservations for you at the Hotel Adlon Kempinski. It's a five-star hotel on a street called *Unter den Linden*. The hotel faces the Brandenburg Gate. It's very upscale. I've stayed at the Adlon Kempinski myself... quite classy. You won't need a car. Take taxis," Jack said.

"My goodness. It sounds like I'm going to be traveling like royalty," Dave replied.

"On a side note, and so you're aware, we'll also be sending a six-man countersurveillance team that will tag along with you," Pete added.

"The reason for that, sir?" Dave asked.

"Primarily, it's our concern over the assassination of Dietzmann. They, whoever they are, felt a reason to place a surveillance on Gunther Dietzmann. They had a line on him. When the two of you met in Munich, they may have also developed an interest in you as well. These six men we're sending along are tough, highly capable, armed individuals. Each one of them has served on several high-level protective details. They would scare the hell out of anybody. Outside the hotel, they won't make any effort to get near you, contact you, or communicate with you. It will be a very discreet countersurveillance. Inside the hotel, you can do so only do it where you won't be observed, in private," Pete explained further.

"Dave, just be there. As I said, explore and sightsee where you can be seen and avoid engaging in anything that could remotely appear suspicious looking on your part. If something does click, we want it to come as approaching you and not the other way around. Sound reasonable?" Jack asked.

"Yes, sir," Dave replied.

"Good. Let's adjourn then. We've covered a lot of ground. Go kill some time at your desk until we meet again for lunch in the senior staff dining room. You're going to have two whole weeks to rest up. It's very good to see you again, and as I mentioned, I am absolutely thrilled about your upcoming promotion to a Principal Assistant position," Jack said.

They all shook hands. Dave and Pete ambled out of Jack's office with Pete's arm around Dave's shoulder. He paused outside in the hallway.

"This is huge for you...Principal Assistant for Special Activities to the DepOps. Wow. It will be a life changer for sure. Dave, I promise you now that I'll give you 100% plus support. You'll be transitioning from being a legend in special operations to a Principal Assistant. Congratulations," Pete said.

"Thanks, Pete. I know I sound redundant, but I'm truly overwhelmed. It's hard to believe it's happening," Dave answered.

Smiling, they shook hands and headed for an elevator.

CHAPTER 25

Pumphrey Drive, Fairfax
Virginia
Monday evening, July 18th

It was five o'clock in the early evening and dinnertime at the
McClure residence. Karen sat on one side of the table cradling
little Carolyn and feeding her with a bottle. She raised the baby
to her shoulder and gently patted her back to burp her. Dave sat
opposite them.

Dave felt that the image of Karen and their new baby girl was
heartwarming. Dave and Karen each had a glass of Cabernet
Sauvignon in front of them on the table but yet untouched. Next
to the wine was a plate of Rigatoni Bolognese.

"You haven't opened up much yet, honey. How was your
day back at the Agency? And your meeting with Jack and Pete?
Was there much discussion about Tony? I apologize for bringing
that up. Don't answer if you really don't want to. You did say
that you had unusual but fabulous lunch with both Jack and Pete
in the senior staff dining room over a bottle of Dom Perignon
champagne. Dom Perignon—that sounds like some serious stuff

happened today. Did it? Can I know about it, or do I owe you any congratulations?" Karen asked, looking up from the baby.

"A lot happened in Jack Barrett's office today, honey. We did discuss Tony, although only briefly. Tony is an emotional topic that I'd like to tuck away for a while. I'm dealing with it mentally and spiritually."

"I understand that completely."

"And yes, there's a lot I want to tell you about today's happenings, sweetheart. All of it is good. In fact, I have to say that some of it was a complete surprise and is astoundingly fantastic...both for me and for us," Dave answered.

"Oh my, now you're giving me goosebumps. Please, tell me everything."

"Come this January 1st, Jack Barrett is retiring. His leaving is going to kick off a shuffle of moves and promotions in the senior leadership positions," Dave said.

Dave went on to explain Pete Novak's remaining in his position as DepOps. Karen nodded, understanding the logic as he explained it. Then he broke the news about the next highest promotion after the directorship, his own approaching promotion on January 1st to Principle Assistant for Special Activities to the DepOps. He related the raise in salary and increase in vacation days. He would have an office on the same floor as Pete Novak.

"Your salary will be practically double what it is now? And you'll receive nearly half again more in vacation days? Wow! Dave, that is absolutely incredible! You're going to be at the executive level at CIA?"

"Yeah, I suppose that's one way of putting it. Jack Barrett said that being in a Principal Assistant position, I'll occasionally be called upon to testify before Congress, the House Permanent Select Committee on Intelligence, the HPSCI, as well as the Senate Select Committee on Intelligence, the SSCI. And also, that

I'll be called to lunches with other agency and military leadership types. He also said that it wasn't him or Novak that made this happen...that the promotion board's selection of me was unanimous. Sweetheart, it all sounds so unbelievable at this point, but they assured me the impending promotion is firm, in concrete."

"No more operations to places all over the globe at the drop of the hat?"

"That too. It's a totally new structure in my career. However, there is one more operation between now and January that they want me to follow up on. Germany. They want me to travel to Berlin in two to three weeks. It will be very low key."

"Oh, I see. One more op. Then the reward."

"Honey, it's not like that. I was already involved in this one."

"That was the trip to Munich you took?"

"Yes. Again, very low key. Nothing to worry yourself about."

"You always say that. And you just came back from Wyoming with a bullet wound and a stab wound."

"All right. I admit that. However, this trip really is low key. They want me to stay in Berlin for a week and sightsee. That's it. They're hoping that I'm approached and given additional information the Agency needs to move forward."

"It does sound benign. Dave, just be careful and know that I love you and always will. So does little Carolyn."

"And I you. Thank you for understanding. How about we attend to dinner? It looks scrumptious."

"Let's do that. This little gal burped, so I'm going to go lay her in her crib."

"Goodbye, Carolyn! Daddy loves you!" Dave exclaimed as Karen rose from the table with the baby against her shoulder."

CHAPTER 26

Brandenburg International Airport
Berlin, Germany
Tuesday afternoon, August 2nd

Unsnapping his seatbelt, Dave pushed himself up from his aisle seat in Business Class and grabbed his leather briefcase bag in the overhead compartment. He moved over into the line of travelers shuffling forward to the front hatch and twisted his torso right and left to shake off the stiffness. The United Airlines flight from Dulles to Berlin had been nonstop and of course, that in itself was a relief, yet his lower back muscles were still taut.

After passing successfully through the *Deutscher Zoll, German Customs,* and glancing around as he rambled along, it was impossible not to notice that Berlin's Brandenburg airport was a large, high-ceilinged, and airy airport. Dave was impressed that it appeared so very well designed and architecturally beautiful. He passed numerous colorful shops on his way to baggage claim carousels.

Minutes later, as he stood near the opening in the wall for the conveyer belts, he noticed several security officers meandering about. Unlike in the United States where there were none at baggage claims, German airports often had them. They were there to watch who was taking what bag off the moving conveyer belt. He grabbed the handle on his large, steel gray Rimowa luggage case and lifted it off the carousel. A security officer walking by him saw the case as Dave twirled it around by its four wheels next to him on the floor.

"Schönes gepäck, mein Herr. Nice luggage, Sir," the officer said.

"Danke sehr. Thanks very much," Dave replied, smiling.

The Germans knew how to make luggage. Rimowa was among their finest brand and near indestructible. With his leather brief bag slung over his right shoulder and pulling his luggage case along by its long, telescoping handle, Dave stepped through the glass exit doors and into the late afternoon sunlight. A long line of taxis was waiting at the curb. He motioned with his arm extended and the first taxi pulled up to him. The driver, who introduced himself as Bashaar from Rabat, Morocco, walked around the vehicle, took Dave's bag and placed it in the trunk. He then opened the rear door for Dave.

"Wohin? Where to?" Bashaar asked, leaning over his seatback.

"Hotel Adlon Kempinski. Pariser Platz und Unter den Linden Strasse. *Kennen sie dass platz? Do you know that place?"* Dave replied.

"Ja, ja. Keine problem. Nicht weit. Wir warden schnell da sein. Yes, yes. No problem. Not far. We'll be there in no time," the driver answered.

The drive was short but interesting. Berlin was an extremely modern city. Blazes of sunlight flashed off the high windows of the skyscraper buildings they passed. Traffic in afternoon

Berlin wasn't all that heavy, fairly moderate, and it seemed like less than ten minutes when they pulled up to the curb in front of the hotel. Bashaar popped the trunk; Dave climbed out from the back seat and lifted his bag. After a generous gratuity, Bashaar grinned and pulled away, waving goodbye.

Dave's eyebrows rose as he entered the lobby of the Adlon Kempinski. Gazing around, all the floors and walls appeared to be constructed of magnificent white and off-white marble. The reception desk, also white-colored, was off to his left. Two young men and an attractive woman stood behind it and smiled as he approached. Glancing further toward the interior, he noticed the lobby gradually telescoped upward into a grand, two-story chamber.

"*Guten Tag, mein Herr, kann ich Ihnen helfen? Good afternoon, sir, can I help you?*" one of the male receptionists asked.

Dave walked up and gave his name. The receptionist tapped his keyboard and brought up Dave's reservation on his computer. He smiled.

Still looking at his screen, the young man offered, "*Aus Amerika? Auf Englisch, Herr McClure? From America? Shall we speak in English, Mr. McClure?*" the young man asked.

"*Ja, bitte. Yes, please,*" Dave answered. Dave spoke German but with the fatigue of the flight still on him, he considered conversing in English would be easier.

"Then, welcome to Berlin and the Adlon Kempinski. I see on my screen that you have a Junior Suite reserved on our third floor. I also notice that you'll be with us for nearly a week...until Saturday. Business?"

"No, pleasure. Just visiting Berlin. Sightseeing. I haven't visited here for years."

"I'm originally from Amsterdam, but I've found I like Berlin a lot. Oh, and if you find you have some free time, just beyond the Brandenburg Gate out the front doors over there is the Tiergarten Park. It's beautiful and a great place for taking a *spaziergang, a walk,* as the Germans call it. Lots of government buildings are in the park, including the new Chancellery and the residence of the President. A great place to visit at any time of the day," the receptionist continued.

"Thanks. I'll try it out. It was a long flight…when does your restaurant open for dinner?" Dave asked, feeling some hunger.

"We have several restaurants. Our prime restaurant, Quarré, is on this floor through those doors over to your right. They open at 6:00 PM, so you have well over an hour to get acquainted with your room and freshen up."

"Super. Thanks very much."

"You'll find that the windows in your suite look down upon the street in front of the hotel, Unter den Linden Strasse. I suspect that you're going to like the room. Here's your room's sweep card, Mr. McClure. Please, enjoy your stay. If you need anything at all, give us a call," the young man concluded.

"Thanks very much. Have a great rest of the day," Dave replied as he backed away from the desk and walked toward the elevators.

As Dave stepped into an elevator, spun around, and briefly stood waiting for the doors to close, he noticed an airport van at the curb in front of the hotel. Six men in suits had already stepped off onto the sidewalk. All of them appeared to be in their mid to late thirties, extremely fit and muscular. Brawny. It was probable that they were his countersurveillance team having arrived and about to check in. He watched them enter the lobby as the doors closed and the elevator began ascending.

In his room, Dave opened the luggage case and put a few things on hangars in the closet. He took his leather dopp kit with him into the bathroom and washed his face and hands. After glancing out his window down to the street and out to the Brandenburg Gate, he kicked off his shoes and plopped on the bed.

The station at the American Embassy would be delivering his Beretta, shoulder holster, and several loaded mags to him sometime during the day tomorrow. Until then, he'd be unarmed, a condition he was not accustomed to. He glanced at his watch—5:20 PM. Dinner would have to wait a bit. He nuzzled the back of his head deeper into the pillow, folded his hands over his chest, and closed his eyes.

Dave made it down to the Quarré restaurant at six-thirty after a short snooze. Half the tables were filled with patrons chattering and picking at their meals. He ordered a glass of Spätlese white wine from the Mosel Valley and glanced casually around the room. He noticed there were three tables spaced throughout the room with two men seated at each one talking, eating, and seemingly oblivious to him—his surveillance team. They'd arrived for dinner and spread themselves out through the restaurant. They had him covered from three angles. During the meal, he would meet their eyes in acknowledgement.

Dave ordered the Geschnetzeltes...a German dish of veal, mushrooms, and a creamy German hunter's sauce over noodles with a side of buttery asparagus. It was lip-smacking scrumptious. After taking time to make eye contact with each man on his team, he finished with a cup of coffee and a snifter of Asbach Uralt brandy. He remembered years ago having his first glass of Asbach at the libation's origins in the town of Rüdesheim on the Rhein River when he first joined the Agency. Dave charged his bill to his room and made his way back upstairs for the night.

The dangle operation would kick off tomorrow. It would be interesting to see if any fish would come to bite.

CHAPTER 27

Unter den Linden Strasse
Berlin, Germany
Wednesday morning, August 3rd

Dave slept soundly through the night like a bear in hibernation due to the fatigue of the air travel that was still on him. He rose out of bed at seven o'clock, and after showering and dressing, he paused at the hotel's Lobby Lounge to pick up a copy of the *Berliner Zeitung,* Berlin's newspaper. He slipped into an easy chair and began reading the front page. Glancing over at the bustle of patrons, he then decided to grab a light breakfast of coffee and a slice of apple strudel. It was enough.

The lobby was abuzz with people snatching their morning coffee and rushing out to the street to hail a taxi. Others were checking out early. He looked out the glass exit doors where several taxis were lined up. His guess was that his countersurveillance team had already dealt with breakfast and was outside spread along the street, waiting. As he was about to stand, a tall, lanky man in a black cashmere coat approached him.

"McClure? Dave McClure?" the man asked.

"Yes, it's that obvious?" Dave asked.

"I had a description of you to go by, Dave. So no, it wasn't obvious. You blend in well. I'm Aaren Engberg. I'm from the American Embassy, the Station. I have a package for you." Aaren said, handing a brown paper-wrapped box to Dave.

"Thank you, Aaren. I'm pleased to meet you. Do you know how many mags are included, and are they all loaded?" Dave asked in a low voice.

"Three mags and a leather double-pouch. All are loaded. Speer Gold-Dot 9mm +P. Also, your slant-rig shoulder holster."

"Super. Thanks again, Aaren," Dave said.

"Most welcome. Have a great day," Aaren replied, turning back toward the lobby doors.

Dave took an elevator up and returned to his room to place the pistol and mags in his suitcase. He locked it. Dave exited the Adlon Kempinski at a little after nine o'clock and turned right on Unter den Linden Strasse. Store fronts of all sorts were beginning to open. Ambling along the treed boulevard, he found Unter den Linden to be a long and glamorous street with shops, cafes, and restaurants that stretched down from near the Brandenburg Gate to the Berlin Cathedral. While he had no intention of walking its entire length, he did walk as far as a branch of the Spree River, passing Humboldt University and the Zeughaus, the oldest building on the street having been built between 1695 and 1706.

He made the effort to enter plenty of shops, examining the shelves filled with collectibles and curiosities, and even stopped at a café for a cup of coffee. Unter den Linden Strasse was a great place to go for a walk on a nice summer morning.

Still, for a dangle operation, he was a little down that

nothing happened. Nothing. No approaches. Arriving at the small bridge that crossed over a narrow branch of the Spree River, he turned around and began meandering his way back to the hotel. Now and then, he caught a glimpse of one of the team members. They were very good at their trade, appearing genuinely indifferent to him and the passersby on the street.

As he passed a shop called Gabriele's that was advertising Bratwurst, Weisswurst, Nürnbergerwurst, and other grilled sausages, Dave caught the aromas coming out of the kitchen and hesitated briefly. He lingered for a few minutes, then decided yes, this was where lunch would be.

After being seated at a window table, he ordered a bratwurst with a pilsner beer. When the owner delivered it to his table with a smile, Dave was pleased to see it came with a brötchen, *a German roll*, and kartoffelsalat, potato salad. The grilled brat was superb as was the German potato salad and roll, and all of it washed down with a smooth pilsner lager beer.

After lunch, he sauntered back up Unter den Linden Strasse to the hotel and up to his room. Having drunk the stein of beer at Gabriele's, he found that he needed to use the bathroom. He threw some water on his face, toweled, and took the elevator back down to the lobby.

Headed once again for the lobby's glass doors, he decided that for the afternoon, he would walk in the other direction, passing through and under the Brandenburg Gate into the Tiergarten Park. The receptionist had indicated it was beautiful and great for a stroll, so why not. He'd give it a shot.

The *Brandenburg Tor* or Gate monument itself was beautiful with long towering columns and a Quadriga, a chariot pulled by four horses, on the roof of the gate. Walking under the gate, Dave saw that Unter den Linden Strasse became

Straße des 17. Juni. An Adlon Kempinski receptionist would later briefly explain to him that the change in street name was to honor the people's uprising in East Berlin on 17 June 1953, when Red Army soldiers and the East German police, the Volkspolizei, struck back with brutal violence and even shot protesting workers.

As one entered the park, tree-lined pedestrian avenues and pathways, manicured lawns, and flower beds began immediately. There were several ceremonial sculptures of Prussian generals and aristocrats. The park was as picturesque as the receptionist had described it. Dave eventually stepped off the main avenue onto a path that wound its way through trees and small open grassy areas. At one left turn, as he glimpsed behind, he noticed a lone figure, a man, walking a discreet distance to the rear of him.

Dave decided to make a few dry-cleaning moves to test the individual's intents, and abruptly walked off the path to stand momentarily by one of multiple streams of water running through the park from the Spree River. The man behind him paused and appeared to be glancing up to watch something in the trees. Back on the path, Dave then walked around the perimeter of a grassy area with benches for sitting around its perimeter. The man hesitated, then broke off from his position to amble in a reverse direction.

It was then that Dave noticed the six men of his counter surveillance team begin to gradually move in on the person from their multiple directions. They had noticed the man's reactions to Dave's movements as well. Dave returned to the secluded, little grassy area surrounded by green shrubberies and trees. He sat down on one of the benches and waited patiently.

The six men slowly closed on the individual to eventually where each of them was no less than twenty feet away from him, forcing him to walk in Dave's direction. The men moved closer, and the man picked up his pace, trying to move away from them. No such luck. They continued to steer him to where he soon found himself standing directly in front of Dave's bench. They patted him down. The team's lead agent, Tom Pellegrino, shook his head...no weapon.

"He's clean," Tom said.

The men in the countersurveillance team began to back off some yards away, watching the man, their hands on the grips of their pistols. The man wore a gray herringbone sport coat, light blue shirt, and dark gray slacks. He stood silent, alternately looking at Dave and over his shoulder at the men still standing a short distance away around him.

"You need to explain yourself," Dave said, making eye contact.

"For what? I'm just taking a stroll in the park," the man answered.

"Let's try that again. Explain yourself. Your name is?" Dave replied.

"Why? What do you want with me?"

"That's not the question, is it? You were following me. You know it and I know it. Now, your name?" Dave answered.

"Devin Connolly. All right, I was following you."

"And why is that? Are you American?"

"Yes, I'm American. However, I live in Berlin. I'm the liaison press officer to the media for the German Federal Intelligence Agency, the Bundesnachrichtendienst, the BND," Devin responded.

"Liaison press officer to the media? Impressive. Your German is that good, Devin?" Dave asked.

"I have a master's degree in German from Vanderbilt University in Nashville, Tennessee. I noticed the BND's employment ad online and applied for the position. After flying to Berlin for an interview, the BND made me an offer and hired me. They told me that, if at all possible, they wanted an American in the job. I've worked for them here for four years now. It's a good job. They pay me well."

"Interesting. All right, come sit here on the bench. Let's chat," Dave said.

"I can't. I have appointments," Devin said.

"I seriously doubt that. Devin, let's cut with the horseshit. You should recognize the situation you're in and come clean with me. You do realize that you're in a rather untenable situation, don't you?" Dave said, motioning to the men in his countersurveillance team.

Devin glanced around him. "Yes, I do. Still, you can't force me to do anything. You have no authority whatsoever," he said.

"But I am doing this to you. And I'm sure that you don't want to wind up like Gunther Dietzmann, do you?"

Devin's face paled at the mention of Dietzmann. He had an instant look of being somewhat nauseous. Without another word, he stepped forward and sat down on the bench across from Dave.

"No. I am afraid of that. This could become somewhat dangerous for me, Mr. McClure. I shouldn't be having this conversation," Devin said.

"So, you know my name. Devin, you live here in Berlin, and you've worked for the BND for four years in a fairly non-intelligence, media-focused position. You must remember however, that first, you're an American. You hold a U.S. passport, don't you?" Dave asked.

"Yes."

"Well, then, at some point you may find you need to choose sides, Devin. I caution you—don't err in making a mistake in that regard. Although, I'm not saying that you need to do that now. So, tell me, why were you following me?"

"The BND knows you're in town, Mr. McClure. How they know, I don't know. They told me that they want to know why you're here. Today, I was supposed to just nonchalantly intersect with you here in the Tiergarten Park, that is, if you came here. Maybe begin a casual conversation. That's it... see if I could find out why you're in Berlin. That's all I know," Devin replied.

"Okay. Much better. By the way, you can call me Dave. I wonder, is this trailing me somehow related to Gunther Dietzmann? Did you know Gunther?"

"Yes, I knew Gunther. He was a nice guy. Fun to be with. We often went to lunch together. I can't understand why he was murdered like that?"

"Really now? I want you to think hard, Devin. Tell me just how well you actually knew Gunther?"

"Okay. I knew that Gunther along with some other BND employees suspected some things were not quite right with the BND leadership's positions regarding our German Defense Minister, Andreas Bachmeier. They gossiped. Gunther should have kept his mouth shut and minded his own business. He'd be alive today if he had done that," Devin said.

"I see. You really feel that way. You held no suspicions yourself regarding Bachmeier like Gunther did?" Dave asked, his eyes squinting.

"Even if I did, I wouldn't be so verbal about it. I concentrate on and do my job, that's about it."

"I think that's smart of you. Does Bachmeier come over to visit the BND?"

"Yes, he does. Fairly regularly. He meets with our director and members of our most senior leadership. They meet in a secure conference room. Something's up, Dave, something big. It has to do with something about future military deployments, that is, armor and infantry movements. I don't want to get involved in it, not in any way. It's too dangerous. My life could be at risk just like Gunter Dietzmann's."

"And we don't want that either. Don't worry, that's not going to happen. I have one more question. Does Bachmeier appear to have anyone senior, perhaps a deputy, who's in charge of whatever this something big is? Someone who he might bring with him to these meetings. Someone who appears to lead the effort and represent him?"

"Yes. General Gerhardt Obermann. Obermann leads the meetings. That's what some of our secure room technicians have said that they've observed."

"How senior is General Obermann?"

"Very senior. Four stars. Obermann used to be just an aide to the defense minister as a Colonel. Apparently, the two of them found over time that they had similar political leanings. Bachmeier realized he liked Obermann a great deal and elevated him to four stars. Bachmeier has that power, that kind of authority," Devin said.

"I see. General Gerhardt Obermann who was promoted from colonel. Good. Anything else you'd like to mention? Anything significant you're aware of that may be coming up on the calendar?"

"There might be, but I don't really know if I should be sharing this with you." Devin mumbled.

"No one is going to know. No one. You have nothing to worry about in that regard, Devin," Dave replied.

"Well, there is one thing. Once again, this is small talk, rumors going around. Word is, there's going to be a high-level meeting in a few days down in Bavaria at the foot of our Alps in Garmisch-Partenkirchen. It's another planning meeting of some sort that they want to hold away from Berlin and its environs. It's to take place this coming Friday, the evening of the 5th."

"Do you have any idea where it's to take place?"

"Yes. I really don't know how these guys find this stuff out, maybe because someone had to make reservations for the hotel and then spoke to someone about it, but they're mumbling among themselves that it's supposed to happen at Bachmeier's usual place. Apparently, that's the Staudacherhof. It's on Höllenstrasse in Garmisch. Bachmeier and his inside group have apparently met there a couple times before."

"The Staudacherhof in Garmisch. Great. Thanks. Look, Devin, this was a productive ten minutes. Thanks for being frank and honest with me and for recognizing your American roots, for choosing sides. I mean that sincerely. And don't worry, we won't do anything to put you at risk."

"Thanks for that, Dave."

"So, you can go back to the BND today and tell whoever sent you that you managed an encounter with me in the Tiergarten Park near some flower beds and a stream. You started up a conversation and I proceeded to engage with you. The story is that I told you that I was in Europe and I'm just here for some rest and relaxation. I thought I might enjoy visiting Berlin again. Sightsee, things like that. Nothing more. Also, that I plan to be here only for a few days and would be leaving soon. Okay? By the way, here's my card. If you feel we need to talk again, Devin, your conscience, call me at this number and just leave a message. I'll arrange a way for us to be in contact," Dave said.

"Okay, Dave. Thanks. I'll be going then," Devin looked over his shoulder as Dave nodded to the countersurveillance team. They moved apart, making a large opening for Devin to walk through and depart.

Devin took the nearest path, walking back toward the main avenue and winding around the trees until he faded from sight.

Dave glanced at each of the men standing around him. A broad grin filled his face.

"Gentlemen, I think we got the best we could today. What we needed. And the way you managed the dangle counter-surveillance op was tremendously well executed. I'll be talking with Pete Novak in a bit, and I will convey that to him."

"Thanks, Dave. That's good of you," Tom Pellegrino said.

"It's deserved, Tom. I'll be leaving soon myself, so, thank you very much for covering me. Please feel free to go back to the hotel, maybe have a last Berlin beer together, and when you can get your flights, head back to Washington and Langley. Thanks, again," Dave said, standing up and shaking everyone's hand.

The countersurveillance team members turned and began walking away through the park, smiling, and chatting softly among themselves. Dave once again sat himself down on the bench.

"This is a nice spot, I think I'll enjoy it for a bit," Dave muttered to himself, settling back into the bench and crossing his legs.

"Garmisch...hmmm."

CHAPTER 28

Hotel Adlon Kempinski
Unter den Linden Strasse, Berlin
Wednesday afternoon, August 3rd

Dave meandered his way through the park, the Brandenburg Gate, and back to the hotel. Walking into the lobby, he approached the receptionist desk.

"Excuse me," Dave said.

"Yes, sir, how may I help you?" a young blonde receptionist asked him.

"I need to make a call back to the United States. It's a business call. Can I do that from a house phone?" he asked.

"And charge the call to your room?"

"Yes."

"'Then just pick the phone in the lobby that you'd like to use, dial zero, and when the hotel operator answers, tell her you'd like an international operator and want to charge the call to your room. That's it," she said.

"Thank you."

Dave walked to one of two easy chairs grouped together in a corner of the lobby with a cocktail table standing between them. A house phone was on the table. He eased himself down in a chair and picked up the phone. He was soon connected to an international operator who made the connection to McLean, Virginia.

"Langley Center. How may I help you?" a male voice answered.

"This is Dave McClure for Pete Novak," Dave responded.

"I'll connect you, Mr. McClure." Dave heard a click and several jingles.

"Pete Novak."

"Mr. Novak, this is Dave McClure."

"Hi Dave. Where're you calling from?" Pete asked.

"The Adlon Kempinski hotel in Berlin. One of many house phones."

"Good choice. This is only day two. Have you already had some success you want to discuss?"

"Yes, sir. Luck of the Irish, I guess. And while I didn't question the man about his heritage, he was obviously an Irish guy. He approached me while I was taking a stroll in Tiergarten Park. The countersurveillance team noticed him and did a fantastic job in steering the man to me. He's named Devin Connolly, and interestingly, an American," Dave said.

Dave went on to explain to Pete about Devin Connolly's situation in Berlin working as an American in a media liaison officer's position with the BND. Also, how Devin knew Gunther Dietzmann and Dietzmann's noticeable phobia about the BND leadership's relationship with the German Defense Minister, Andreas Bachmeier. Devin was asked by the BND to try making a casual encounter with Dave and determine why he was visiting Berlin. And finally, Dave related what

Devin had said regarding an upcoming meeting at the behest of Bachmeier at the Staudacherhof Hotel in Garmisch as well as General Gerhardt Obermann, the name of Bachmeier's apparent lead man for the project.

"Excellent collection effort, Dave. The BND didn't waste any time in tagging you. How do you feel about perhaps renting a car and driving down to Garmisch, and if you can, attempt to garner some info regarding this meeting of Bachmeier's. Especially, whether this project actually concerns what we think it does?" Pete asked.

"I'm good with that. I can check out of the Kempinski hotel Friday morning, take a taxi to the *Hauptbahnhof, train station*, and take a one of those Inter-City Express, ICE, fast trains to the Frankfurt airport. I'll rent a car there and drive down to Garmisch in Bavaria. I can search around a bit and find a place to stay."

"You released the countersurveillance team today. They reported that they're headed back to Langley. Are you sure you wouldn't want them with you in Garmisch? Do you think that's a wise move?"

"I don't think it'd be a good idea to bring the team down to Garmisch. Garmisch isn't a big city. It's primarily a ski town in winter and in the summer months, an attractive village-sized town where tourists can take a ski Bahn car up to the Schneefernerhaus at the summit of the Zugspitze. I skied the Zugspitze myself many years ago."

"The Zugspitze?"

"Yes, it's the highest mountain in the German Alps and the back side, the south side is a glacier-type ski area, no trees. The Germans built a pretty large structure on the summit called the Schneefernerhaus. It has a small restaurant and is sometimes used as a hotel as well as a research facility, meteorological."

"I see. Okay, finish your thoughts about the countersurveillance team?"

"What I was getting to, Mr. Novak, is that Garmisch is a small town, almost a village. And I expect that Bachmeier will have his own intel types out interspaced on the adjoining streets. If we put six of our own men on the streets as well, something might eventually appear off, seem wrong."

"I see. That's good thinking, Dave. I agree with that. You think it might possibly be a worthwhile trip? I suppose we really have nothing to lose with you going down there to just be casual, sniff around. By the way, Barb just handed me a page from our international resource directory. We have a hotel in Garmisch-Partenkirchen that we've used before on a couple of occasions. It's a nice place. It's the Hotel Koenigshof on St. Martin Strasse. We'll go ahead and book you there for three nights, Thursday, Friday, and Saturday nights. You can go down tomorrow, Thursday morning, and you'll have some time to wander around and get acclimated to the town. I assume you'll go operational on Friday night. Then you can stand down on Saturday and leave Sunday, depending on when your flight is. How's that sound?" Pete asked.

"I like that. Yes, sir. That's great. The Hotel Koenigshof on St. Martin Strasse. Thank you. It might be worthwhile, one never knows. Worst case, I might even be able to glean some information from the hotel staff. However, maybe things will work out and I can collect some direct intelligence myself. As you said, we really have nothing to lose," Dave said.

"Good. Take care and if you discover something that you feel is urgent, call me. Otherwise, I'll take your report on Monday morning when you're back in the area. I'll block a time for you and ask Jack if he wants to sit in. I assume that afterward, you'll be flying back to the States out of Frankfurt?"

"Yes, sir. I think that would be easiest to manage. In any case, I'll need to return the rental car there."

"Right. It's a go. Dave, check your six and keep a round in the breech. And remember, if it comes to it, shoot first. Fire the first bullet…first bullet. Always," Pete said. The line clicked off.

Dave rose from his chair and walked to the elevator bank. He wanted to get back up to his room and pack up before dinner.

CHAPTER 29

Hauptbahnhof Central Train Station
Europaplatz 1, Berlin
Thursday morning, August 4th

Dave rose early from bed at five o'clock in the morning, managed a shower and quick breakfast in the lobby lounge, and checked out from the Adlon Kempinski at seven o'clock. He took a taxi to the train station where he bought a ticket on a fast Inter-City Express, ICE, train to Frankfurt which would make a stop at the airport on its way to its final destination. The ticket clerk had commented that the ICE trains travel at about 300 km/hour, or 186 mph. His trip would take three-hours, thirty-nine-minutes. Yes, Dave thought, that was indeed fast.

Once in the train station and after checking his suitcase, Dave had time to walk along the train up to its bullet-shaped nose. It was sleek indeed. All the train cars were colored white with a red stripe down the middle. The acronym 'ICE' was stamped in large, gray letters on the engine's car. Once inside, Dave found the interior of the train more than just a bit classy.

It sported high-backed, comfortable seats and was pristine in its cleanliness.

Dave's choice was an early train and at departure time, no one was seated next to him or across from him. As he always did with the airlines, he had chosen an aisle seat. After what seemed only minutes, the train began to pull ever so smoothly away from the platform and the station. Rolling through the city of Berlin and to the edges of its suburbs, the ICE train began to accelerate rapidly. Dave could feel the speed increasing briskly.

Within a short time, a white-jacketed waiter came by to take lunch orders. Dave ordered a small *aufschnitte*, a German dish comprising a wooden platter with sliced meats, cheeses, crackers, and a few deviled eggs. He also asked for a chilled glass of Spätlese white wine to wash it down.

When lunch was delivered, he was impressed with the layout of the offering and wasted no time devouring it. Glancing occasionally to the window, the countryside whizzed by at such a swift rate that Dave felt the term 'high-speed' describing an ICE train was an understatement.

The blur of the passing towns and forests was such that trying to watch the sights through the window could be a bit disorienting. So, after lunch was done and the tray had been taken away, Dave studied the maps showing the highway route he'd take from the airport to Garmisch. It was pretty much a straight shot—Autobahns E41/E42 and A3/A5/A9 would eventually transition to even more numbers, yet take him directly into the town center of Garmisch.

Putting the maps away, Dave slipped in and out of a light sleep. His thoughts were of Pumphrey Drive back home, Karen, little Carolyn, and Tony. His contemplations grew solemn at his thoughts of his lost partner, Tony.

Dave was awakened by the sound of a crisp male voice emanating from the speaker system. They were approaching Frankfurt airport. The train slowed as it approached the structure and cruised moderately along its platforms. As it stopped, Dave pulled his luggage ticket from his dark blue blazer and rose from his seat. Twenty minutes later, with his Rimowa suitcase in tow, he walked through the passenger departure area, baggage claim, and to the *Sixt* car rental counter. In just minutes of registering, he ambled away with a set of keys to his rental, a silver Audi A4, and headed for the garage.

Dave climbed into the Audi, exited the garage, and left the airport area to begin the drive. Heading due south, he would have to circle the outskirts of the city of Munich. Then farther south to Bavaria. The drive to Garmisch in its entirety would take him about 4 hours. Not too bad. He found the silver Audi A4 was peppy and handled well, but it was no match for his shiny black Audi A6 back in Virginia.

The drive was steady and, in a lot of ways, tedious. The autobahn just seemingly stretched on forever. Occasionally, he squirmed in his seat to stretch and adjusted his shoulder holster several times. That was a habit. At one point, he shuddered at a painful cramp in his left shoulder, the one he'd been shot in. It was probably because his arms were elevated for so long on the steering wheel. At almost five o'clock in the late afternoon, he stopped for gas before entering the town limits of Garmisch. He was soon cruising south on the main drag, *Hauptstrasse, Main Street.*

Dave gave streets to his right a hard look, searching for Bahnhofstrasse and soon spotted it. He took the right turn. After a short stint, to his right, the Hotel Koenigshof stood at the corner of Hauptstrasse and St. Martin Strasse. He pulled into the lot, switched off the ignition, and grabbed his suitcase and leather briefcase bag. He strolled through the sliding glass doors to the receptionist desk.

The receptionist was an older but pleasant gentleman. Probably a night shift volunteer. He registered Dave and gave him the sweep card to his room on the third floor, once again a junior suite, but this time with a balcony facing the mountains. On his way to the elevator, he passed their restaurant, *Das Königliche, The Royal*. He saw it was already open. So, after he threw his bags on his bed, that's where he was headed next. He was starved.

Once down in the restaurant, it didn't take Dave long to order. He asked for an old favorite of his...a *Jägerschnitzel, Spätzle, and Rotkraut...a Hunter's Schnitzel, noodles, and red cabbage* as well as a glass of Spätlese white wine. The meal was delicious, so he finished with apple strudel and a cup of coffee. He charged dinner to his room, then checked his watch—six thirty.

After freshening up back in his room from the drive, he had plenty of time to take a stroll and attempt to locate the Staudacherhof Hotel. He'd already determined from the maps that it was on the same side, east side, of Hauptstrasse and about eight blocks farther south. It shouldn't be too difficult. On the way through the lobby, he stopped to check at the reception desk.

"*Guten abend. Kann ich dir helfen? Good evening. Can I help you?*" the middle-aged receptionist asked.

"*Ja, bitte. Die Staudacherhof Hotel, ist es in der Nähe. Yes, please. The Staudacherhof Hotel, is it nearby?*" Dave asked.

"*Ja, ja. Es ist nicht weit von hier. Yes, it's not too far from here,*" the man answered.

"*Ein Freund von mir wohnt dort. Wie komme ich dorthin? A friend of mine is staying there. How do I get there?*" Dave said.

"Gehen Sie von hier aus einfach nach Süden. Es geht um sieben Blöcke. Just walk south from here. It's about seven blocks."

"Danke," Dave said.

"Bitte," the man concluded.

At almost seven o'clock and outside his hotel, Dave found the evening in Garmisch to be a gorgeous Bavarian night. A great night for a walk. He headed straight south from the hotel. All around him the streets were a mix of shops, hotels, and residences, and all upscale. A nice neighborhood. And Dave found the blocks were short blocks, no more than one to three buildings on each one.

Standing on the corner across from the entrance to the Staudacherhof Hotel, Dave's eyes scanned and considered it. It was a great looking hotel, older, a very traditional hotel in Bavarian style, having three floors, outside exterior doors to the rooms, and carved wooden balconies that ran along the length of the building. There were two large attractive turrets with windows and mosque-like roofs built into the corners of the hotel on the north side that gave the Staudacherhof a majestic appearance.

Those balconies could be key, Dave thought. The balconies on the higher floors were no more than seven and half feet above from the lower floor balconies. Tomorrow, Friday night, he could initially approach the hotel from the rear to avoid any security that he assumed would be focused on the front entrance. If he could watch for a bit and determine which rooms weren't occupied, he might be able to climb up using those balconies to a room on the third floor, pick the lock, and enter.

First however, he would need now to enter the hotel, ostensibly for a cup of coffee and strudel. He might be able to determine where Bachmeier's meeting room might be. Yes, he'd do that now, rather than risk going inside the hotel tomorrow.

Dave entered the hotel and walked past smiling receptionists. He veered to his right and into what appeared to be the dining room, *Hochwiesen Café, High Meadows Café.* He sat in a booth against the wall. A waitress approached him.

"Guten abend. Auf Deutsch oder Englisch?" she asked.

"Englisch, bitte," Dave replied.

"Good. What would you like," the woman asked.

"Just desert and coffee. Apple strudel with whipped cream?"

"Yes, we have that. Anything else?"

"Well, I'm sort of doing some scouting for my company. Do you have meeting rooms in this hotel?"

"Yes, we do, but just the one, really. It's on the first floor down the main corridor to near the rear of the hotel. There's also a small balcony above the conference room on the second floor for observers, if any."

"Outstanding. Thank you," Dave said.

"You're welcome. Coffee and strudel coming up," she replied with a grin.

Dave smiled. That meant that tomorrow night, all he would need to do is manage to climb quietly up the balconies to the third floor and pick the lock on an unoccupied room through its exterior sliding door. He'd then come down a floor by a stairwell and search for the door to the small balcony the waitress mentioned. He might be able to hear voices from below in the conference room well enough from there.

With a slight smile across his face, Dave eased back in the seat and awaited the coffee and strudel. He rubbed his left shoulder and winced at a slight spasm. This was the one Sigmund Degler had put a bullet into weeks ago out in the forest in Wyoming. Afterward in his recovery exercises at home, that shoulder appeared to be 100%, however there were still some random aches. He knew his shoulder would need good to be for his climb tomorrow night.

CHAPTER 30

Koenigshof Hotel
St. Martin Strasse, Garmisch-Partenkirchen
Friday, late afternoon, August 5th

Dave sat at one of the tables covered with an umbrella outside the hotel, a half empty glass of Spätlese wine resting in front of him. He stared up at the colossal, regal peak of the Zugspitze and remembered skiing down its southern slope many years ago. At the time, he had been finishing up his master's degree in the late Spring at Case Western Reserve University in Cleveland, Ohio, when he decided to take a ski break and fly to Germany to visit Garmisch. It was a year before he'd met Anne and they'd eventually married. It was before his son, Michael, came along. And it was before he ultimately lost both of them in that horrific collision with an 18-wheeler in a late November micro blizzard on I-70 near Eagle, Colorado. His face turning somber at the thought, Dave shook his head as images of Anne and Michael flashed across his mind and then slowly faded.

Yes, he'd been a free spirit in his visit to Garmisch way back then, and he still had memories of that trip. In any event, he was now married to former NCIS agent, Karen, whom he truly loved, and they had a beautiful, newborn little girl, Carolyn. Still, he knew in his heart that he would never, could never, forget his first wife, Anne, and his son, Michael. Never! He thought it was strange how life could twist you around and yank you in directions you never dreamed possible. It was also extraordinary how a loving God could grab someone, pull him from a dark, crippling grief, and thrust them once again into a bright light of happiness. He nodded his head at the thought, his eyes continuing to gaze at the summit of the Zugspitze as winds blew wisps of snow across its crest. He took a sip of wine.

Dave glanced at his watch. Almost five o'clock. He got up and walked into the hotel, then into the restaurant. It would be an early dinner tonight. He ordered the Beef Rouladen which came served with dark gravy, grilled potatoes, and red cabbage. To drink, he asked for an iced tea. No booze tonight. He finished the meal with just a cup of coffee.

Up in his room, Dave changed into a dark blue shirt, black jeans, and dark gray Nike hiking shoes with sponge-like soles. He laid back on the bed and turned on the television to watch the news – it was a large, Samsung 48-inch screen. The only thing of note was North Korea's still launching of missiles into the Sea of Japan. He smiled to himself, thinking that eventually, the Japanese were going to take just so much. And someday ole Kim Jong-un was going to get his ass handed to him.

At seven o'clock with the sun slipping behind the mountains and daylight dimming, Dave rose from the bed and walked into the bathroom to wash his face and hands. He took a pair of black leather gloves and slipped them into his left pants pocket. From his leather briefcase bag, a lock pick set was stuffed into his right pants pocket. The only weapon he'd carry with him tonight was a SOG flip knife with a five-inch, razor-sharp blade. He left the room and took the elevator down to the lobby.

As he left through the front doors of the Koenigshof, Dave skipped down the stairs and steered off a block to his right. Tonight, he would walk the distance down to the Staudacherhof from a block to its east. That would take him past the front entrance to the hotel and well out of sight of any security posts. He'd end up across from its rear parking area. According to his map, it would be south on Mittelfeld Strasse, then south to St. Martin Strasse, and farther south to the cross street of Hausbergstrasse. After making a final left turn onto Höllenstrasse, he would slowly work his way back north to the rear of the Staudacherhof where he'd begin his routine of checking for lights in third floor rooms.

Almost to the corner at Hausbergstrasse and Höllenstrasse, Dave noticed the gray sky had transformed to a deep black but filled with millions of sparkling orbs of stars. Streetlamps had switched on with an orangish glow. He stood silently on the corner across from the Staudacherhof watching the row of third-floor rooms.

With the time now approaching eight o'clock, Dave was growing increasingly fatigued from constantly scanning the windows of the rooms. Perhaps the entire hotel was booked, he thought. He decided to give it another twenty minutes and, gazing upward, he realized that the lights had yet to turn on in one third floor room.

The room of interest was located in the middle of the stretch of rooms along the west side of the hotel. That could be the one. Checking first to his left and right, he jogged quickly across the street to the rear of the hotel.

He glanced around the rear corner. Nothing. No security. Given that this was to be a limited and low-key meeting, any security presence was most likely focused on the main entrance, Dave thought. He walked tentatively and quietly on his Nikes along the side of the hotel. The unoccupied room on the third floor was coming up. He was soon just below it. He glanced around. There was no one that he could observe in the area.

The ground floor room had its lights on, but the curtains were drawn. Dave eased himself up onto the railing running along the first-floor deck. He raised himself up to standing erect. It would be just a short leap to grasp the flooring of the second-floor balcony. He took a deep breath and shook his arms and legs, gathering his strength.

He flexed his legs at the knee and abruptly jumped directly upward. The rubbery, soft soles of his shoes enabled a silent leap off the railing. He made it—his fingers and the palms of his hands grabbed onto the floor of the balcony. He ever so slowly pulled himself up, his forearms resting on the floor's edge. He took another deep inhale of alpine air and thrust himself higher, his right knee planted on the border of the balcony's floor. Dave paused, listening. The lights were also on inside the second-floor room, but again, the curtains were closed. There were no shadows moving near the sliding door. It was nighttime and the visitors were probably focused on the TV.

Dave's arms reached up and over the balcony's railing. His arms tightened around the railing, so he could heave himself up to his first knee. He then rose, standing on the brink of the floor that extended a few inches outside the railing. He gulped in several deep breaths of air. A few minutes passed. He climbed up onto the balcony's railing, swayed, and after wobbling a bit, was able to steady himself. This climb up the side of the hotel was a tad more difficult than he initially thought it would be.

He glanced upward to the wooden lip of the third-floor balcony. Just one more hop. Just one. And the room above was empty and still dark. He instantly sprang upward, his fingers and palms clutching the edge of the balcony's wooden floor above him. He exhaled and inhaled.

Hanging precipitously from the edge of the floor, Dave instantly froze, his body rocking gently back and forth. Voices. Male voices not above him but below. Hanging by his fingers and palms of his hands, he glanced down.

Two men were slowly ambling along directly below him and paused. From their German chit-chat, Dave knew they were security personnel, and therefore most assuredly they were armed. The men were looking along the side of the hotel to the rear parking lot.

Dave's left shoulder, the one that had taken a bullet several weeks ago, began to ache with a passion. His fingers and palms of his hands strained painfully to continue to hold onto the edge of the rough wooden floor. Beads of perspiration broke out across his forehead, and a trickle of sweat seeped down his left cheek.

Dave continued to stare at the men below. His fingers and palms had numbed to the pain. He could no longer feel them. Seeing nothing of interest, the security duo on the walkway down below spun about and began traipsing back toward the front of the hotel. Not wanting to make the slightest noise, Dave waited seconds more even though the searing pressure in his hands, arms, and left shoulder was now excruciating. The men soon turned the corner at the front of the hotel and were gone from sight.

Hanging precipitously from the third-floor balcony, with every ounce of strength he had left in him, Dave yanked himself upward. He managed to place his right forearm on the floor's edge. He breathed a sigh of relief. His left forearm followed. He lifted his right knee to where it was soon resting on the wood of the edge. Wasting no time and in a tremendous effort, he hauled himself up and over the railing, making a slight thump as he dropped, crumpling on the balcony's wood floor. He gasped for breath.

"Shit. Now that was fun," he whispered to himself with a slight chuckle. He turned to his side and rolled onto his back. His hands shoved him to a sitting position where he continued to breathe hard. He knew that if it came to it, climbing back down would be a whole lot easier. Dave swiveled around on his knees and moved toward the sliding door.

He plucked the lock pick set from his pocket. The lock on the door was old, so it took several minutes of moving the steel pick around inside it. It sprung loose with a click, and Dave slid the door open. He rose to his feet and walked through the room. There were no suitcases lying around and nothing in the closet. He looked in the bathroom where there were fresh towels, bars of hotel soap, and shampoo. He had guessed correctly…this room was empty.

Dave eased the room's interior door open and looked down the hallway to the right, then left. No one. The hall was empty. He stepped out into the hallway, leaving the door to Room 317 ajar. He might need it later. He walked slowly along the rooms on the other side of the hall, looking for one that might indicate that it was not entrance to a room, but to the conference room balcony. Four doors down the hall he found it. He gently cracked it open and instantly heard voices, all male voices.

Dave glanced left and right again, then got down on his knees and squeezed through the doorway, carefully ensuring it didn't open so wide as to be noticed. He closed the door, then slid on his belly down the carpeted balcony stairs to the first row of seats. The voices below were all in German and Dave understood what was being said, just not who was saying it. Still, he could guess at the speaker if it was Bachmeier or Obermann. He settled into a supine, resting position and listened.

"All right, then, good. When do you think the bunker will be completely finished?"

"Three to four weeks at the most, Andreas."

"Good. Refresh my memory. I may want to drive by it. Where exactly is it located," most likely it was Defense Minister Andreas Bachmeier who spoke, asking the question.

"The Bunker is of course east from Berlin, first on highways B5 to B1, then north on Strasse des Friedens to the intersection with Diedersdorf Strasse where one takes a final right. It's there, in the woods southeast of Görlsdorf. On one's left," the person most likely speaking was the project manager, General Gerhardt Obermann.

"Excellent, Gerhardt, your progress is superb and right on target. I congratulate you," Bachmeier said.

"Thank you, sir. As a concluding remark and as I mentioned earlier, all of our armored and infantry forces have advanced GPS technology. Their progress will be monitored and controlled from our new bunker at Görlsdorf. That's where you, I, and the senior staff will be located from the very onset after giving the order to begin the assault. And all of our fighter and bomber air forces will be controlled from the new base we've constructed at Fürstenwalde Air Base. Fürstenwalde is also east of Berlin off Highway L36 and Strasse der Freundschaft," General Obermann said.

"As I said, Gerhardt, superb work. One more question... How will we handle the Chancellor?

"As I mentioned that I would ensure some time ago, we have already handpicked twelve men from the Bundeswehr special forces. We held very detailed interviews with each of them. On the night that the operation begins, they will travel to the Berlin Chancellery residence on Willy Brandt Avenue and arrest him. He will be temporarily incarcerated until trial. We're ready, sir."

"Again, Gerhardt, outstanding. All right, enough for tonight. We'll meet again in two weeks. Let's go into the tavern and toast a beer," Bachmeier explained.

The group rose from their seats still chatting and walked to the conference room door. Their voices soon faded as they strolled down the hallway.

Dave slowly raised himself, glancing over the conference room balcony's railing. The room was empty. The group had left the lights on, and the entrance door was ajar. The long conference table was bare. Any papers had been removed.

Dave stood, turned, and walked up the few steps to the hallway door. He glanced right and left and entered the hallway. Walking down to room 317, he decided that he'd leave the same way he'd come...on the exterior side of the hotel. However, climbing down would be much easier than climbing up had been.

Dave considered what he had learned. It was timely information, but not urgent. Information that he could wait until Monday to brief Peter Novak. And that meant he had another whole day to cruise through town and explore Garmisch.

Above all else, General Gerhardt Obermann was an inherently suspicious man, even paranoid to a fault. As the others in the Bachmeier's group walked away for a beer, Obermann lingered behind.

Leaning against the wall just outside the entrance door to the conference room, Obermann's face bore an angry scowl as he stared through the narrow open space of the doorway. His hands clenched in fists, he watched as Dave walked back up the stairs of the conference room's second-floor balcony.

CHAPTER 31

Koenigshof Hotel
St. Martin Strasse, Garmisch-Partenkirchen
Saturday morning, August 6th

Dave was awakened by his alarm clock at seven o'clock in the morning on Saturday. He showered and then headed to the Königliche restaurant for breakfast. He had thrown on a black and gray herringbone sport coat, jeans, dark blue shirt, and his Nikes. His flight didn't leave until 1:00 PM tomorrow, Sunday, so he had another day in Garmisch. He planned to walk the length of Hauptstrasse to see all the sights…the shops, cafés, and bistros. Maybe for lunch he'd have a brat, brötchen, and a beer just like a Bavarian would.

Sitting in his usual booth, the waitress set a plate of scrambled eggs, bacon, fried potatoes, and toast in front of him. He smiled, took a sip of coffee, and rubbed his left shoulder, rotating it gently around. The shoulder still ached from last night's climb up the side of the Staudacherhof hotel. His fingers, hands, and arms had a slight discomforting tension in them as well.

ANDREW CERONI

On the plus side, he had gleaned what he thought was some significant information that he would soon relay to Pete Novak and Jack Barrett. From what he had heard, Dave believed a dark cloud was gathering to hover over Europe. And at some point, it would need to be dealt with.

Finishing breakfast, it was still a bit early for Dave to begin his walk. He grabbed a copy of the German magazine, *Der Spiegel, The Mirror,* in the lobby and plopped in an easy chair in a sitting area by the lobby's far wall. The magazine was filled with the usual news about the federal government, crime in the large cities, and sports. It was interesting enough to occupy his time and brush up on his written German. A man in a white dinner jacket came by and offered to pour him a cup of coffee. Dave took him up on the offer and tipped him generously.

He flipped to the last page of Der Spiegel at a little after nine o'clock. Dave felt it was late enough to begin his stroll down Hauptstrasse. He rose from his seat and then exited through the front doors. Dave walked from the hotel, taking a left, another left, and then a final left southeast onto Haupstrasse. He entered many curio shops and liked the carvings, Hummel figurines, and Bavarian crafts he saw. He wished he could tote many of the offerings back to Karen and Carolyn in Virginia with him but there was just too many. Choosing would be too difficult.

By ten thirty in the morning, Dave had walked nearly the entire in-town length of Hauptstrasse. While it was a bit early for lunch, he did pause on the sidewalk to savor the aromas coming off the grill of one bistro.

His senses alerted. It was then that he noticed them. There were two of them. Both men appeared in their early forties, loitering, and appearing to window shop, but also moving along with Dave about a half block behind him. Although it was a pleasant, midmorning day in August, both men had on light shell jackets. Perhaps to conceal pistols?

Dave picked up his pace. Crossing one block further down, as he took a casual glance around him, Dave noticed the two men were walking a bit faster as well. Keeping up with him. Dave continued along Hauptstrasse. He saw signs coming up for the Tyrolean Zugspitzebahn, the cable car up to the summit of the Zugspitze. Perhaps he'd have his brat, brötchen, and beer up in the Schneefernerhaus' restaurant. He quickened his gait even more.

Noticing a cable car was about to close its doors and depart. Dave broke into a jog up to the young ticket clerk and handed him the money for the round trip. The young man gave him a ticket and allowed Dave to hop on. As his mountain bahn car rose over the trees, Dave looked out the rear window as the two men stood next to each other on the platform below, glaring up at the ascending car. Dave managed a slight smile but briefly wondered if they would follow him up the mountain. He doubted it, as the Zugspitze summit's views over the Alps and the Schneefernerhaus itself drew lots of tourists who would be witnesses to whatever occurred.

Dave sat in the restaurant munching on a brat and brötchen and looking out the window at the mountain scenery. Lunch was delicious and the views gorgeous. Afterward, he walked into the little souvenir shop and bought a paperback book with lots of photos regarding construction of the structure on the peak of the mountain. He had to kill some time. His plan was to take the very last cable car back down near the end of the afternoon and see if the two had the fortitude to hang near the platform all day.

Near four o'clock in the late afternoon, Dave stood on the Tyrolean Zugspitzebahn peak platform watching as cable cars filled with people swung around in a large loop and headed out in midair down the mountain. No one but Dave was left standing on the platform when the last cable car swung around and paused. Dave didn't see an operator in the car and turned to the ticket clerk.

"There's no operator on this car," Dave said.

"No, not on this last one, sir. Johan sometimes stays the night up here. He's also an electrician and a mechanic. He cares for the hotel through the night when there's no more than just a couple occupants. And that's the case tonight. It doesn't matter though. The cable car will take you directly to the platform down in Garmisch. This is the last car, so, hop on," the ticket clerk replied.

Dave stepped into the car and moved along the wall just behind the operator's wooden stool. As the car began to lurch ahead, two men brushed past the ticket clerk, handing him tickets, and sprang onto the car. It was the two men Dave had noticed earlier on Hauptstrasse. Apparently, they'd taken another Zugspitzebahn car up the mountain and decided to wait Dave out.

One of the two, the older one, who also had a couple days' growth of beard, smiled at Dave. The car lurched ahead, continuing its loop around the platform and then out into the air above the trees and mountainside.

Dave suddenly kicked the wooden stool toward the doors. The two men watched in curiosity as the cable car doors tried to close but instead jammed against the stool from its top seat pad to its bottom wooden rungs. The doors left a gap of nearly two feet between them.

The man with the slight beard was quickly caught by surprise, lurching backward as Dave unexpectedly lunged at him. He reached for a pistol he had tucked into his belt. Dave's right hand came down hard on the man's wrist. The pistol clattered to the floor of the cable car. The car swayed with a slight vibration to the rapid movement inside the car. The pistol slid across the floor, under the wooden stool, out the jammed doors, and into the air. Dave smiled.

The man grimaced, reaching into a jacket pocket. He pulled out a hunting knife and yanked the knife from its sheath. The sheath fell to the floor. Dave's right hand reached into his back pocket and jerked out his SOG flip knife. At the sight of the impending action, the second man wedged himself backward into a corner of the cable car.

Dave and the man with the beard circled each other around the inside of the car, winding past several floor to ceiling chrome hand bars. Dave noticed there were also several chrome parallel hand bars positioned up near the ceiling. The man suddenly sprang forward, his knife plunging in a downward slashing motion. It caught and sliced through the sleeve of Dave's jacket. Dave countered with an upward stab that pierced the man's wrist. The man winced and lurched backward from the strike, his blood dripping onto the metal floor.

"*Amerikanisches schwein! American pig!*" the man exclaimed.

"*Sagt du, arschloch! Dieses Amerikanische Schwein wird dir in den treten! Says you, asshole! This American pig is going to kick your ass!*" Dave shouted back.

The man again leaped forward and snapped a front kick that caught the right side of Dave's jaw. Dave recoiled at the blow, stepping backward to recover. The man followed with a reverse kick that caught Dave in his neck. Dave stumbled back farther, shaking his head.

The man rushed again, this time going for Dave's neck. Dave abruptly ducked, the blow missing its target. Seeing the opportunity so near, Dave rammed his SOG knife's blade into the man's knee, slashing it fiercely backward, slicing tendons. The man screamed at the stab and staggered backward near the door.

Dave leaped forward at the man's retreat and in a violent forward thrust, plunged his blade into the man's abdomen. The man moaned. His hands reached down to the deep wound he now had in his stomach. With his right hand, he waved his knife in the air, slicing back and forth at Dave.

The man unexpectedly lunged forward. With a downward slash, the man slit a gash down Dave's chest. Blood immediately began to seep across his shirt, oozing downward onto his jeans. Dave flinched at the pain. He needed to end this fight and now.

Dave stuffed his knife in his pocket. He jumped up, his hands wrapping around a parallel chrome hand bar near the ceiling. He swung rapidly forward, both of his feet hammering into the man just below his neck. The man fell backward at the pounding, tripped over the stool behind him, and with a look of sheer horror across his face, tumbled through the cable car's doorway into the air. There was no sound, no scream, just the rush of air and wind outside the cable car.

The second man, still leaning hard against the corner of the cable car, drew his own knife, a flip knife like Dave's. He flicked it open. Dave cautiously approached him, his SOG knife again in his right hand. Dave glanced down at his chest. The knife wound was most likely not deep, but it drew a lot of blood. The man in the corner charged Dave, his arm raised for a downward slash. Dave leaped to his right, thrusting his blade into the man's right shoulder as he rushed by.

The man groaned at the stab wound, turned, and ran at Dave again, this time with a horizontal hacking move. Dave's left arm blocked the thrust, and he plunged his knife into the man's left shoulder. His blade sunk in deep, tearing through muscle and sinew, its razor point striking bone. The man grunted, backing up to the rear of the car.

Dave walked slowly toward the man.

"English?"

"Ja," the man whimpered.

"You have a choice. This," he said, raising his knife, "Or this," he said, pointing to the open jammed doors. Now, who sent you?" Dave asked.

"I can't tell you that," the man replied, cowering against a rear window.

"Then it's your time," Dave answered, raising his knife to his hip, and continuing to approach the man,

"General Obermann sent us. He said to find you, to tail you, and when the time appeared right, to kill you," the man whimpered.

"Good. Well, your choice is what?" Dave said, his SOG knife raised and pointing toward the doors.

Seeing how quickly Dave had dispatched his partner, the man knew he had no chance against McClure in a knife fight. Both of his shoulders already had deep wounds. He moved from the corner along the side of the car, dropping his knife as he went. He approached the jammed doors and stepped his right leg over the wooden stool.

As the man's left leg rose over the stool, Dave rushed forward and grabbed him by the back of his collar. He tugged the man violently backward. The man fell over the stool and onto his back on the cable car's metal floor. He stared up at Dave. A look of puzzlement washed across the man's face.

Dave kicked the stool out from the car. It flipped end over end into the air. The doors slid closed with a thud. As the cable car descended to the floor of the Zugspitzebahn platform, it wound around in a circle over the platform and stopped. Dave looked down one last time at the man on the floor, then exited the car.

As he walked briskly back up Hauptstrasse, questions flooded his mind about what had just happened. Like the first man who he had pummeled to his death from the cable car, the second man was also an assassin sent to kill him. Yet something happened in Dave that wouldn't let the second man, even though he was obviously willing, take a dive to his own death from the cable car's jammed doors.

Dave rubbed his forehead, searching for an explanation. Why had he acted the way he did? Why had he shown that assassin mercy? He couldn't see the logic of it.

Dave buttoned his sport coat to conceal the blood on his shirt. He would buy some bandages at a pharmacy, patch himself up, and open his suitcase to change shirts. Maybe take some painkillers. That would have to do for now.

More importantly, it was clear that somehow General Obermann knew Dave was in Garmisch. That was a puzzle. And one thing was certain—since it was Obermann himself who had sent the duo to kill him, Dave was convinced that others would be following.

Dave sensed it was time to check out of the Koenigshof hotel, begin the drive north to Frankfurt, and leave the charming town of Garmisch behind him.

CHAPTER 32

Pumphrey Drive, Fairfax
Virginia
Sunday evening, August 7th

It just before six o'clock in the evening when Dave's flight pulled up to the gate at Dulles International. Dave was beat, utterly fatigued. He didn't sleep at all on the plane as his chest throbbed with pain. It hurt like hell. The good thing was he got through customs at both Frankfurt and at Dulles without questions or any issues because he had concealed the wound well.

Walking to the baggage area, he called Karen to let her know he was back in the states. She was ecstatic and eager to see him. He told her he was going to first make a stop at the Emergency Room at Inova Alexandria Hospital off Fairfax Boulevard before he came home. Karen was concerned about that and wanted to know what was wrong, but Dave told her to not worry about it… it was a minor issue.

Forty-five minutes later, a nurse brought Dave into an examination room. It was only a few minutes before a doctor arrived. He had Dave remove his shirt.

"Mr. McClure, I'm Dr. Frank Hamilton. This cut across your chest looks at least 24 hours old. And it's over 12 inches long. Why didn't you have this wound treated earlier? It looks like a knife wound. So, my question is, do I need to call the police? We're supposed to, you know, if we suspect foul play. What do you say?" the doctor asked.

"Dr. Hamilton, this happened yesterday in Garmisch, Germany. Down in Bavaria. Two would-be robbers. I patched myself up afterward as best I could and flew back to the states. The reason is I didn't go to a hospital over there was that I didn't want to be detained by the German police, miss my flight, and end up spending another week in Germany. It was a robbery gone bad."

"I see," Dr. Hamilton replied.

"And in any case, I ended up beating the living shit out of the perpetrators. I have no doubt that they'll think twice next time, that is, if there is a next time. Please, Doctor, can you just suture the areas that need it and put butterfly bandages on those areas that don't? I really don't need or want any police involvement," Dave replied.

"Hmmm, well, all right, since you ended up beating the living shit out of the criminals who tried to rob you, and along with me feeling really generous tonight, we'll just stitch you up. No police. Mr. McClure, this laceration across your upper torso must be really painful. It doesn't look infected yet though," the doctor said, chuckling.

"It is painful. Extremely so. And thank you very much, doctor. I appreciate this," Dave said.

"You should. I'm giving you a break because I think you deserve one. By the way, I'll use self-absorbent stitches, so you don't have to come back here to have them taken out and end up having to explain things all over again. I'm going to give you a tetanus shot and an antibiotic shot. You'll also get a prescription for some antibiotics that you'll need to take to a pharmacy. Don't fail to do that. You'll need the antibiotics."

"I will. Thank you."

Dr. Hamilton stitched the gash closed. The doctor administered an anesthetic shot before he sutured the more deeply slashed flesh. All in all, Dave had thirteen stitches and a host of butterfly bandages on his chest. Dave thanked the doctor for cutting him some slack and left the hospital around seven-thirty. He winced a little as the flesh around the stitches stretched when he squeezed into the front seat of his black Audi A6.

He pulled into the driveway on Pumphrey Drive about twenty minutes later. Karen came to the door holding Carolyn. Seeing Karen and the baby, Dave's eyes lit up. Karen grinned after watching Dave approach with his suitcase in tow and opened the door for him. In the foyer, she tried to hug him, but he held her off. The anesthetic was beginning to wear off.

"Honey, I have a cut on my chest. It'll hurt a bunch if we hug. Please don't," Dave said.

"A cut? Serious? How bad is it?" Karen asked.

"It's long, but not too deep. I have some stitches and butterfly bandages on it. I'll explain it all to you later. Can I have something to eat? I'm starved."

"I already made your favorite sandwich, a BLT. It's waiting for you in the fridge with some potato salad and a slice of kosher dill pickle."

"Oh jeez, that sounds wonderful. Thank you, sweetheart."

Dave sat at the table and Karen handed him Carolyn. He kissed her forehead and snuggled her against his chest. The little gal smiled at him and nestled her head on his shoulder. On her way to the fridge, Karen glanced over her shoulder and saw them cuddling.

"Oh, Carolyn can hug her Daddy, but I can't hug my husband!" Karen exclaimed.

"Honey, she's just a tiny thing. She doesn't even hug—her arms aren't long enough yet."

"I know. I'm kidding," Karen replied.

Karen brought over the BLT and potato salad and set it in front of Dave along with a ginger ale to wash it down. He handed Carolyn to her and took a bite of the sandwich. He grinned.

"Karen, this is great. Thanks!"

"My pleasure. Now show me this chest wound of yours," she said as she sat across from him holding Carolyn in her lap.

Dave slipped off his sport coat and laid it on his lap. He slowly unbuttoned his shirt. There was no undershirt since it had been soaked with blood and Dr. Hamilton tossed it in a trash bag.

"Oh, my goodness! That's a huge, long wound. How did that happen?" Karen asked him.

Dave explained that for this op, he had been eavesdropping on a meeting at a hotel in Garmisch and had gleaned some important intelligence. He then described the attack by two men in a cable car the next day that ended in a knife fight to the death. He assumed the assault was to keep him from revealing what he'd heard the night before. Somehow, they knew he had the details.

"A knife fight in a cable car coming down a mountain. That sounds like a scene from a James Bond movie. I thought we were finished with all that stuff...pistol wounds, knife fights, hand-to-hand combat. I'm very glad you survived it. And you tossed a guy out of the cable car?" Karen asked.

"I kicked him out of the cable car. He had to be in so much shock that he didn't even scream as he tumbled into the air. And my promotion is not until January 1st," Dave answered.

"Well, same result. That guy's at the bottom of a mountain in the German Alps. Who knows if they'll ever find his body."

"I can't allow myself to worry about things like that."

"And then you saved the second assassin from leaping from the cable car. That's interesting, Dave. Something in you couldn't let him jump to his death. I find that very interesting."

"I've thought about that myself. I'm not completely sure why I did it," Dave replied.

"You did it because you're human. And you're a good human at that, that's why. And I love you so much for who you are, and so does Carolyn," Karen said.

"Thanks for that. Now you know about the wound. I have to brief Pete Novak and Jack Barrett on all this tomorrow. Honey, I want to devour this sandwich and potato salad. After that, we can talk while I unpack upstairs. Deal?"

"Deal. I'll put Carolyn to bed in her crib," Karen said as she turned and began to walk from the kitchen.

CHAPTER 33

Langley Center, McLean
Virginia
Monday morning, August 8th

Pete stopped speaking when Jack's intercom jingled. Jack set down his mug of coffee and seeing it was Barb calling, he picked up the phone.

"Yes, Ma'am?"

"Mr. Barrett, Dave McClure is here. He said he had an appointment with Pete, but Pete wasn't in his office. So, he wants to brief you on the trip," Barb answered.

"Send Dave in. Both of us want to hear what he has to say," Jack replied.

"Sorry about that, Jack. Time got away from me," Pete said.

"No biggie," Jack responded, as Barb opened the door for Dave.

"Good morning, Dave. Have a seat. Pete and I understand from Dave Stratton that you have another wound. A chest wound?" Jack asked.

"Yes, sir. The wound is long in length, but not that deep. The doctor at Inova Alexandria Hospital in Fairfax said he had to put sutures in less than a third of it. Butterfly bandages cover the rest," Dave said.

"This was the result of a deadly knife fight with two male assassins in a cable car coming down from the Zugspitze, the highest peak in the German Alps?" Pete interjected.

"Yes, sir. That's about it," Dave answered.

"It sounds like a scene from a James Bond movie!" Pete exclaimed.

Dave smiled, chuckling, before he spoke, "Mr. Novak, that's exactly what Karen said last night."

"Stratton also said that during the fight, you kicked one of the would-be assassins out of the cable car. He fell to his death. How in the hell did you get those cable doors open?" Jack said.

"As the cable car left the station on top of the Zugspitze, I kicked the operator's wooden stool over to where it jammed between the doors as they closed. That left a large, open gap between the doors. And that's right. That man was very capable in hand-to-hand combat and knife fighting. I had no choice," Dave answered.

"Yet you spared the second assassin's life?" Pete asked.

"Yes, I did. That second man was far less capable. I wounded him badly. Really, it was no match between him and me," Dave responded.

"Stratton said you had related to him that you'd given the second assassin a choice...a knife fight or the cable car doorway. Dave said that the second man walked over and stood in the doorway of the cable car and was about to jump to his death, but at the last minute, you pulled him back in? Correct?" Jack asked.

ANDREW CERONI

"Yes, Mr. Barrett. I'm still trying to figure that one out, sir. The man did tell me that it was General Gerhardt Obermann who had sent them to find me, tail me, and when the time was right, kill me. Anyway, it was all happening so fast, that I... well, I really don't know why I did that," Dave said.

"Compassion. It was compassion, Dave. That second assassin had already been defeated in his mind and knew that you would kill him. He decided to end his life himself, a choice you gave him. And you stopped it. Compassion. You're a very skilled yet complex man, Dave. I've seen that in you on several occasions and I find I like it. Now, go ahead and tell us what you learned," Jack said.

Dave described waiting until it was dark to walk the eight blocks south to the Staudacherhof hotel and then scaling the wall up to the third floor at the side of the hotel. He took the staircase to the second floor and searched down the hallway, ultimately finding the room to the small balcony above the large conference room where Andreas Bachmeier's meeting was being held.

You scaled the outside wall of a hotel up to a third floor balcony? Jeez. That's another James Bond scene," Jack chuckled, "Please continue."

Dave went on to relate that apparently, General Obermann was in charge of the project. He led the briefing for those present regarding the project's current status and took questions afterward, mainly from Bachmeier. Obermann mentioned that their command bunker was near completion. This bunker is where Bachmeier, Obermann, and the senior staff would be on the night the operation begins. From there, all ground forces of armor and infantry would be controlled. Also, the new air base they built at Fürstenwalde would control the fighter and bomber forces.

230

"This is getting serious, Jack," Pete said, looking at Jack.

"I agree. Please continue, Dave. Anything else?" Jack asked.

Dave nodded and mentioned that Obermann had also briefed Bachmeier that they'd interviewed and handpicked twelve men from the Bundeswehr special forces. Those men would arrive at the Berlin Chancellery residence on Willy Brandt Avenue on the afternoon of the night that the operation was to begin and arrest the Chancellor. He would be incarcerated until his trial.

"Shit. Pardon my language, gentlemen. This is getting hard to believe. Dave, do you have the location of the bunker and the air base with you?" Jack asked.

"Yes, sir," Dave replied.

Jack picked up his phone and dialed the intercom.

"Yes, Mr. Barrett," Barb answered.

"Barb, please see if you can get hold of Rod Bailey and ask him to come up to my office armed with paper and a pen," Jack said.

"Will do, sir," Barb replied.

Jack glanced at Pete, then focused on Dave.

"Rod Bailey is our liaison to the National Reconnaissance Office, the NRO. The NRO owns and operates our satellite reconnaissance platforms. He'll be here in a bit. Dave, how's the baby?" Jack said.

"Little Carolyn is doing fine. She's captured both our hearts. You'd love her if you saw her," Dave said.

"I bet I would. I can only imagine. Hearing you speak of those things, well, it brings back memories. Those are great years, so be sure to cherish them," Jack said.

"Oh, we do, Mr. Barrett, we do. We find something new about the little one each time we play with her."

"That's fantastic," Jack said, turning to the door as Barb let Rod Bailey in.

"Hi, Rod. I think we have something that we're going to need the NRO's take on. We need you to ask them to move, reposition some satellite reconnaissance platforms for us in order to take a look at a couple things on the ground. In Europe," Jack said.

"Okay, sir," Rod said, taking a seat next to Dave.

"Dave, give Rod the locations of the bunker in Görlsdorf, Germany, and air base at Fürstenwalde so he can write it down," Jack said.

"Rod, give those locations to the NRO. We'd like to know what they see, the specifics," Jack said.

"Right. I'll do that as soon as I get back to my office, Mr. Barrett," Rod replied. Finished writing, he stood, nodded to both Pete and Jack, and left the room.

"Dave, once again, excellent work. On the one hand, I have difficulty believing that this is actually taking place in Germany, however secret. On the other hand, given what happened two years ago with the eighteen arrests the German police made concerning plans that were apparently in place to overthrow the German government, I find myself forced to believe the possibility. And now, in my mind, what was once only a possibility has transformed to a probability," Jack said.

"I know what you mean, Jack. Another imperialist Germany? A Fourth Reich? Really? It doesn't sound possible. However, we appear to be uncovering more and more intelligence that leads us to assess it as possible, and as you said, even probable," Pete said.

"What's next, Mr. Barrett," Dave asked.

"Let's see what the NRO determines. Assuming worst case, I'll need to brief the president regarding where we are in all of this. No doubt we'll need to begin some planning of our own. Pete, what say you?" Jack replied.

"Ditto on everything you've said, Jack," Pete replied.

"Anything for me, sir? Orders?" Dave asked.

"Not really. I think the bottom line here, Dave, is that we're going to wait to see what the NRO says and take it from there," Jack concluded.

The men rose and shook hands. Dave and Pete walked to the door.

CHAPTER 34

Langley Center, McLean
Virginia
Friday afternoon, August 12th

Reg Hartwick, Deputy Director of the NRO, walked through the glass doors of Langley Center. He had salt and pepper hair and looked every bit like a senior executive... dark navy blue pin-stripe suit, white shirt with French cuffs, and a blazing gold tie. He was met immediately by a male escort in a gray suit who escorted Reg through the turnstiles and over to the bank of elevators.

"I'm Tom Dougan, sir. I'll be taking you up to Mr. Barrett's office," the escort said. The young escort did his best to sound and look professional. They walked together and stepped into the first elevator that opened. The doors closed.

"I'm pleased to meet you, Tom. You look sharp in that suit. Nordstrom, Chevy Chase? How long have you been with the CIA?" Reg asked.

"Yes, sir. It was on sale. I've been here just over two years."

"Like it?"

"Yes," Tom answered.

"Well, when you have the time, you might take a hard look at the NRO. We do exciting things with our space platforms. We can read a license plate from 60 miles in space... how about that?" Reg said.

"Well, that's great, sir, if you're being attacked by license plates," Tom replied with a slight chuckle.

Reg squinted his eyes and then broke out in a laugh, "Tom, you tell me that you've only been at Langley for two years and you're already a smartass! It usually takes longer for the CIA guys to get to that point! Hah!" Reg exclaimed laughing, surprised at the young man's coarse but hilarious answer.

"I apologize, Mr. Hartwick, but you did leave the door open though," Tom said.

"That I did. You have a sharp wit, young man. That may come to play greatly to your benefit as you move up in responsibility. And it was funny. Don't lose it," Reg said with a low laugh.

"Thank you, sir," Tom responded as the elevator doors open. He escorted Reg to Barb's desk. She rose and picked up her phone.

"Mr. Barrett, Reginald Hartwick is here," Barb said.

"Send him in, Barb!" Jack answered.

Barb took Reg to Jack's door and opened it for him. Inside, Jack and Pete both stood.

"Hi, Reg! Come in and have a seat! It's great to see you!" Jack blurted out.

"And you as well, Jack! Hi to you too, Pete. I heard something lately in the rumor mill. Is it true?" Reg asked.

"If the rumor is about my plans to retire after the first of the year, then yes, it's true. It's time for me," Jack answered.

"Damn. We are going to miss your formidable self in the lineup, Jack, that's for sure. Other than that, I understand. Truth is, I've been thinking a lot about that myself," Reg replied.

"Whoa…and pass up a shot at the Director's job?" Jack asked.

"Yeah, that too. Being a Deputy Director at the NRO is a fine way to go out. It's enough of a prestigious position for me. I don't know, but I'm thinking about it. With you leaving, I'll probably be taking the possibility more seriously. Anyway, Godspeed, Jack. You've been a super ally and I will miss you dearly. Maybe you and I can have a drink together occasionally," Reg said in a lower tone of voice.

"I would sincerely like that, Reg. Let's not forget," Jack said.

"Okay. Can we get to business? Please tell me…what the hell is going on at that huge new air base at Fürstenwalde in eastern Germany. Jack, Pete, in my time at the NRO, I've seen a lot of reconnaissance satellite photos of air bases and army posts, but until yesterday, I've never seen so many fighters and bombers crowded onto one base. Wingtip-to-wingtip… all over the tarmac parking areas. It's probably that way in the hangars too. And they've built what looks like a large double fence around the perimeter of the base. What the hell's going on there?" Reg asked.

"I see. So, it's true. And the bunker?" Jack asked.

"From an overhead view anyway, a bunker is a bunker. This one is also in eastern Germany in the middle of a large patch of woods and it looks new, modern. There's a lot of activity, trucks, workmen moving around. Other than that, though, nothing really stood out. Can you share with me what's going on? Does it have to do with Russia and Ukraine?" Reg asked.

"Well, you see, Germany's Defense Minister, Andreas Bachmeier, would like you to think that, Reg, but in truth the air base and bunker have nothing at all to do with Russia," Jack answered. Pete nodded to Reg in agreement.

"Then what? That's a shitload of airpower at Fürstenwalde Air Base. Why? Why's it there?" Reg asked.

"Reg, this is very highly classified. It can't go beyond this room," Jack replied.

"Okay, I swear. Do you need a Non-Disclosure Agreement, an NDA signed by me?" Reg asked.

"Not from you, no, Reg. Your word is good enough. You've done us so many great favors, including this one. So, here it is — there's a plot by the German Defense Ministry to arrest the Chancellor and overthrow the government," Jack responded.

"Shit. In order to do what?"

"Establish a Fourth Reich," Jack replied.

Reg Hartwick's face went pale. His hands clenched, balled into fists, then laid flat on his thighs. He glanced from Pete to Jack, a look of sheer astonishment across his face. He swallowed hard.

"A Fourth Reich? World War III? Oh, my God. This is no kidding," Reg said.

"No kidding," Jack replied.

"Dammit, not again. A colonial, imperialist Germany. A Fourth Reich. That's hard to digest, Jack, but I do believe you. What are you going to do? What plans are in the works?" Reg asked.

"Ultimately, the president will decide what's going to take place. My own take is that if we can manage to, that is, without being noticed, convince the Chancellor about what's being planned, and obtain his approval, his request, to provide military support, we'll have some options," Jack said.

"I see. Wow. You've hooked a big one this time. If you need any support in this from the NRO, please know that you'll have it in spades, and pronto," Reg said.

"Thank you, Reg. We might," Jack said.

"That it? As if this isn't enough," Reg asked.

"That's it, Reg. Thanks for coming over," Jack said standing. He walked around his desk.

"And Pete, I suspect the Special Activities Division will be heavily involved in whatever ends up taking place, so good luck and break a leg," Reg reached out and shook Pete's hand.

"Thanks. Sincere thanks," Pete replied.

Jack and Reg shook hands as Reg shook his head back and forth. He grasped one of Jack's hands with both his hands and squeezed gently.

"God bless you, the Agency, and the United States in this," Reg concluded.

"Thanks, Reg. I suspect we're going to need all the prayers we can get," Jack said, watching Reg walk through the door.

CHAPTER 35

Federal Ministry of Defense
Berlin Office, Stauffenbergstasse 17
Saturday afternoon, August 25th

Andreas Bachmeier rose from his chair at the long table. He walked to the front of the conference room. A screen began to descend on the wall behind Bachmeier, and he abruptly moved to the right side of it. He smiled at those present around the table.

This meeting of Bachmeier's was held on a Saturday, a non-workday, so the building they were in was nearly completely empty. They were meeting on the top floor, fourth floor of the Bendlerblock building in Berlin. The Bendlerblock building had originally served as the former Supreme Headquarters of the German Wehrmacht High Command in WWII. The large structure now housed a memorial recognizing the German military resistance to the Nazi regime during WWII and the attempt to assassinate Hitler at his Wolf's Lair headquarters in 1944.

Bachmeier turned to Devin Connolly, the BND's liaison press officer, who was standing by the door.

"Devin, you can go ahead and leave now. Thanks, however for setting everything up, and thanks to the BND for allowing you to assist us. What we're going to discuss at our meeting this afternoon is not something that we'll be releasing to the media. So, no worries there," Bachmeier said.

"Thank you, sir," Devin said, opening the door behind him and leaving the room.

What neither Bachmeier nor Obermann knew was that Devin had seen the opportunity and viewed all their briefing charts and photographs for the meeting while he was in the process of setting up the conference room. Obermann's leather briefcase that held the briefing charts had been inadvertently left unlocked.

Devin ambled down the fourth-floor corridor to the bank of elevators, his head filled with thoughts of what to do now or if he should attempt to do anything. What he had seen in the charts gnawed at him. He believed that he needed to contact Dave McClure. And as soon as possible.

He walked from the Bendlerblock building onto Unter den Linden Strasse and began walking toward the Brandenburg Gate and Tiergarten Park. He passed the Adlon Kempinski hotel on the way. Once in the park, he walked off the main path to an area secluded by trees, undergrowth, and flower beds. He pulled out Dave McClure's business card from his wallet and chose the mobile number to dial.

"Dave McClure," Dave answered.

"Dave, this is Devin Connolly, in Berlin. We need to talk," Devin replied.

"Devin, great to hear from you. I assume you've done your research that I asked you for and have a list of places that I should visit on my next trip to Berlin. Tell you what, you go home and call me again from your place, okay?" Dave said, concealing that anything suspicious was involved.

"Okay." The line clicked off.

Dave pulled out his maps of Berlin from his desk at Langley and began studying them…looking for what might be the safest place to meet with Devin. Believing he'd found it in the Grunewald Forest on the far west side of Berlin, he called Pete Novak about Devin's urgent call. He detailed the location of where he and Devin would most likely meet. Pete liked what Dave had researched and approved it.

Pete said his office would make airline reservations for Dave leaving tomorrow morning out of Dulles airport and find the best hotel on Berlin's west side for room reservations. Pete said he would brief Jack Barrett and for Dave to go home and pack for a couple days' stay in Berlin. Dave's weapon, mags, and shoulder holster would come to him tomorrow at the hotel by diplomatic pouch, just like for his last trip.

Dave closed up his office and minutes later climbed into his Audi A6 in the parking lot, headed for home. Pulling into his driveway twenty-five minutes later, his cell rang.

"Dave McClure," Dave answered.

"Dave, this is Devin," Devin replied.

"All right. Devin, what I want you to do is to go into the lobby at the Adlon Kempinski hotel. Tell the receptionist that you want to make a long distance, international call, from a house phone and that you'll pay for it immediately afterward. Call me after that, okay," Dave said.

"Yes, sir. I'll do that now. I don't live too far from the hotel, so it won't be long."

"Great. I'll be waiting," Dave said.

Ten minutes later, Dave's cell jingled again.

"This is Devin," the caller said.

241

"Devin, are you familiar with the Grunewald Forest on Berlin's west side?" Dave said, sitting in his study at their house on Pumphrey Drive.

"Yes. I go there often on weekends to stroll or occasionally jog. Dave, what I have to tell you I...I think it's crucial and also urgent."

"Actually, that's great. I assumed that. What I'm going to refer to now is the area in the Grunewald Forest around Schlachtensee Lake, the southernmost and largest lake Grunewald's chain of lakes," Dave said.

"I know the area around that lake very well."

"Good. The spot I'm thinking of is off Heerstrasse where the stream from Krumme Lake flows under the bridge to the south and eventually into the Schlachtensee. The jogging and walking path is there. There's a place not far down the path where the two fences, the one on the side of the path and the other one around the lake almost touch. That's where I would like for you and me to meet," Dave explained.

"I know that spot. I've walked past it many times. What time do you have in mind for us to meet?"

"Tomorrow, Sunday, around 5:30 p.m. Is that workable?" Dave asked.

"Yes."

"Great. While you're in route, be careful and act casual, especially when you get in the forest and you're walking to our meeting location," Dave said.

"Dave, I'm worried. I'll be at risk after this," Devin said.

"I understand. Tonight, write a resignation letter to the BND. Say in it that you've got an outstanding offer from a television station in the United States, in Chicago, and that you've accepted it. Also, say that because of the timelines in the offer, you need to leave Berlin right away," Dave said.

"Wow. And after that?"

"Pack some clothes along with anything you don't want to—or can't—leave behind. Drive to Brandenburg International Airport and at the information desk, ask where the diplomatic flights arrive and depart. They'll direct you. I'll make the arrangements. You'll be met at the entrance doors and ushered inside. Ultimately, one of our jets will fly you here to Dulles International Airport in Virginia. Don't worry about money, Devin. We'll have a safehouse for you to stay at temporarily until we find the right place to get you settled. How's that sound?"

"Wow. It sounds fantastic. All right, then, I'll see you in the Grunewald Forest tomorrow," Devin replied.

"Take care, Devin, and thanks very much for your assistance," Dave said.

Dave walked into his house. He had to tell Karen about this impending trip, as well as pack a few things for the travel.

CHAPTER 36

Abba Berlin Hotel
Lietzenburger Strasse, Berlin
Sunday afternoon, August 26th

Unable to find an early morning flight, Dave had taken an
Agency jet to Berlin. Outside the departure area at the
Brandenburg airport and with his suitcase in tow, he grabbed
the first taxi that pulled up to him. It was a near-twenty-minute
drive to the Abba Berlin Hotel on Lietzenburger Strasse at the far
west side of Berlin. He glanced at his watch…four-thirty in the
afternoon. There wasn't much traffic at that hour on a Sunday.

Once in the lobby at the Abba hotel, Dave checked in at
the reception desk and took an elevator up to his fifth-floor
room. He saw that once again the Agency had reserved a junior suite for him. That was certainly nice of them—it was
probably Barbara who made the reservations. The room itself was fairly spartan but like most German hotels, extremely
well kept and clean. He felt it would work out fine for the few
days he'd be in Berlin. He threw his suitcase on the couch and
plopped on the bed.

FIRST BULLET

Several minutes later, there was a knock on his door. Dave sprung from the bed, walked to the door, and stared through its peephole. A man in a suit stood at the door holding a package in his arms.

"Who is it?" Dave asked.

"Mr. McClure, I'm George Takura. I'm from the Embassy, the station. This package for you just arrived by diplomatic pouch. There was an accompanying note with it that said it needed to be passed on to you at the earliest time possible. So, here I am," the man said.

Dave opened the door. The man handed Dave the package and stuck his hand out. They shook hands.

"Godspeed, Mr. McClure. And check your six," the man said, turned, and walked back down the hallway.

"George, thank you. And take care yourself," Dave said as the man walked away. George waved back over his shoulder.

Dave had an hour to get to the meeting place in the Grunewald Forest. He opened the package and removed the shoulder holster, mags, and pistol. The mags were loaded…good, that would save time. He wriggled out of his sport coat and slipped on the shoulder holster, then secured the Beretta and mags. He left the room, pulling his arms through the sport coat as he walked down the hallway, and took an elevator to the lobby.

Outside the Abba hotel, Dave hailed a taxi. It promptly pulled to the curb. Dave asked and the driver replied that he was familiar with the Grunewald Forest. It was just fifteen minutes later when they crossed the bridge at Heerstrasse and the taxi pulled over onto the shoulder. Dave gave him a generous gratuity and began walking down the pedestrian path, the Havelchausee. It was not a long walk.

In just under ten minutes, he found himself at the spot where the two fence lines, the one on the side of the path

245

and the one around the lake, almost touched. The views of the Schlachtensee from that spot were beautiful. It was a picturesque lake surrounded along its shoreline by thick green woods. He paused and leaned against the fence at the side of the path. He would wait here for Devin.

It seemed that large bodies of water always had certain aromas associated with them. Oceans did…the sea air near oceans and seas is invigorating. And large lakes like the Schlachtensee did also. The scent of the lake water was potent and, at the same time, pleasant to experience.

Not much time had passed when he saw a man approaching around the curved pathway. Dave pushed off the fence. It was Devin Connolly. They waved at each other as Devin approached. Devin stopped by the fence and stood to the left of Dave.

"How did you get here so quickly, Dave? A commercial airline couldn't have been able to do that."

"No, it was an Agency bird, Devin. Our jets don't fly the commercial air routes. They got me here as quick as they could. How are you? Are you okay?" Dave asked.

"I suppose. I'm just nervous as hell," Devin replied.

"Don't be. We'll take care of you, Devin. Go ahead and tell me what you've learned. What's the critical information you've gathered, as you implied on the phone," Dave said.

"Right. Well, Bachmeier and Obermann have selected a date. It's three weeks from now. September 11th."

"September 11th…9-11. That's strange," Dave said.

"It's deliberate. They believe that this operation will not only demonstrate to the world how incredibly powerful Germany's military forces are but kicking it off on 9-11 will also represent an intentional slap in the face to the United States. That is, another failure by the U.S. to detect an imminent threat," Devin said.

"Assholes. Do you mind if I record what you have to report, Devin, instead of attempting to memorize it all?" Dave asked.

"No, go ahead," Devin answered.

"Shoot," Dave said as he switched on his pocket recorder.

"Okay. In the early evening on that date, Bundeswehr special forces will arrive at the Berlin Chancellery residence on Willy Brandt Avenue and arrest the Chancellor. He'll be incarcerated until his trial. Next, there's going to be a motorcade that will depart at 12:00 a.m. midnight on September 11th from the Ministry of Defense on Stauffenbergstasse 17 in Berlin. Andreas Bachmeier and General Obermann will be traveling in that motorcade. They will follow the highways east on B5 to B1, then north on Strasse des Friedens to the intersection with Diedersdorf Strasse, take a right, and enter the grounds of the bunker in the woods southeast of Görlsdorf at about 01:30 a.m. For security, the motorcade will have a lead vehicle of well-armed shooters as well as a follow car of shooters. On Bachmeier's cue, Obermann's order to begin the offensive will be given at 03:00 a.m. In that way, the German forces will have the early morning hours and all the entire next day to roll across Poland and the Czech Republic to their eastern borders. The armor, mostly tanks but also armored personnel carriers, will follow the highways, not veer off into the countryside. Trucks with infantry will follow. They will halt at the borders, aligning their formations on Poland's eastern border with Russia, Lithuania, Belarus, and Ukraine. In the Czech Republic, the forces will form up on the eastern borders with Slovakia and eastern Austria. That's what I learned by scanning the briefing charts for General Obermann's last meeting at the Bendlerblock building in Berlin. And without his knowledge," Devin explained.

"I see. Devin, sincerely, thank you. You have done your country a great service. I will see to it that..."

Dave froze in alarm and disbelief as the first round struck Devin in his neck below his left jaw, exploding through his larynx, trachea, and upper esophagus. The high-powered rifle round burst from the other side of Devin's neck, spewing out blood and flesh.

Not more than two seconds later, a second round followed, piercing Devin's left temple. A spray of red blood, bone, hair, brain matter, and other gore gushed from the top of Devin's head into the air around him. Devin was propelled backward and thudded to the ground. He'd died instantly.

Dave immediately dove for the ground as a third round slammed into the tree directly behind him, breaking off a large piece of its bark. A second round followed, bashing into the same tree, but lower on the trunk as Dave lunged to the ground. He immediately rose in a crouch and ran as fast as he could to his right into the treed area of the Grunewald Forest. Due to the speed of the sequence of shots, Dave felt certain there were at least two shooters with scoped, high powered rifles.

As he ran, several more rifle shots followed, bashing into the trees around him. After he'd covered about thirty yards, Dave rose to an erect position and began to sprint as rapidly as his legs would take him. In his dash, he bore slightly left, making a huge arc in that direction. His intent was to circle his attackers, completing his arc just behind them.

The rifle shots slowed to an occasional shot every ten seconds or so, the rounds hammering into trees near him as he raced by. Dave suddenly sensed the pounding of feet. The sound was coming directly toward him on an intersecting course. His pistol drawn, the safety off, and the hammer cocked, Dave dove for the undergrowth. Taking a glimpse from under a bush, he could see a pair of legs rushing at him. With a two-arm grip on the Beretta, he fired repeatedly at the man's legs.

One round of Dave's bullets struck the man in his right kneecap, shattering it, and two rounds banged into his left thigh. The man shrieked as he fell forward, face down. Dave carefully aimed and fired three more rounds. All three rounds smashed into the top of the man's head, blood instantly spurting out and onto the ground.

Dave rose to his feet and continued his sprint along the arc to his left. Running as fast as he could, he dropped out the mag and thrust a new one into the grip's chamber. He soon broke out into the forest's pathway, his feet skidding to a stop.

Dave looked down the path. The second shooter was facing the woods, his back to the lake. Upon seeing Dave, the shooter spun about and began raising his scoped rifle to his shoulder.

Dave dropped abruptly to a prone position and again with a two-hand grip, began firing first.

"Take this, you sonofabitch," Dave muttered to himself.

Dave emptied the magazine plus the round that had been loaded in the breech. The rounds stitched up the man's torso, plunging into him from his groin to his neck. Sprays of blood erupted from the impacts. The assassin stumbled backward, dropping his rifle as he staggered, the ten or so rounds that hammered into him taking their toll. He fell to the ground, lying motionless on the path.

Dave shoved himself to his feet. He holstered his Beretta, spun about, and began jogging back on the pathway toward Heerstrasse. Upon reaching the street, he found himself totally out of breath. Gasping for air, he began to hail passing taxis. One soon pulled over.

"Wohin? Where to?" the driver asked.

"Das Abba Berlin Hotel. Kennen-Sie dass? The Abba Berlin Hotel. You familiar with that?" Dave said, still breathless.

"Ah, ja. Nur fünf Minuten. Sure, just five minutes."

And sure enough, in five minutes the cab pulled to the curb in front of the hotel. Dave gave him a nice tip, turned, and walked to the hotel's entrance, pushing through the revolving glass door. He walked straight to the elevators and took one to the fifth floor.

In his room, he began throwing clothes and his shaving kit into his suitcase. He locked the suitcase and left the room, locking the door behind him. He took the same elevator down that he'd ascended on. Dave paid for the room and nodded in agreement at the receptionist who commented they were sorry to see him go.

Outside the hotel on Lietzenburger Strasse, after a few minutes of trying, Dave finally hailed a taxi and told the driver to take him to the Brandenburg airport. The taxi swerved from the curb and entered the traffic flow. It was growing dark in the early evening and traffic had picked up on this Sunday night. Still, they made it to the airport in less than twenty minutes, and Dave tipped the driver who smiled and waved good-bye.

Inside the airport, Dave stood, watching the departures screen. He saw that a United Airlines flight would be leaving in an hour and a half. Approaching a ticket clerk, he purchased a Business Class ticket and checked his suitcase. Walking as fast as he could manage, he found the departure gate in ten minutes.

Glancing around him, he saw that there was a bar across the concourse from his flight's gate. The signs read that it served German fare. He walked over to it, sat at the counter and downed one beer. He ordered another along with a brat and potato salad. Sipping at the second beer, he reached up to wipe the beads of sweat from his brow. He did his best to calm himself, to chill out.

Goodness' sake, Dave thought, the man who he had promised he would save and fly to the States, Devin Connolly, had been killed by snipers' bullets. Apparently, Devin didn't check well enough to determine if he had tails on him while traveling to the meet site. Dave felt remorse at that, but there was nothing he could do. The man was dead. At least, Dave had confronted and wasted both assassins. There was some gratification in that. Those two bastards had gone to their maker; their chosen careers were suddenly over.

His flight began boarding. Dave found his seat and strapped on the seatbelt. As the stewardess came by for drink orders, Dave ordered what had been Tony Robertson's favorite — a vodka and sprite. He smiled, remembering how much Tony had loved vodka. And he noticed that they had a good pilot — the takeoff was smooth as could be. Roughly fifteen minutes later, as the airliner passed through 30,000 feet in altitude, Dave pulled his cell phone from his belt. He dialed Langley.

"Pete Novak," Pete answered.

"Mr. Novak, this is Dave McClure," Dave replied.

"Dave, wow. I didn't expect to hear from you so soon. Where are you? Have you met with Devin Connolly yet?" Pete asked.

Dave described the meeting with Devin in the Grunewald Forest on Berlin's west side. He explained how two assassins with high-powered rifles had shot and killed Devin, but not before Devin had revealed to Dave all that he had learned. Then, he went into the short-lived but frenzy-of-a-chase he had with the two shooters pursuing him through the woods and how he'd shot and killed both. He related that it was then he'd decided it was time to leave Berlin, and as fast as he could.

"Damn. No wounds?"

"No, sir, I'm fine."

"Dave, I'm glad you're okay. Superb work on your part in whacking both those assholes. I'm truly sorry about Devin Connolly. It sounds like he missed a surveillance that they, probably that General Obermann you spoke of, had on him. There was nothing you could do. When does your flight get in?" Pete asked.

"About one-thirty in the morning. I took the first one I could get,"

"Then, go ahead and sleep in. How about 2:00 p.m. tomorrow afternoon in Jack Barrett's office. Will that work for you, give you enough to catch up on rest?"

"Yes, sir. Thanks for that break. It's much appreciated."

"You deserve no less. I'll see you then," Pete said as the line clicked off.

CHAPTER 37

Pumphrey Drive, Fairfax
Virginia
Monday morning, August 27th

It was 02:30 a.m. when a very tired Dave McClure pulled his Audi into their driveway in Fairfax. Not wanting to have the garage opening and its noise waking Karen, he dragged the suitcase alongside him up the walk with his leather brief-case bag slung over his shoulder and unlocked both the screen door and wooden door. He paused in the foyer for a second, catching his breath. He was dead tired.

"Stand where you are! You try to move and I'll shoot!" Karen bellowed, holding her Smith & Wesson Model 60, five-shot, .357 magnum revolver thrust out in front of her with both hands.

"Karen, sweetheart, don't shoot! It's me, Dave!" Dave answered in a nervous voice, letting go of the suitcase, both of his palms facing outward.

"Dave? Is that you? You just left here in the morning! Did you fly all the way to Germany and back already?" Karen asked, lowering the revolver.

Karen reached over and flicked on the foyer light switch and approached Dave. She wrapped her arms around him and rested her head on his chest. Dave smiled and enveloped her in his arms.

"Yes, I did. Honey, but look, I am absolutely dead tired. I'm drained beyond belief. Please, let me go and get washed up, then crawl under the covers in bed. I don't have to be in the office tomorrow until two o'clock in the afternoon. I'll explain everything to you. How's Carolyn?" Dave said.

"She's fine. She missed her Daddy."

"Well, Daddy's home…he's just really pooped."

Dave and Karen walked from the foyer through the living room and down the hallway to the bedroom kissing every couple seconds. Karen walked around the bed and put the revolver back into its holster in the top drawer of the nightstand. Dave threw his suitcase on the bed, opened it, and retrieved the shaving kit. He took that with him into the bathroom and began washing up.

Twenty minutes passed before the lights were finally out when Dave and Karen were each lying on their pillows. Karen turned on her side to face Dave. She reached out so her fingers could touch his face.

"Why did you come back so unbelievably fast? Was it hard?" Karen asked in a near whisper.

"Hard? Hard beyond belief. Extremely difficult. And I felt I was at high risk, in great danger. I had to leave Berlin and leave it as fast as possible," Dave replied also in a low voice.

"Well, you recognized it and then acted. I'm thankful for that. You had told me that you were meeting with a man you'd met previously in Berlin. Did that meeting end up going as planned?"

"No, that man is dead. He was standing only about three feet from me as I watched his head blown off by two high-powered rifle bullets. We were in the Grunewald Forest in west Berlin. After that, I ended up in a chase, racing against two assassin snipers. In separate instances, I shot both of their asses dead."

"My God, Dave. You really were in great danger. You killed both of them? I'm so glad you made it home safe. So, do you expect this German operation to still remain active?" Karen asked.

"Yes. In spades. It's a very scary situation with significant international impacts. That's what I have to brief Pete Novak and Jack Barrett on later this afternoon. I'm certain that Barrett will ultimately be taking this to the president," Dave said.

"Wow. My goodness. It's that big?"

"Bigger. Karen, you have to keep this to yourself. You can't mention it to anyone."

"I understand. I'll sign an NDA for you if you like."

"No, an NDA won't be necessary. I trust you," Dave said with a chuckle.

"Thank you," Karen said.

Dave reached over and pulled Karen to him. Her head lay lightly on his chest. She looked up at him and smiled.

"I like this. I miss you so much when you're gone. You can't imagine," Karen said.

"I'm home. We're safe. There's still some work to be done, some very important work to keep this thing in Germany from happening. Don't worry, I'll be fine. And remember, at the end of the year, I have a huge promotion coming up that will change our lives forever. I won't be engaged in ops abroad or at home anymore," Dave explained.

"Thank God for that. Sweetheart let's snuggle. I like this a bunch. And I want to watch you drift off to sleep. You're cute when you sleep," Karen said, stretching her arm across Dave's chest.

"I thought I was cute when I was awake, too," Dave said.

"You are. And just a tad conceited as well," Karen said, giggling.

Dave smiled and closed his eyes.

CHAPTER 38

Langley Center, McLean
Virginia
Monday afternoon, August 27th

As he always did at random times throughout the day, Jack Barrett stood by his eastern windows. He watched a light drizzle descend over the green forest between Langley Center and the George Washington Parkway near the rocky headwaters of the Potomac.

"Damn, I'm going to miss this view. It's so lovely, so serene," Jack mumbled to himself.

"We'll take photos and send them to you, Jack," Pete said, stepping quietly through the office door.

"Oh, please do," Jack replied, turning around to face Pete, "Come on in and have a seat, Dave should be arriving any minute now."

"In fact, we ought to have a photo of you standing there and frame it. A framed photo of you standing pensively by those windows. Hang it in the hallway. We've all seen you in that pose when you've felt you need to do some serious thinking," Pete said.

257

"I suppose that's true. But no, I don't want anything remaining of me in some sort of memorial spot that could interfere with the new DCI establishing his own style. That wouldn't be fair of me. I wouldn't want to do that," Jack said, as his intercom jingled. Jack walked back behind his desk.

"Yes, Barb," Jack said.

"Mr. Barrett, Dave McClure is here," Barb answered.

"Please, bring him in," Jack replied.

Dave walked through the doorway as Barb quietly shut the door behind him. He stepped forward and stood by one of the leather chairs in front of Jack's desk. Pete was sitting two chairs over.

"Have a seat, Dave. Yesterday had to have been a hard day for you — all the way to Berlin and back. We're eager to hear what intelligence you've gathered. And please know we're very sorry about the death of Devin Connolly. That poor man was trying to assist us. That he ended up dying in the process is incredibly sad. I mean that from my heart. I know you have to feel bad about that," Jack said.

"I had promised Devin Connolly that we would protect him, bring him to the States, and resettle him. And after that, in less than a minute, I watched him die by two high-powered rifle shots to his neck and head. The top of his head was nearly blown off," Dave said, a look of sadness on his face.

"Dave, I understand what you're saying. You couldn't possibly have known that two assassin snipers had followed Devin to your meeting location in the Grunewald Forest. There's no way you could have known that. Unfortunately, you had to witness his death close-up, but there was nothing you could have done to stop it. And then, with your own formidable skills, you killed both snipers. I'm continually amazed at your combat expertise…how lethal you can be. But don't continue to carry Devin's death on your conscience," Pete said.

"I agree one hundred percent with what Pete just said," Jack interjected, still looking at Pete and nodding, "You should let this go, Dave. In no way could you have prevented Devin Connolly's death."

"I know that sir, it's just...I promised him. And with the very last breaths he breathed, he believed me. I'll get over it. At least those two bastards who killed him won't take another breath either," Dave answered.

"Indeed," Pete replied.

"Ditto," Jack said. "Dave, do you feel okay enough now to relate what Devin shared with you? Are you okay to do that?"

"Yes, sir. I recorded everything Devin told me. I've memorized it since then," Dave replied.

"Then please, let us have it," Jack said.

"Yes, sir. A date has been chosen to begin the German offensive across Poland and the Czech Republic. It's September 11th. The first thing that will occur is that in the early evening hours on that date, Bundeswehr special forces will arrive at the Berlin Chancellery residence on Willy Brandt Avenue and will arrest the Chancellor. He will be incarcerated until his trial. The order to begin the offensive will be given at 03:00 a.m. in the morning from the newly constructed bunker in the woods at Görlsdorf. Bachmeier and Obermann believe that the German forces will then have the early morning and all the entire next day to roll across Poland and the Czech Republic to their eastern borders."

"Damn. This is hard to believe. Hard to think that this is really going to happen. Dave, please continue," Jack said.

"German armored forces will follow the highways, not move across the countryside. Trucks with infantry will follow. They will halt at the borders — Poland's eastern border with Russia, Lithuania, Belarus, and Ukraine, and the Czech Republic's borders with Slovakia and eastern Austria."

"On September 11th — 9-11?" Jack asked.

"Yes, sir. I asked Devin about that. He said it was purposeful, that Bachmeier believes the operation would not only demonstrate to the world the power of Germany's military, but it will also serve as a slap in the face of the United States for failing to detect yet another imminent threat," Dave said.

"Damn. Bachmeier and Obermann are not only Neo-Nazis, but assholes to boot," Pete said.

"Do you know how Bachmeier and Obermann are going to travel to the bunker?" Jack asked.

"Yes, sir. There's going to be a motorcade with Bachmeier and Obermann departing at 12:00 a.m. midnight from the Ministry of Defense on Stauffenbergstrasse in Berlin. It will follow the highways east on B5 to B1, then north on Strasse des Friedens to the intersection with Diedersdorf Strasse, and then after a last right, enter the grounds of the bunker in the woods southeast of Görlsdorf at about 01:30 a.m. The motorcade is supposed to have a lead car of shooters and a follow car of shooters," Dave said.

"A motorcade. That's interesting. A motorcade which we know what route it will take," Jack said, glancing at Pete who nodded back.

"My goodness, Jack. This could end up being the start of World War III. And once again, it's Germany," Pete said.

"That it could. I agree. I have to take this to the President. And very soon, like tomorrow morning," Jack said.

"And offer what?" Pete asked.

"I'm going to say that I'd like to ask our Ambassador in Berlin to arrange a meeting at the U.S. Embassy for the Chancellor to meet with me. I'll ask the President to allow me to represent him at this meeting. I'll explain to the Chancellor what we know. And I'll ask the Chancellor to make an official request to the President of the United States for the support of the U.S. military in quelling this treasonous rebellion and precluding another world war. He can't very well go to the defense ministry, can he?" Jack said.

"No, no way," Pete answered.

"And further, that sometime in the late afternoon of September 11th, we will transport the Chancellor from his residence to a safehouse somewhere on the outskirts of Berlin. When the Bundeswehr Special Forces group arrives at the Chancellery, they will be immediately apprehended, arrested, and handcuffed by a couple of our SAD Spec Ops teams."

"Wow. You're actually going to propose that to the President?" Pete asked.

"I am. And with an official request from the Chancellor for U.S. military support, we can then develop plans to intercept that motorcade, arrest both Bachmeier and Obermann, and seize the bunker at Görlsdorf, as well as the air base at Fürstenwalde. Obviously, this will be a joint operation by our own Special Activities Division and Department of Defense special forces. I think it will be doable," Jack said.

"It's huge. Those are the only words I have at this point. But I'm with you, Jack. I think it could succeed," Pete said.

"We will prevail," Jack said, turning his attention to Dave.

"And you, young Skywalker, you will have greatly assisted the United States in preventing another world war. The three of us will meet again two days from now, on Wednesday," Jack declared.

"Thank you, Mr. Barrett," Dave said.

All three men rose from their seats and shook hands.

CHAPTER 39

U.S. Embassy
Clayallee 170, Berlin
Tuesday afternoon, September 4th

U.S. Ambassador Allan Breitinger leaned across the conference table to Jack Barrett, his face filled with concern.

"After what you've just told me, Jack, and knowing it comes from the Director of the Central Intelligence Agency who's officially speaking for the president, this scares the hell out of me," Allan said.

"You're not alone, Allan. I'm convinced myself of its reality. However, if the Chancellor decides to give us an official request for U.S. military assistance, I think we'll be able to fix it, stop it in its tracks," Jack said.

"I surely hope so. I would hate to implement our evacuation plan. It would be a nightmare. So now, I'll be downstairs in the lobby...I'll bring Chancellor Kalbach up when he arrives."

"Thanks, Allan."

As the ambassador left the room, Jack remained sitting at the conference table and sipping from a cup of coffee. It was almost two-thirty in the afternoon, the time of the day they had set for the meeting. The Chancellor had sensed a gravity in the ambassador's phone call and readily agreed to the request for a meeting.

After learning of the German Chancellor's concurrence, Jack's black Cadillac limo subsequently picked him up at his residence and drove him to Dulles. He took an o'dark early company jet from Dulles airport to Brandenburg airport, arriving an hour and a half ago, at one o'clock. As a result, he was rather fatigued. Jack looked up at the ceiling, then at the clock on the wall. And he yet again began going over in his mind what he intended to relate to the German Chancellor.

Four black Cadillac Escalades pulled from behind the Chancellery at 2:10 p.m. They rolled down the drive, each vehicle having a well-dressed man in the back seat who was about the size of the Chancellor. The men sitting in the singular surveillance vehicle parked down the street on Willy Brandt Avenue were at a loss for which one to follow. They chose the second one. Their Mercedes E-450 swerved from the curb to begin trailing the Escalade from a discreet distance.

All of the Escalades headed for various highways leading out of Berlin except for the third Escalade. That vehicle, the third Escalade with Chancellor Verner Kalbach riding in the rear seat, drove to Clayallee and the U.S. Embassy. Security personnel stepped from the embassy doors and surrounded the Escalade on the street and sidewalk as the Chancellor climbed out and walked to the glass doors.

After escorting the Chancellor up to the second-floor conference room, Ambassador Breitinger introduced Jack Barrett to the Chancellor Kalbach. After some additional pleasantries, the ambassador bid goodbye to the Chancellor and left the room. Jack and the Chancellor took seats opposite each other at the table.

"Mr. Barrett, I'm fluent in English and the ambassador told me that you aren't fluent in German. That being the case, we'll speak in English. The only other thing that Allan told me about our meeting today was that our democracy may be at risk. And that of course gave me the shivers. Is that what this meeting concerns?" the Chancellor said.

"Chancellor Kalbach, I find that I'm meeting today with a head of state. That doesn't happen often with CIA directors. So, please, feel free to call me Jack."

"That's nice of you, Jack. If I can call the director of the CIA by his first name, then he can certainly call me by mine. It's Verner."

"Thank you, Verner. I like that," Jack said. Jack loosened his necktie.

"Nerves?"

"Somewhat," Jack said, "It was a hurried and long flight this morning.

"I bet it was. Well then, Jack, as you Americans say, let's cut to the chase. I'm more than just a little anxious to hear what you have to say," Verner said.

"All right. Verner, we have had excellent, multiple intelligence sources who tell us there is a high-level plot within your cabinet with plans to overthrow you and the German Government. And further, that plot, using the Russia-Ukraine situation as a false justification, will also involve an invasion by German armed forces of Poland and the Czech Republic that will only come to a halt when reaching their most eastern borders. You yourself will be arrested by Bundeswehr special forces, incarcerated, and tried for treason. All of this is scheduled to occur one week from today, September 11th. There are lots of other details such as a newly constructed command bunker Görlsdorf as well as the abundance of fighters and bombers gathered at the new Fürstenwalde air base. I can address that later if you so choose," Jack explained.

"*Mein Gott! My God!* Excuse me, but this is horrific news. Who is behind this plot?" Verner asked.

"There are two primary culprits...first, Defense Minister Andreas Bachmeier, and his operations manager, General Gerhardt Obermann."

"Bachmeier? In my time as Chancellor, I have never completely trusted that man. He has always appeared to be concealing something from me. If Bachmeier is so damned dissatisfied with our government, do you have an idea of what it is that he intends to establish as a replacement for our government?" Verner said.

"Yes, I do. A Fourth Reich," Jack said.

Verner gasped, raising a hand to his mouth and shaking his head in disbelief.

"You might not be aware of this, Verner, but Bachmeier's grandfather, Klaus Bachmeier, worked directly for Heinrich Himmler in the Schutzstaffel, the Nazi SS, as a member of Himmler's immediate staff here in Berlin. In the last days of the war, die Spinne, 'the Spider' was able to move Klaus safely out of Germany, first to Malta, and then to Argentina. Klaus' son, Andreas' father, Conrad Bachmeier, was raised in Argentina in a milieu of his father's continued verbal support for Nazi ideals."

"No, I didn't know that. I've heard of the organizations of Odessa and the Spider, but my knowledge ends there. It explains a lot, doesn't it? Jack are you really certain of all this?" Verner asked.

"Yes. So much so that the President of the United States has authorized me to accept an official request from you for

U.S. military assistance. With such a request from you, I can assure you that we can bring this treasonous revolt to a sudden halt and ensure the continued integrity of the current German government," Jack said.

"What is the U.S. prepared to do? How will that happen?"

"That's a fair question. So, early on the 11th, our forces will escort you from your residence at the Chancellery to a safehouse, another residence that we lease in northern outskirts of Berlin. We will then intercept the motorcade carrying Bachmeier and Obermann on their way to the bunker at Görlsdorf, arrest them, and transport them to GITMO at Guantánamo Bay in Cuba until you request their extradition. And we know the route that motorcade is to take. Our special operations forces with support from the US military will then seize the bunker at Görlsdorf as well as Fürstenwalde air base. The German population is no doubt familiar with a lot of noise at the air base. Finally, when all is safe, you will be escorted back to the Chancellery where you may choose to make a statement to the German people. And that's due to the likelihood that there may be leaks to the media," Jack explained.

"My goodness. Jack, if all this is true, and you've done an excellent job in convincing me that it is, I don't see that I have a choice. Not if I want to preserve our nation and our democracy. I assume that in all of this, there will certainly be some casualties and fatalities," Verner said in a somber voice.

"I agree. I don't see how that can be avoided. It all depends on the reaction of your own forces, those in the Bundeswehr special forces and those defending the bunker and air base. That's not within our control. Nevertheless, the bottom line in what I'm offering is that your office of the Chancellor and the German parliamentary system of government will be preserved," Jack said.

"Then, let's move ahead. I'm prepared to request U.S. military assistance to stop this, as you correctly called it, treasonous revolt."

"Verner, I don't wear a uniform, but I salute you in your decision. I happen to have a bottle of Asbach Uralt in my briefcase along with two crystal glasses. Shall we toast this event?" Jack asked.

"Indeed, let's!" Verner exclaimed.

Jack and Verner stood, reached over the table, and shook hands. Jack placed the Asbach Uralt on the table with the two glasses beside it and poured.

Verner lifted his glass and smiled.

"*Auf die Vereinigten Staaten! To the United States!*" Verner said.

Each man raised his glass and took a sip with a grin.

CHAPTER 40

Langley Center, McLean
Virginia
Wednesday, September 5th

It was seven-thirty in the morning on Wednesday, and Jack Barrett was back at his desk in his office at Langley. He took a bite of the croissant he'd picked up on the way into the campus and followed it up with a gulp of his first cup of coffee.

Jack found himself blinking his eyes often, having had very little sleep during the night before after returning from Berlin. On his desk was laid out an oversized chart of U.S. Army commands. He picked up his phone and dialed Barb's intercom.

"Yes, sir?" Barb answered.

"I know you just got in a few minutes ago, Barb, so give me a buzz when you're settled in enough to make a couple calls for me," Jack said.

"Five minutes, Mr. Barrett. That's all I need."

"Great."

The five minutes passed. Barb's desk was now all arranged for her day as Jack Barrett's executive assistant. Barb's face crinkled in a smile as she raised her phone.

"Ready, Mr. Barrett," Barb said.

"Barb, I want to speak with General Howard Anderson down at the U.S. Army Special Operations Command. They're at Fort Bragg, North Carolina. Please call Fort Bragg and get me routed to the General. And please also tell him to use a secure phone. He and I need to go secure," Jack said.

"Will do, sir."

Minutes passed. Finally, Jack's intercom jingled again. He set down his coffee mug and picked up the phone.

"Mr. Barrett, General Anderson is on the line. I'll connect you," Barb said.

"Jack Barrett," Jack replied.

"Jack, you old spook! It's been what, almost two years, since I saw you last at that intelligence symposium in Washington, DC. How're you doing? And by the way, I'm on a secure phone," Howard said.

"I'm doing fine, Howard. And between you and me, please, I've decided to retire the first of the new year."

"What? You're leaving us? I don't know if the nation can carry on without you, Jack. You've been the pivotal point in so many crises. How the hell can we go on without you in the lineup? Jeez, that's a huge decision!"

"Oh, don't I know it, but I'm convinced the time is right for my departure, Howard. How about you? Have you given it any thought?" Jack asked.

"One year from now. It's a mandatory retirement. So, in that regard, I won't be far behind you, Jack. I plan on moving back to northern Virginia. That means you and I can play golf and support the whiskey business. Other than that, well, you called me, so please, tell me what's on your mind," Howard answered.

"Indeed. Howard, I need a favor. A big one," Jack said.

"You spooks always need favors, and big ones at that. What is it this time, may I ask?" Howard said.

"I need about 150 of your rangers. We have a request from Germany's Chancellor, Verner Kalbach, to the President of the United States for military assistance in stopping an attempt to overthrow their government. The president has approved our support. We need those rangers and maybe a tank company in Germany and ready to go to work by next Tuesday, September 11th. The mission for the Army is to seize the new air base at Fürstenwalde, Germany. With our own special operations forces, we'll be seizing a command bunker at Görlsdorf and engage in some other related operations. But Fürstenwalde Air Base is too big for us to handle. We need your support," Jack explained.

"Why the hell doesn't Kalbach use his own military forces to take care of this?" Howard asked.

"Because Germany's Defense Minister Andreas Bachmeier and General Gerhardt Obermann are behind this plot to overthrow the government and also to invade Poland and the Czech Republic," Jack said.

"I see. I'm familiar with that short, fat shit General Obermann. I never liked him. Okay, you have our support, Jack, for 150 rangers to seize that airbase. As for the armor, I'll send two companies of M1A3 Abrams tanks to you. They're already in-country at Wiesbaden, Germany. Everything will be there—just outside of Berlin, operational, and ready to go by September 11th. As soon as we hang up, I'll call Major General Ken Bennett at Fort Benning, Georgia. Ken is the commander of the 75th Ranger Regiment. He'll be providing the forces. Jack, those guys in the 75th are experts at kicking ass," Howard said.

"If you say so, then I believe it. Fantastic. Thank you so very much, Howard. I'll buy the first round of drinks when you and I meet up after your own retirement!" Jack exclaimed.

"And believe me, I'll drink it! Take care, Jack. Anderson out," Howard said, and the line clicked off.

Jack picked up the phone again and called Barb.

"Barb, please track down Pete Novak and tell him I want to see him as soon as possible," Jack said.

"Shall I interrupt Mr. Novak's Monday morning staff meeting, Mr. Barrett?"

"Yes, please go ahead and interrupt Pete's staff meeting. Tell him it's urgent. He'll understand," Jack replied.

Jack poured himself another cup of coffee and walked to his eastern windows facing the green forest. Several minutes later, Pete walked through the door.

"Uh-oh, this has gotta be significant. Jack Barrett is standing at the windows again and in deep thought," Pete said with a smile, walked in, and seated himself in front of Jack's desk.

"You already know this is significant," Jack said, returning to sit at his desk, "Pete, do we have at least four of those, EMP, Electromagnetic Pulse, rifles in our inventory?"

"Yes, I believe we actually have a dozen of those left. The Army took the rest. What are you thinking, Jack?" Pete asked.

"That's how we're going to stop the motorcade. By positioning four of our guys with the EMP rifles hidden in the woods along the roadway, they can each fire several EMP bursts to stop the lead car's engine. After that, we'll be turning the spotlights on the entire motorcade from the woods. They'll be lit up like an NFL stadium on a Sunday night. At that point, our Spec Ops teams move in and take control. By the way, Dave McClure will be leading the assault on the motorcade with two of our Special Activities Division, SAD Spec Ops teams."

"Well, four or more bursts from those EMP rifles will surely stop the lead vehicle's engine. And I agree one hundred percent with Dave taking the lead. He's a born leader. God help those Germans if they try to fuck with our ambush with Dave in charge. How about Bachmeier and Obermann? Are we taking any special actions with them?"

"Bachmeier and Obermann will be separated from everyone else. They'll be taken to a regional airstrip that NRO identified for us and flown by a C-17 Globemaster III to Ramstein Air Base. From there they'll go to GITMO until Chancellor Kalbach makes an extradition request," Jack said.

"All right. Do you already know where to place this ambush where it can be most effective?"

"Yes, I do. It'll be on the route where the motorcade reaches the intersection with Diedersdorf Strasse. There's forest on the side of the road there, and the motorcade will also be slowing down to make the turn. I had the Berlin station check the location out."

"Not that it matters all that much in an operation of this size, but will the EMP bursts also kill the men in the lead car?" Pete asked.

"No, you have to hit skin for an EMP burst to be that effective, that is, to stop a heart. I seriously doubt that will happen to the men sitting inside the vehicle. And in any case, the German protective security detail will be neutralized by both our blinding spotlights and by our Spec Ops forces moving in and surrounding the motorcade—and armed with full auto assault rifles. They'll have no option but to fold and surrender."

"Wow. I have to say you are a master strategist, Jack. I understand that before that, in the afternoon, a couple of our men will drive to the Chancellery, pick up Chancellor Kalbach, and take him to our safehouse off Greifwalder Strasse near Volkspark Friedrichshain, yes?"

"That's correct. It's a large residence and well protected. Then, in the evening, we will have erected spotlights in the landscaped areas of the Chancellery. When the Bundeswehr special forces arrive, exit their vehicles, and approach the residence to arrest the Chancellor, our spotlights will be switched on...that will blind them. One team of our SAD Spec Ops with additional agents will move in to arrest and cuff them. All will be heavily armed — Sig Sauer M5 assault rifles and SAW M250 fully automatic rifles. If the Germans fire on us, they'll be mowed down. Survivors will be transported to the German prison at Tegel."

"And the bunker?" Pete said.

"I think that three of our SAD Spec Ops teams would be a little overkill — however, a serious advantage in numbers is what I want. From the NRO photos, we've had a partial view of the main doors to the bunker. Some heavy metal is involved. So, to begin with, once surrounding the bunker, our teams will fire three FGM-148 Javelin missiles at the entrance to blow open the doors. I'm confident those missiles will do the job. The personnel inside will be instantaneously blinded and deafened after those earsplitting explosions. After that, it shouldn't be too hard for our teams to take control," Jack said.

"The German personnel?" Pete asked.

"They'll be disarmed, cuffed, and taken by bus to the prison that the German correctional system has at Karlsruhe. Two buses will be standing off the roadside, waiting on Highway B5 until the bunker is under our control."

"Sounds like a plan, except that the actions at the Chancellery, motorcade, and the bunker will have consumed all of our Spec Ops forces. That being the case, how do we handle Fürstenwalde Air Base?" Pete asked.

"We don't. The U.S. Army has that mission. General Howard Anderson, commander of the U.S. Army Special Operations Command at Fort Bragg, is sending 150 rangers from the 75th Ranger Regiment at Fort Benning. In addition, two companies of M1A3 Abrams tanks from Wiesbaden will be supporting the rangers. The tanks' first objective will be to take the control tower down and then proceed to crater the runway. After that, there will be no flight operations at Fürstenwalde. The tanks will also scare the shit out of the German air force personnel. Air base personnel taken prisoner will be disarmed, cuffed, and bused to Tegel, Stammheim, and Karlsruhe prisons." Jack concluded.

"Damn. The way you describe it, Jack, this sounds all very doable." Pete said.

"It is doable, and we're the ones — with the support of the United States Army — who are going to do it," Jack said.

"You have me convinced."

"Good. By the way, I know it's early, but I have this bottle of Redbreast 12-year-old single-still Irish whiskey in the buffet table behind me. Would you care for a toast to our impending success?"

"I would indeed, sir."

CHAPTER 41

Langley Center, McLean
Virginia
Thursday morning, September 6th

Dave sat twiddling his thumbs in a chair in front of Jack Barrett's massive desk. He passed up on Jack's offer for coffee. Jack walked back to his desk carrying another fresh cup of coffee and eased into his chair.

"Pete should be here any minute, Dave. Are you sure you won't have a fresh cup of coffee?" Jack asked.

"Thanks, but no thanks, Mr. Barrett. I've already had two," Dave replied.

The door to Jack's office abruptly opened and Pete stepped through it. He walked into the office and took a seat next to Dave. His hair was disheveled.

"Sorry I'm a bit late, Jack. I've been playing catch up this morning," Pete said.

"Car trouble? Everything okay at home?

"It's our Labrador, Sheila. She's been sick as anything and at fourteen years old, we were concerned. We took turns, watching her all night. She was better this morning, but I don't think she has much time left. Poor gal," Pete said.

"That's okay, Pete. I've been late for several reasons before myself. Been there, done that," Jack said with a chuckle.

"You didn't include a subject in your voice mail to me this morning, Jack. I assume this is about events that will occur on September 11th?" Pete asked.

"It is indeed. I wanted us to be together when I briefed Mr. McClure on his role that evening, as well as other events that will be occurring that night."

"Right," Pete replied.

"Dave, this is a large operation coming up, but I'll try summarizing it as briefly as I can. It all occurs on September 11th, which is now only five days away. In the midafternoon on the 11th, our agents will pick up the Chancellor at his residence and drive him to a safehouse in a suburban area north of Berlin. The next four events I'll mention will be occurring nearly simultaneously.

"Okay, sir."

"First, in the evening when the Bundeswehr special forces arrive at the Chancellery, they will be blinded by spotlights we will have erected and they'll be confronted by one of our heavily armed SAD spec ops teams. They will be apprehended, cuffed, and transported to Tegel prison in Berlin. Second, Dave, you will lead two spec ops teams to ambush the motorcade along their route at the wooded intersection with Diedersdorf Strasse. Four of your men will be trained and armed with EMP, Electromagnetic Pulse, rifles. They will fire bursts to stop the engine in the lead car. Then, with spotlights that will have been erected beforehand to blind the Germans in the motorcade, your teams will surround the motorcade and force the Germans to leave their weapons inside and exit the vehicles. You'll need to separate Bachmeier and Obermann from the other personnel. Your teams will be armed with Sig Sauer M5 assault rifles and SAW M250 full auto rifles. German personnel from the motorcade will be disarmed, cuffed, and transported to the prison at Karlsruhe. You will accompany Bachmeier and Obermann to a pre-identified general aviation, civil airstrip where they will board a C-17 and be flown to Ramstein Air Base at Kaiserslautern. At that time, you yourself can then return to Berlin. Sound good to you?" Jack said.

"Yes, sir. Thanks for giving me a lead role in one of the mission areas. Where do you want me to report when I return to Berlin? The embassy?" Dave asked.

"No. You don't need to report in at all. We'll have reservations for you once again at the Hotel Adlon Kempinski. After this operation is complete, we may want you to be met at the hotel by some of our agents protecting Chancellor Kalbach and taken to the safehouse. That way, you can be representing the Agency in accompanying the Chancellor back to the Chancellery where he will reassume leadership of the German government. Okay?" Jack said.

"Yes, sir. That actually sounds exciting. I do have one more question...any special courtesy, deferential treatment that I should consider providing to Defense Minister Bachmeier and General Obermann?" Dave said.

"Negative. None. Those two bastards are the ringleaders of this effort to overthrow Chancellor Kalbach, the German regime, and invade Poland as well as the Czech Republic. We owe them nothing. When you apprehend them, cuff them like the others, load them into one of the Mercedes Sprinter vans, and transport them to the airfield where the C-17 will be waiting. Your driver will have directions to that civil airfield. Okay on that?" Jack said.

"Yes, in spades, sir. And the other two missions?" Dave answered.

"Right. Third, three of our SAD Spec Ops teams armed with three FGM-148 Javelin missiles for blowing off the bunker's main metal doors will surround and seize the bunker at Görlsdorf. Fourth and last, 150 rangers from the US Army's 75th Ranger Regiment at Fort Benning joined by two companies of M1A3 Abrams tanks from Wiesbaden will assault and seize the air base at Fürstenwalde. That's it in a nutshell," Jack said.

"This is huge, Mr. Barrett," Dave said.

"It's slightly bigger than huge. I'd say near mammoth. Enormous. We're going to shut this damn thing down with a bang. Fourth Reich, my ass. The President has approved our actions. It's a go," Jack concluded.

"It gives me gooseflesh to hear you talk like that, Jack. If you don't mind me saying, you sound like General George Patton. And in a way, it's exciting," Pete said.

"Well, since you raise George Patton, my most favorite quote of Patton's is this: 'May the Lord have mercy on my enemies…because I won't.' In this operation, the enemies of the chancellor and his parliamentary German government are our enemies. We will defeat them with shock and awe," Jack said.

"We will indeed, Jack," Pete said, his hand balled into a fist, pounding the armrest.

Dave looked at Jack and Pete in wonderment at the scope of what was to come.

CHAPTER 42

Berlin Chancellery
Willy Brandt Avenue, Berlin
Tuesday afternoon, September 11th

Two shiny black Escalades veered to the curb in front of the Chancellery on Willy Brandt Avenue. With the engines off and the windows rolled down, the men inside sat immobile, listening intently and scanning the street with their eyes. In the rearview mirror, the lead agent, Ron Cardoso, saw a car parked several buildings down the street with two men sitting in the front seat.

"Paul, that vehicle down the street that's parked against the curb is most likely a surveillance vehicle. Let's lose them," Ron said.

"Got it, Ron," Paul replied.

All four men from Paul's Escalade climbed out of the vehicle. Grouped together, they began walking directly toward the suspect vehicle and unbuttoned their jackets, moving their hands inside. The driver of the suspicious vehicle didn't like what he was seeing, his face wrinkling. He started the engine on his Mercedes E 450, yanked the sedan from the curb, and did a U-turn down Willy Brandt Avenue. The Mercedes took a right turn at the first intersection and disappeared from sight.

"Nice work, Paul. We're going to go up to the front door now and get the Chancellor," Ron said.

Ron and two of the men in his Suburban walked up the steps to the Chancellery and rang the bell. The Chancellor, his wife, and son walked out toting overnight suitcases behind them. Ron's men took the suitcases from their hands and walked down the steps to load them into the vehicle. Ron opened the rear door for Chancellor Verner Kalbach and his family. They climbed into the back seat. Ron's men walked back to the second Suburban and clambered into the third-row seats.

"I can't tell you how much we appreciate this. Thank you so much," Chancellor Kalbach said, smiling.

"Our honor and pleasure, sir. I think you'll like the safehouse, Chancellor. It's in a very nice area."

"Thanks again to you all," Verner said.

"Okay, let's roll," Ron said. The two Suburbans swung away from the curb, moving quickly up Willy Brandt Avenue.

Hours later, at almost ten o'clock in the evening, two Mercedes Sprinter vans turned onto Willy Brandt Avenue and barreled up the street. They rapidly swerved against the curb in front of the Chancellery. Twelve men in black tactical dress exited out the back of the van, bent over, and in a low crouch, began moving up the steps, spreading across the lawn, and creeping like alley cats. As they reached the entrance to the mansion, spotlights from both the sides of the Chancellery and the landscaped areas switched on, illuminating the Bundeswehr special operations team with intense, blinding light.

"Sie sind umzingelt! Lass deine Gewehre und Pistolen fallen und Knien Sie sich auf den Boden! Jetzt! You are surrounded! Drop

your rifles and pistols and kneel on the ground! Now!" George Landry, SAD Spec Ops team leader, shouted out.

The Bundeswehr troops stood in place stunned, blinded by the light. However, one of them, standing by the front door to the Chancellery, raised his rifle and opened fire at a spotlight. He then fired at the area just below it. Sparks and glass burst out from the spotlight while his assault rifle rounds ricocheted off its metal stand.

Six SAD Spec Ops team members armed with SAW M250 full auto rifles opened fire. A horrific scene abruptly followed as the German was pummeled by tens of rounds, his body exploding in a spray of blood and gore, nearly severed in two. He was propelled backward off the porch, tumbling into an adjacent landscape bed.

Watching in terror as their teammate was shot to death, the Germans nervously began dropping their weapons. They kneeled on the lawn.

The SAD Spec Ops team, their weapons at the ready, stepped out from the shadows into the light and approached the Germans. Several of them pulled out handcuffs from their web belts and began cuffing the Germans. Cuffed, the Spec Ops team pulled the Germans to their feet. Minutes later, an olive-green colored bus drew up on the avenue in front of the Chancellery. That bus would transport the prisoners to the Tegel prison recently reopened for business at the direction of the Chancellor.

At one o'clock in the early morning hours, the three-vehicle motorcade carrying Andreas Bachmeier and General

Gerhardt Obermann slowed down on the dark road of Strasse des Friedens in its approach to the intersection with Diedersdorf Strasse.

"Almost there, Gerhardt. This time, this Reich, the Fourth Reich, will succeed! This is the rise of a new Germany, a Germany with unmatched military power, a Germany that will strike fear in NATO, the U.S., Russia, China, and the rest of the world," Andreas said.

"That's for certain, Herr Bachmeier! What...?" General Obermann exclaimed as the spotlights switched on, illuminating the motorcade with glaring light.

The men with EMP rifles stepped from behind trees and fired bursts at the lead vehicle. Its engine shut down instantly. The second vehicle jolted into the bumper of the lead vehicle and the third vehicle smacked into the bumper of the second. The driver of the lead vehicle slumped over against the steering wheel, unconscious, but still alive, from the effect of an EMP burst.

The shooters leaped out from the lead and follow vehicles, raising their rifles, firing at the spotlights and at random into the woods. Spotlights exploded, glass bursting outward. Bullets ricocheted off their metal stands and shredded bark from trees.

As the SAD Spec Ops teams lunged behind trees for cover, Dave tugged his Beretta from its holster, fired three shots into the air, and turned his head back and forth.

"Return fire!" Dave yelled out, "Fire!"

"Twenty-four team members armed with Sig Sauer M5 assault rifles and SAW M250 full auto rifles opened fire in a blazing clatter of gunfire. The blistering rate of fire from Dave's teams' weapons blasted into the German security personnel, smashing into them, ripping limbs from their bodies after the impacts of multiple rounds. The fray in front of the motorcade was over in just minutes. A deafening silence engulfed the roadway, smoke rising from the SUV's engines. Bodies of Germans lay strewn around vehicles. The roadway itself was swathed in blood.

The singular surviving German security agent rapidly surveyed the gore around him and tossed his Heckler & Koch assault rifle to the ground. His pistol followed as he raised his hands in surrender.

Dave and the two Spec Ops teams moved in, surrounding the motorcade. They pulled Bachmeier, Obermann, and the three drivers from the vehicles. The drivers were separated from the two senior defense ministry officials.

As the drivers were being handcuffed and led away, Dave stepped from the woods, his pistol still at his side. He walked up to Bachmeier and Obermann.

"This is an outrage! You are interfering in the activities of a sovereign nation. You will all be tried and executed!" Obermann barked, stepping forward, his hands on his hips.

"General, isn't that what intelligence agencies do on occasion, meddle in the activities of sovereign nations?" Dave asked, moving through the crowd and up to within three feet of the General.

"Not here! Not now! You American pig! You murdered my men! And you will die for it! Especially you! And now!" the general shouted, yanking his pistol from his belt holster.

"Not likely, you Neo-Nazi bastard," Dave said, his pistol still slung by his side. Dave abruptly raised his right arm and fired three rounds at point blank range into General Obermann's chest.

His eyes at first glaring at Dave, then rolling up in their sockets, the general groaned. Obermann slumped to his knees, dropping his pistol, and collapsed sideways. He thudded to the road surface.

"Take his body and throw it in the back of a van. He'll get a proper burial later," Dave said as he gestured at the general's corpse.

Bachmeier looked on in total shock, his eyes opening wide and forehead furrowing. He glanced down at Obermann's corpse and then up at Dave.

"What do you want?" Bachmeier said, gasping at the sight of Obermann's dead body lying on the ground in front of him.

"Your arrest, Herr Defense Minister. Come with me. You're going to take a plane flight from a civil airstrip not far from here. You'll be heading first to Ramstein Air Base in Kaiserslautern. They'll tell you where you're eventually going once you land there. And I'll be accompanying you to the airfield. Walk to that first Mercedes Sprinter van, climb in, and step to the rear. I warn you, if you resist in any way, you will regret it. Do you understand, Herr Defense Minister?" Dave said, moving up to handcuff Bachmeier.

"I understand," Bachmeier replied in a meek tone. He abruptly placed his hands behind his back.

"Good. Then, let's take a drive," Dave answered.

At 01:30 hours in the morning, concealed by the forest east of the air base at Fürstenwalde, twenty M1A3 Abrams tanks and 150 rangers were lined up near the edge of the woods. Colonel Mike Selman, commander of the combined armor and infantry force, stepped forward to the front of the group and spun about, facing them.

"Men, we will move in to assault and seize this air base at 01:45 hours. That's ten minutes from now. Rangers, the tanks are in front of you. Let the armor take the lead. Tankers, blow the parallel perimeter fences and roll forward into the base. Your first target is the control tower. Take it down. Continue to blast it until it collapses. Then move forward, align yourselves near the runway, and crater it. Crater it so badly that no planes can take off. After that, return to support the rangers as they rush to the hangars, dorms, and administrative buildings. We are going to storm this base and take control of it as quickly as we can. Any resistance you encounter, that is, if any Germans fire at you, return fire and keep firing until they stop, or they've gone to meet Jesus!" Colonel Selman exclaimed.

A large cheer rose from the group.

"Men, I ask you...are we ready?" the Colonel shouted.

"Hooahhh!" a booming, boisterous shout arose into the night air from the rangers and the tank commanders. They raised their arms, waving them high above their heads with their hands balled into fists.

The Colonel counted down with his fingers as the strike hour approached. At 01:45 hours, Colonel Selman raised his right arm and slashed it downward through the air. With a blaring roar, the line of twenty tanks started their engines and moved forward, circling the woods to their right. The rangers followed behind them, their assault rifles at their hips.

In the meadow on the west side of the forest, the tanks formed a skirmish line and opened fire with their 120 mm cannons on the fence line. Mangled sections of fence blew up into the air with clumps of weeds as the explosions blew the fencing apart. The tanks rolled over the demolished segments of fence, crushing it into the earth, and entered the air base.

The 150 rangers spread apart as they followed the armor into the base.

Minutes passed as the ranger force and armor advanced, approaching the base buildings where interior lights had begun switching on. German airbase personnel scrambled to get dressed, then rushed down hallways, and exited doors. Some had pistols stuffed in their belts, others had reached for their rifles.

The line of M1A3 Abrams tanks opened fire on the control tower, their cannons firing repeatedly, erupting in thunderous blasts that cratered the tower's middle and lower structure. The tower walls slowly began to lean to the right, its midsection crumbling. Unable to withstand the tremendous battering, the tower finally thundered to the ground in a smoking pile of metal, concrete, wood, and glass. The tanks rolled forward and began firing a barrage of salvos at the runway, cratering it.

The rangers dashed for the hangars and buildings. A rattle of gunfire erupted from three open windows in what appeared to be a dormitory. Several rangers were hit and fell to the ground.

The turrets of four Abrams tanks rotated and opened fire on the windows of the building. Explosions of brick, cement, and wood burst out from the building along with the remains of the German shooters. Its roofline teetered, its support beams demolished, then collapsed on the rubble.

A deafening clatter of gunfire ensued between German security forces rushing forward from several buildings and the attacking rangers. The Germans' standard weaponry was no match for the rate of fire from rangers shooting SAW M250 full auto rifles. The Abrams tanks' 120 mm cannons took their toll on the administrative buildings, dorms, and hangars. A near slaughter followed, the carnage among the German forces overwhelming.

After a little over a half hour of constant battle, dozens of Germans emerged from buildings and hangars, their hands raised above their heads in surrender. The rangers moved forward, some gathering the Germans together and moving them to the quadrangle lawn adjacent to the base headquarters. There they were handcuffed. Other rangers continued to search the hangars and buildings. Colonel Selman stepped up to the center quadrangle.

"This announcement is for the German personnel. In several minutes, you will board buses and be transported to the prisons at Tegel, Stammheim, and Karlsruhe. I warn you... any resistance on your part will be met by harsh punishment," Colonel Selman said, turning to his tank commanders and rangers.

"Men, this was a superbly executed operation. Absolutely fantastic. I congratulate all of you for your bravery and courage in the line of fire. After our prisoners are loaded onto the buses and depart, other conveyances will arrive and we will begin our own departure, eventually returning to our assigned bases in the U.S. So, for a job well done, I salute you!" Colonel Selman exclaimed, coming to attention and saluting. A loud cheer arose from the armor and ranger forces.

At precisely 01:45 a.m., simultaneous with the attack on Fürstenwalde Air Base, three FGM-148 Javelin missiles blasted into the main metal doors at the command bunker in Görlsdorf. The colossal explosions of light, fire, and smoke

287

were deafening. Huge, jagged shards of metal blew out from the doors. At that early hour of the morning, only two security personnel were posted at the entrance. Those two guards were instantly incinerated, fragments of their bodies vanishing into the ball of fire and black smoke emanating from the front of the bunker.

The SAD Spec Ops teams rushed forward and threw several flash-bangs into the huge, smoking hole in the bunker's front wall. Blasts of light and sound burst out from the hole.

The Spec Ops teams slipped on oxygen-fed masks and rushed into the bunker to find German personnel lying on the floor shrieking in pain, holding bloody ears and noses. Caustic smoke spread throughout the bunker from still burning and melting electronics. The mission to seize the command bunker was over in less than fifteen minutes.

Team members helped the Germans rise to their feet and walked them out from the bunker. Outside, two medics applied antibiotic cream and bandages to areas of burned flesh. The Germans were treated as well as was possible at the site, cuffed, and loaded onto buses headed for the prison at Karlsruhe.

CHAPTER 43

Hotel Adlon Kempinski
Unter den Linden Strasse, Berlin
Wednesday afternoon, September 12th

Dave McClure washed his face and combed his hair in the bathroom of a junior suite on the third floor of the Adlon Kempinski hotel. He'd been dropped off by a Spec Ops Mercedes Sprinter van an hour earlier. After climbing out of the Sprinter van, and before approaching the doors of the hotel, Dave had walked down to a men's shop just three doors down from the hotel where he ended up buying a few things. And then he'd returned to the hotel and checked in at the receptionist desk. Dave glanced at his watch—twelve-thirty in the afternoon. He was fatigued and hungry.

Still in the bathroom, Dave donned a brand new light blue shirt, gray slacks, and blue blazer he had purchased at the men's shop. He walked into the living area and glanced out the windows to the street below. It was packed with pedestrians walking and chatting during the lunch hour. There was a knock at the door. Dave spun around.

"Who is it?" Dave asked, having just pulled his pistol from its holster.

"Joe Marchetti, Mr. McClure. Ron Cardoso asked me to come over to the hotel and pick you up. We're headed to the Chancellor's location," Joe said.

"Okay," Dave answered, uncocking the hammer on his Beretta and flicking the safety back on. He opened the door.

"Pleased to meet you, Mr. McClure. I've heard a lot about you. We're parked at the curb, so we should hurry a bit downstairs."

"Sure. Have you met the Chancellor, Joe? Anything I should know?" Dave asked as they stepped from the hallway into an elevator.

"I've been around him, but I haven't actually met him or talked to him myself. Ron says he's a nice guy, very personable, and easy to chat with. The two of them seemed to chat a lot together in the safehouse," Joe said.

"That's good. How long is the drive to the safehouse?" Dave asked in a low voice as they walked through the lobby.

"About twenty-five minutes. That's what it took to get here," Joe replied.

Outside the hotel, Dave climbed into the backseat of a black Cadillac Escalade. There was a driver and one shooter in the front seat he'd never seen before.

"Thanks for the lift, guys," Dave said.

"Our pleasure, sir. It's good to meet Mr. David McClure, the real guy," the driver said, leaving the curb and entering traffic.

"Call me Dave, please, and don't believe half the stuff you hear about my antics. Most of it is most assuredly baloney and the rest are things that any of you would also do in the same threatening situations," Dave said, chuckling.

"Oh, I doubt that. Anyway, it's not what we hear, Dave, but I understand your meaning. By the way, I'm Lee Thorne and I'm pleased to meet you. I've been through the defensive driving school. I found it both interesting and fun, so I chose to stay in this line of work as a protective detail driver," Lee said.

"Likewise, Lee. And that's good to hear," Dave said.

The right front seat shooter introduced himself as Sean O'Connor and leaned over the seat back to shake Dave's hand. The drive took twenty-five minutes just as Joe Marchetti had predicted. As they eased to the curb in front of the stately residence, Joe excused himself and exited, saying the Chancellor and his wife would be in the second row with Dave.

As Joe left the vehicle, the front door opened at the stately residence and what he assumed were agents stepped out, carrying luggage to the rear of the suburban. Chancellor Kalbach, his wife, and son, followed. They were flanked by two shooters walking alongside them, but on the lawn.

The son, Gerard. climbed into the third row of the vehicle. After the son had his seatbelt fastened, Chancellor Kalbach and his wife squeezed onto the second-row seats next to Dave.

"Chancellor, I'm Dave McClure. I'm pleased to meet you, sir," Dave said.

"It's I who am pleased…"

Several bullets suddenly ricocheted off the windshield's bullet proof windows. Cracks ran across the glass. A Chevy Suburban racing down the street in front of them, then rushed at them on the right, windows open and pistols blazing. Bullet impacts began to riddle the side windows as the attacking Suburban veered into the curb opposite them.

"Fire it up, Lee, pull ahead, and back into them. Ram them! Now! Go Lee!" Dave shouted at the driver.

The Escalade's engine roared to life. Lee swung the Escalade from the curb, crossed into the center of the street. Lee then thrust the SUV in reverse, turned the steering wheel hard, and accelerated. With its engine bellowing and the tires spinning and burning rubber, the Escalade's rear end slammed ferociously into the Suburban's side doors.

The men inside the Suburban were at first violently propelled forward thumping against the doors and windows, then boosted backward, pounding them into the flooring.

Dave threw his door open and fired his Beretta repeatedly into the side doors of the Suburban, emptying his magazine. Spurts of blood sprinkled up onto the Suburban's side windows. He rammed in another mag and lurched back inside the Escalade.

"Great work, Lee! Let's go! To the chancellery, we have a team there! Lights and siren on! The agents at the residence will call this in," Dave shouted.

With its tires spinning hard and blue smoke rising from the wheel wells, the Escalade lunged forward and barreled down the street. Dave swiveled in his seat and glanced out the rear windows. The Suburban wasn't moving.

"Are you okay, Chancellor? Mrs. Kalbach?" Dave asked as the Escalade flew down streets and rushed through turns in intersections. Dave glanced at their son in the back seat who had a broad grin on his face.

"I'm fine. My, that was stressful but also exciting, Mr. McClure! You sure know how to deal with situations like that. And your driver, Lee, is superb," Mrs. Kalbach blurted out in response.

"Yes, it was! Can we do it again, Mom?" Gerard, their son, asked from the back seat.

"Dave, my compliments. Quick thinking. By the way, my wife's name is Sarah," Chancellor Kalbach said.

"I'm pleased to meet you, Sarah," Dave said.

"And I you, Dave. I feel like I've just driven away from a scene in a James Bond movie," Sarah said.

"We have a full Special Operations team at the Chancellery. No one will try anything with us there. You're safe," Dave said, glancing at the driver. James Bond was coming up so much in discussions that maybe he should apply for a screen test, Dave thought, chuckling.

"Again, Lee, great execution!" Dave declared.

"Thanks, Dave. I think we nailed them well," Lee replied.

"Somehow, some way, the safehouse was most likely compromised. I'll put that in my report. What do you plan to do first, Chancellor, if I may ask," Dave said.

"Good question. I'm going to order all armor and infantry forces to return to their bases. Then I'm going to write out a brief speech that I'll give through the media to the German people that briefly explains what happened. In very general terms, that is," The Chancellor said.

"Sounds appropriate, sir. Congratulations and good luck," Dave replied.

"Congratulations and thanks are due the United States and men like you, Dave. Thank you," the Chancellor said.

The black Escalade continued its quick cruise down Berlin's avenues and streets. The Chancellery was now just five minutes away.

CHAPTER 44

Langley Center, McLean
Virginia
Monday morning, September 17th

Jack Barrett had intentionally moved quickly through his staff meeting's agenda and was now back in his office. He glanced from his desk to the eastern windows, then turned to face both Pete and Dave.

"The President called early this morning. He's extremely pleased with our support, that is, the manner in which we emphatically crushed the intended overthrow of the German government. The President said he received a communication over the weekend from Chancellor Verner Kalbach that was filled to the brim with laudatory comments specifically about you, Dave, as well as our special operations forces. I've already called General Howard Anderson down at Fort Bragg, North Carolina, early this morning and passed on the President's accolades. Gentlemen, this turned out to be a superbly executed operation. Well done," Jack said.

"Thanks, Jack. Another feather in your cap. And Dave, I can't say enough good things about your performance. It was stellar," Pete said.

"Thanks, sir," Dave answered.

"Dave, the only regret I have is we didn't take General Gerhardt Obermann alive; however, at the same time, I want you to know that I understand the circumstances surrounding the incident where you shot him. You really had no choice," Jack said.

"Thank you, Mr. Barrett. I didn't have a choice. He would have shot me," Dave replied.

"I believe that. In my estimation, it was you or him. I'm just sorry that idiot did what he did and forced the issue. I understand that the general is having a quiet and unattended burial at one of Berlin's cemeteries today. Oh, and State Department also called early this morning. The Chancellor has also already sent an official request for the extradition of Andreas Bachmeier. I expect that Bachmeier will be tried, convicted, and ultimately end up dying in prison. A Fourth Reich...Jeez, what the hell was he thinking," Jack said.

"If not for us and the U.S. Army, that might have ended up being a reality, Jack," Pete said.

"That's true, and we have to remind ourselves about that possibility. It seems almost anything is possible, even probable, if you let it fester," Jack answered. He turned to Dave.

"Dave, given your performance on this enormous, manpower-intensive operation, we want to accelerate things a bit. Your promotion to Principal Assistant to the DepOps is now only three months away. Pete and I have decided to move you up to Pete's floor and give you a temporary office with a secretary. Your new secretary, Margarite Esposito, is already at her desk outside your new office. So, once again, please accept my congratulations. Today, take some time to move into your new, but temporary, office. Pete's going to take you there, show you where it is," Jack said.

"Wow. My own office? I'm at a loss for words again, Mr. Barrett. Thank you so much," Dave replied.

"That's all I have to say for now. There may be some awards coming to us from The White House. I'll keep you informed on that. Oh, and by the way, Dave, with your new temporary office, you've also been given access to the executive dining room. Use it. It's great. Take care and have a great day," Jack said, standing. He shook hands with both Pete and Dave.

Two floors down, Pete and Dave stepped out of the elevator. Pete put his right hand on Dave's left shoulder.

"It's this way, Dave. If you find you need anything, anything at all, please call me. You're going to find that your visibility in the Agency has increased dramatically. People are going to want to see you, talk to you, get your opinion on things. Be prepared for that. At first, it may seem like an assault on your time, but it's not. People are just going to want to talk to you. Use Margarite as your security guard. She can schedule meetings for you and remind you of them. This is going to be a new experience. Not necessarily more difficult, just different. Okay?" Pete said.

"Sure, I'm just nervous," Dave said, as Pete steered him to his left off the hallway.

"That's to be expected. So was I when my own promotions moved me to this floor," Pete said as they rounded a corner.

In front of them was a large desk behind which was seated a woman with jet black hair and big brown eyes, Margarite Esposito. Margarite looked to be in her mid-thirties.

"Hi, good morning, Mr. Novak. Can I help you with something?" Margarite asked.

"Margarite, meet your new supervisor, Dave McClure. Dave's going to be moving things into his office today," Pete said.

"I'm pleased to meet you, Mr. McClure. If you need anything, anything at all, call me, knock on my desk, or tap my shoulder. That's why I'm here," Margarite said, smiling and focusing on Dave's electric blue eyes.

"Likewise, Margarite. Thanks, Pete, for introducing me," Dave said.

"I'll leave you to your moving in activities, Dave. By the way, I forgot to mention it, but your windows face east over the forest to the headwaters of the Potomac just like Jack Barrett's. I think you'll like that. So, get settled and call me if you have any issues," Pete replied, turning to leave.

"Thanks again, Pete," Dave said.

"Don't worry, you'll get used to it," Pete said, chuckling. He disappeared around the corner.

"Well, Mr. McClure, any initial orders for me. Would you like a cup of coffee?" Margarite said.

"No orders, no requests, not yet. You and I will play this by ear, Margarite. Oh, and while I do appreciate the coffee pot being on in the morning, however I can get my own coffee. Your duties will be more substantive than that," Dave said.

"Thank you, sir," Margarite answered.

"I only have a few things on and in my desk that I'll be toting up here, so I'll begin with that. Please just take phone messages and advise callers that I'm busy for an hour or so."

"Thank you, sir," Margarite said. She was encouraged by Dave's personable demeanor. This was going to be a great relationship, she thought.

Dave went down to the cafeteria for lunch and chose the meatloaf and mashed potatoes with gravy. Staring out the glass walls to the landscaped quadrangle, he wondered about how fantastic life was turning out to be for him. He marveled, imagining the change of processes that would now consume his time.

Back in his office at a little past one o'clock, Dave worked at the minor tasks of placing things on his desk and shuffling things in the drawers. He was startled when his intercom jingled...the four walls of his office had an echo effect on the ringing sound.

"Yes, Margarite?" he answered.

"Mr. McClure, you have several visitors. Can I send them in?"

"Several? Ah, sure, show them in," Dave said, somewhat in wonder that he had several visitors all at once.

Margarite opened the door and ushered three men into Dave's office. There were three leather chairs in front of Dave's desk.

"Gentlemen, have a seat, please. How can I help you?" Dave asked.

"Well, it's sort of the other way around, sir. We want to help you settle in, gain an understanding of what we do, even though you don't take over as Principal Assistant until January 1st. By the way, I'm Dan Callahan, Chief of Land Division," Dan said.

"And I'm Gerry Albrecht, Chief of Naval Division," Gerry said.

"And last but not least, sir, I'm Al Dixon, Chief of Air Division," Al said.

"Well, I'm impressed that you decided to visit with me so soon, guys. And by the way, since you will be my go-to guys, my deputies, let's dispense with the formalities. I'm 'Dave' to you, and you'll be Dan, Gerry, and Al to me. And I know you,

Dan, as I worked in your section. So, I ask, between us, will a first name basis work?" Dave asked.

"Yes, it will, and that's superb of you, Dave. Thank you. Do you think you'll be holding regular meetings with us?" Dan said.

"I'm sure I will, but I don't know on what day or time. I have to see how I myself will be tasked in that regard. I'm sure I'll have a handle on that fairly soon," Dave replied.

"Great. We just wanted to come in and meet you. I think this is going to run smooth. One thing for future planning," Al said.

"Yes?" Dave responded.

"Are you a fisherman, a fly fisherman, perhaps," Gerry asked.

"When I was a young fella, I fished with my father, but I haven't fished in any form in over ten to fifteen years. Why do you ask?" Dave said.

"Once a year, usually in the early fall, September time frame, the three of us go fly fishing for a week somewhere in the states. It's enjoyable, and it sheds any stress you might be carrying. It's fun. And about once every five to six years, we go fishing during a black moon. It's our black moon fishing trip. And next year in September, there's a black moon. We'd like to invite you to come along. We'll teach you how to fly fish," Dan said.

"Black moon? That sounds spooky," Dave said.

"It's not. It's an astronomical term. When a second new moon occurs in the same month, it's called a black moon. That's all. And next year we're going to Montana in the Selway–Bitterroot Wilderness," Dan replied.

"The Bitterroot Wilderness? Montana? Wow. Any concern for grizzlies there?" Dave asked.

"There is, but encounters are rare, and we all carry handguns. Whaddya say, Dave, might you be interested, operational activities not withstanding?" Dan asked.

"I'll say yes for now. It might be interesting, even though I still think black moon sounds spooky," Dave said.

"Great. Then we're pleased to meet you and we'll be on our way. We know that on your first day in the new office, you have things to tend to," Dan said.

"Great. Thanks for stopping by, guys," Dave said, standing and shaking hands with each man. The men turned and left his office.

Still smiling from the visit, Dave returned to shuffling things and straightening his desk. Once again, his intercom jingled.

"Yes, Margarite?" Dave answered.

"I know you just had a visit, Mr. McClure, but there's a gentleman here to see you. Shall I bring him in or reschedule?"

"Go ahead and bring him in, Margarite. I have time," Dave said, thinking how Pete was right about visitors.

Margarite ushered the man in and quietly closed the door behind him.

"Good afternoon. You are? And how may I help you?" Dave asked, noticing the man was young, very young, maybe in his twenties.

"My name is Dennis Stone, Mr. McClure. Most people call me Denny," Dennis said.

"Where do you work, Denny?"

In the SAD, sir. I'm a special operations agent, Land Division. I went to Dan Callahan's officer earlier, but he was out."

"That's because Dan was here in my office along with the chiefs of the naval and air divisions. How can I help you, Denny?" Dave asked.

"Well, I have my first mission coming up that's out of the

country…Bangkok, Thailand. It will be upcountry, not far from the Laotian border. I was hoping for a little advice, that's all. Maybe I shouldn't have elevated this to you, Mr. McClure," Denny said.

"Don't worry about that. What kind of advice are you seeking, Denny?"

"Well, basically rules of engagement, sir, on an op like this."

"I see. Well, I have an idea. Let's take you back to your training days. My question number one for you is: what's the first commandment of intelligence, Dave?"

"Be offensive, sir."

"That's exactly correct. Great. Be offensive. Denny, if our senses are fine-tuned—then you know when something bad is coming your way. Do you feel you have that ability, that gut sense?"

"Yes, sir. My coworkers say I actually have an uncanny sense that way, that I'm very good at that," Denny replied.

"Then I don't anticipate you having any issues on this Thailand op. Still, in any armed confrontation, the man who hesitates and fires the second shot is often dying or he's already dead. So, my advice to you, Denny, is this—if you sense something lethal may be coming at you, shoot first. Fire the first bullet. First bullet."

"First bullet. Got it. Thanks, Mr. McClure. I appreciate it. Thanks for seeing me," Denny said, rising with Dave to shake hands. He turned and left the office.

Dave eased himself back into his seat. His face bore a look of wonderment. He had just given a young Spec Ops agent advice. It was the same advice that Jack Barrett had once given him. This job was going to be like that. That's what Jack and Pete were attempting to explain to him. Dave smiled and folded his hands in front of him on his desk.

So, this was how it was going to be.

CHAPTER 45

Pumphrey Drive, Fairfax
Virginia
Monday evening, September 17th

Dave took a sip from his glass of Merlot wine, then returned to munch on the lasagna that Karen had prepared. She'd also worked up a great salad in a vinaigrette dressing as an accompaniment. Karen laid her fork down and looked across the counter at Dave.

"Dave, honey, you've been mum since you came home. And you haven't said anything all weekend either. The Germany trip—so, what was going on? What happened? Was it bad?" Karen asked.

"Have you already fed the baby?" Dave replied with a question.

"Yes, I have. She's taking a short nap since we're eating so early. And don't change the subject—please answer my question. What's going on?" Karen said, persisting.

"I've been gathering my thoughts, sweetheart. Getting it together on what I want to tell you and what I can tell you," Dave answered.

"No time like the present. Tell me, Dave, did everything go okay today?"

"Sweetheart, that's been my trouble in thinking how to relate it to you. It's beyond okay. It was absolutely phenomenal," Dave said, watching Karen's face light up.

Dave continued, "You'll hear about it soon enough... maybe on the news tonight. There was a plot to overthrow the German government and establish a Fourth Reich," Dave said.

"A Fourth Reich! You're kidding!" Karen exclaimed.

"No kidding. It was an enormous operation. We had the assistance of the U.S. Army for two companies of Abrams tanks and 150 rangers. It was huge. Within the operation itself, there were four mission areas that involved firefights. I led one of them although I can't give you the specifics. Not yet anyway," Dave explained.

"Wow. And it will be on the news, you think?"

"Germany's Chancellor Verner Kalbach is making a speech to the German people, explaining to them in general terms what took place. He's already ordered all German military forces, armor, and infantry, to return to their assigned bases."

"Return to their bases? Where were they?" Karen asked.

"Along with the process of planning to arrest the Chancellor and overthrow the government, there was also a planned invasion by armor and infantry of Poland and the Czech Republic," Dave replied.

"My goodness. This sounds like the start of World War III."

"It could have been. We stopped it," Dave said.

"And today?"

"Jack and Pete are accelerating things somewhat. Those were their words. Since it's three months to my promotion as a Principal Assistant, they're assigning me a temporary office on Pete's floor with a secretary, Margarite Esposito," Dave explained.

"Dave, that's fantastic! Congratulations! I am so proud of you," Karen said, rising from her seat, circling the table, and planting a kiss on Dave's forehead.

"Well, it was truly a remarkable and totally unexpected event. I just..." Dave interrupted himself, "What was that?"

"What was what?" Karen said with a look of concern.

"It was something like a yelping sound. It came from the hallway," Dave said, rising from his chair.

Dave walked down the hallway, Karen following with a timid expression on her face. While the door to the nursery was already open a crack, he gently pushed it open all the way. Little Carolyn was sound asleep in her crib.

Dave's eyes opened wide. He inhaled deeply. At the base of the crib, curled up in a ball, with its eyes now focusing on Dave...was a puppy.

"A puppy!" Dave exclaimed. Dave bent down. The puppy jumped up, ran to him, and leaped on his legs.

"Yes, I confess. I have a bed for him in the living room, but it's a little strange in that he always ends up here at the bottom of Carolyn's crib. It's like he believes he's protecting her," Karen said.

"What's his name?"

"Just 'Puppy' for now. We were leaving the naming to you."

"Well, it can't be Plato. That wouldn't be right. Plato was a great puppy, but he's gone. Ah, I think this puppy's name is going to be 'Socks' for 'Socrates.' How does that sound?" Dave said, the puppy nuzzling up his chest.

"Socks. I like that. Or Socrates when he's been a bad boy," Karen said.

Dave lifted the puppy into his arms and walked into the living room. He plopped on the sofa, stroking the puppy's head.

"Are you done with your lasagna, Dave?" Karen asked.

"Yes, thank you. It was great, honey. And thank you for your loving heart that went and got us another puppy. So, where was he all this past weekend?"

"I loaned him out to a neighbor to keep it a secret," Karen said.

"Bless your heart. I love you to death, Karen," Dave said, "Can you see how things are changing for us, Honey? Big time. New job. New hours. New pay. New baby. And now..."

"A new puppy, Socks," Karen said, finishing the sentence. Karen headed into the kitchen, grinning.

Dave placed the puppy on the sofa cushions and rose to his feet. Socks watched Dave as he walked to a cabinet, opened it, and poured himself a thumb of Redbreast Irish whiskey. Dave returned to the couch. The moment Dave sat back down, the puppy hopped back into his lap.

"Socks, I think this is the beginning of a fantastic friendship," he said, stroking the puppy's ears.

The puppy bent his head to the side, his ears flopping, as though wondering what Dave had just said.

Dave looked to the ceiling. He began to mutter in a low voice.

"Lord, thank you so much. Tony, my best buddy, please know that I will miss you forever, but I am certain in my heart that the Lord has taken you into his arms and embraced you," Dave whispered, his eyes misting.

Dave glanced down at Socks lying in his lap, then turned to look down the hallway toward the nursery where little Carolyn lay asleep, and finally glimpsed toward the kitchen where Karen stood at the sink amidst a clatter of dishes.

Smiling, Dave glanced upward again. A tear slid down his cheek.

"Thank you."

The End

ACKNOWLEGEMENTS

While I have been to the locations where this story takes place, Ocho Rios, Jamaica; Berlin and Garmisch-Partenkirchen, Germany; and the mountains of Wyoming, this book required a great deal of research. I owe great thanks to my developmental editor, Joyce Ragle. In his book, On Writing, Stephen King notes that "To write is human, to edit is divine." Joyce has accomplished a divine job in both syntax and plot adjustments so that this book would be at its best for publication. I thank my reader-editors, Tom Inks and Joe Dalton. I am sincerely grateful for their recommendations to regarding the plot and sentence structure. This is my seventh novel published with Outskirts Press and there is a good reason for that. They are the best in the business. Period. Their support of the author is top-notch. And they Design fantastic front and back covers as well as superb interior formatting. Most of all, I thank my lovely wife, Trudi, for her loving support of my writing.